PRAISE FOR WILLA DREW

Willa Drew's writing style blew me away.

Highly recommend this author and book without a doubt!

My first book by Willa and it won't be my last!

I look forward to reading other books by this author in the future. Because I went into this one with hope and promise, and it absolutely delivered! Now it's your turn!

This is a great story written by two clearly talented authors. The characters have been put front and centre of this book, with their story and development being what it is all about.

This is the first time I have a read a book by these authors and I enjoyed the collaboration. The book flowed well, seamlessly moving through the story.

I am glad I stumbled on this book and these authors, and I will definitely be adding them to my list of authors to keep my eye out for.

The authors did a wonderful job of writing the characters in a way that I felt connected to them right away.

DISTANCE, LOVE, & US

FALLING FOR THE LIAR BOOK FIVE

WILLA DREW

MOVING WORDS PUBLISHING

Published by: Moving Words Publishing
www.movingwordspublishing.com

FALLING FOR THE LIAR SERIES

One night to bring them together.

One lie to tear them apart.

Five holidays to fall in love.

What starts out as a lie, turns into a passionate and heartfelt romance story about finding oneself and love. Each book revolves around one holiday in Sarah and Nick's romance.

Christmas Eve: Kisses, Lies, & Us

Valentine's Day: Misses, Hearts, & Us

Independence Day: Crushes, Friends, & Us

Halloween: Passions, Hopes, & Us

New Year's Eve: Distance, Love, & Us

If you like secret identity, movies, soulmates, friends-to-lovers, and a right person wrong time new adult romance, the *Falling for the Liar* series is for you.

CONTENTS

The story so far...

In *Kisses, Lies, & Us*, Nick Stavros, a film student, finds himself at a swanky bar in LA on Christmas Eve. While his father is in a meeting, Nick orders an Old Fashioned using a fake ID with the name Shawn Rosstav. Sarah Connor, the bartender and an aspiring script writer, inspires Nick to drop his hockey-jock persona and be his true self—aside from the fake name. Sarah and Nick spend Christmas Eve together eating tacos, talking movies, and sharing a romantic kiss, but are split apart before exchanging contact information.

In *Misses, Hearts, & Us*, Sarah is on the way back from Toronto after attending her grandmother's funeral when her plane makes an emergency landing. Sarah not only finds herself in Chicago on Valentine's Day, but she discovers Shawn Rosstav's ID in the leather jacket he placed on her shoulders on Christmas Eve. With an address and time to spare, she decides to take a chance on love. Unfortunately, the address on the ID belongs to Nick's ex-girlfriend, who greets Sarah at the door. No matter how quickly Nick realizes what happened, he doesn't catch Sarah as she runs away, left only with her Toronto Maple

Leafs hat. Certain that the guy she kissed on Christmas Eve omitted having a girlfriend, an upset Sarah flies to LA alone. Unbeknownst to each of them, Sarah and Nick are both notified they have been accepted into the Starlight Foundations' Film competition that begins in the summer in LA.

In *Crushes, Friends, & Us*, Nick's lie is exposed on the first day of the Starlight Competition. In front of Sarah, a screenwriter on the project, Nick, the director and leader of the Blue Team, is introduced under his real name. Sarah and Nick are forced to work together as they write, direct, and film a short movie. Nick is working at a coffee shop and sleeping on his estranged father's couch to save money while struggling to keep his team on track. Sarah decides to give Nick a chance at friendship, but just as she is giving in to her attraction, her friend reveals more skeletons in Nick's closet. In a heartwarming grand gesture, Nick lays out his full story for Sarah on film, lies and all. Sarah accepts his apology and seals their renewed relationship with a kiss. When Sarah needs a new roommate, Nick moves in and is certain that, together, their life will be perfect.

In *Passions, Hopes, & Us*, Nick and Sarah are just roommates as they get ready to attend the Starlight Foundation Gala. Nick wins Best Director, but Sarah loses Best Screenplay to her friend Karina. Nick and Sarah celebrate the end of the competition and give into the attraction boiling between them for eight months. Nick is happy to finally call Sarah his girlfriend, but living together as they each navigate jobs, school, and opposite schedules doesn't leave much time together.

Nick gets an offer to film a documentary with his father, filming interviews with inmates about to leave the low security prison where his father was incarcerated for five years. Saying yes to the offer means Nick will miss time with Sarah, including Thanksgiving in Canada with her parents. Sarah insists he accept the offer, but silently is frustrated she has not received any similar opportunities. While Sarah is home in Toronto, Karina calls her with an offer to work as assistant screenwriter on an exciting new show, Vampire Club. Sarah rearranges her schedule and agrees to start right away—so quickly, she forgets to tell Nick about her decision.

Nick's hopes to get to know more about his father's past are dashed when the only talking his father does is with the inmates they interview, reading the same five questions off index cards. Sarah's bright-eyed view of her new industry gig dims, though she hides her disappointment from everyone, especially Nick. The night before Nick's twentieth birthday she puts together an elaborate celebration, including a hockey game and a night at a fancy hotel. During dinner, Nick's father gives him an envelope with index cards, just like the ones he used to interview the inmates. Later, Sarah reads the cards to Nick at his request, and together they learn what happened to his dad during and after his incarceration. Sarah consoles Nick as he processes what his father's life has been like and the impact on his family.

Their schedules continue to clash. Sarah is busy at work, and Nick feels sidelined but stays quiet, even when Sarah moves his things into her room as a surprise. To prove herself to the head writer, Sarah agrees to visit the Vampire Club set on Halloween. When Sarah doesn't show up for a party, Nick confronts her about the lack of communication. Their fight escalates and Nick runs away to his father's place, where they have a heart-to-heart.

To help a friend, Sarah and Nick reunite to shoot a music video. In the parking lot of the Griffith Observatory, the site of their first kiss, they talk about their issues, but Nick is not ready to come back to their apartment and instead returns to help his dad finish the documentary. As Sarah commiserates with her friend and roommate Ryan, he points out that Sarah has been treating Nick like a boyfriend, but not a partner.

Sarah surprises Nick by moving all their things out of her room, promising to make decisions together from now on. She finally opens up to Nick, answering his father's same five questions on index cards and explaining how much Nick means to her. They reconcile and Nick tells Sarah that he loves her. But is she ready to say those words back?

For those who believe in love

ONE

NICK

It's official. Sarah and I are a couple. I might've thought that was true the day she invited me to be one of her roommates. Or when she moved me into her bedroom without asking. Or when we spent two days rearranging furniture and making her room our room. But it's today. Because today I get to meet her parents. My hand is shaking as I clutch Sarah's. Or at least I think it is my hand. Is it me or is it her?

Sarah's lips tremble, and her eyes are wide and full of unease. Her dread creeps through our connected hands on the armrest between our seats. The cabin of the Airbus shrinks to the two of us. The red-eye flight was my idea. A way to attend my Thursday classes and maximize our long weekend in Canada. Sarah was fine with the plan, and she's been on plenty of planes before.

"What's going on?" I ask.

She's not worried about me meeting her parents and brothers; she made that clear.

"Nothing." She grabs my hand tighter and looks away from the flight attendant demonstrating the proper way to put on a life vest in case of an emergency.

"You can tell me anything," I whisper into her ear.

"The emergency landing in Chicago, on Valentine's Day"—she clamps her eyes shut—"I think it was the same flight attendant. That can't be, right?"

"It's an LA to Toronto flight. And you were on Toronto to LA. Quite possible. You want me to ask her?"

"No." Sarah tugs my hand, as if I'd stand and interrupt the rehearsed spiel. "Unlikely it's her. But I'm having a flashback. Or a premonition. Like something bad is about to happen. My stomach is revolting. I shouldn't have had that second cup of coffee."

"This is an easy flight." I try to infuse confidence into my tone. "Just enough time to finish the pages you promised Karina, so she can work on them while we're celebrating with your parents." I wiggle my fingers in her grip. "A short nap, and we'll be there."

No nap for me. I'm behind already. I pound the space bar with my free hand. This weekend away is bad timing. I need to outline my essay, edit the last prisoner interview for the documentary, and, if there is time, do the research for my Econ 101 project due on Monday.

Sarah nods. "Karina's right. We need to finish the screenplay before *Vampire Club* starts again. If it gets picked up. She'll have new pages for me by the end of this weekend, and I'll have nothing if I don't do it now."

Sarah fiddles with her seatbelt. "This'll sound weird, but . . ."

Between the talk after our Halloween reconciliation, and the times she has cried out in pleasure because of my body parts exploring hers, there cannot possibly be anything she doesn't feel comfortable telling me.

"The only weird thing is that you think there might be a weird thing between us. What is it?"

"Could you give me your driver's license?"

Not an embarrassing request, but a bizarre one. No one needs a driver's license on a plane.

"Sure." I struggle to unearth my wallet one-handed. "Care to explain why?"

"Last time"—her gaze flies to the flight attendant then back to me as I pull out the plastic card—"as we were making the emergency landing in Chicago, I found your fake ID in the pocket of your jacket." She takes my real ID and pushes the corners into the pads of her fingers. "Looking at your photo made me calmer. Maybe I can recreate the feeling." She peers at my flat rectangular image on the card.

I cup her cheek with my palm and turn her to face me. The sunshine she brings into my life spreads through my brain synapses, sparking the love that grows every day. Every second. "You don't need my driver's license." I kiss her nose. Her light flows through my veins. "Because you have the real thing." I kiss the knuckles of her hand and slip the ID out of it. Our gazes meet and I jump into the ocean of her eyes. "And if you need me to stab you with something pointy, I have a better idea." I can't get enough of how easy being next to her is. How fun. All sorts of fun. I poke my finger into the ticklish place in her side. It's one of the sensitive spots I've discovered during my favorite activity: exploring Sarah's body.

Her lips quiver, but not because she's on the verge of tears anymore. She squirms in her seat to escape my sneak attack. "Stop it." She playfully slaps my hand. "There're people."

"So what?" My pulse in my throat, I bite my lip and drop my gaze to her mouth. Sarah's trapped between the window of the airplane, the seatbelt, and my hand that's no longer tickling but is making steady progress up her ribcage.

She giggles. "Nick." She throws a glance at the woman sitting on the other side of me, who's intently *not* looking at us. I'm sure she's very aware of what's happening next to her.

"I'll behave." I steady my breath and reluctantly return my fingers to the waist of her jeans under her sweater. In case I need to poke her again.

Sarah wraps her arm around mine and tugs on my shirt for me to bend closer. Our sign that she's in as much as I am, even if she's not ready to say the words. The air between us crackles when we kiss. Her lips linger much longer than airplane PDA police might find appropriate. We're setting the cabin on fire, but I'm not gonna complain. I'll never complain about her kisses.

"You are better than the card." She nuzzles her face against the cotton of my long-sleeved polo. "And warmer." She pokes my bicep with her finger. "And just as hard."

"You know it." I grin at her glare and the pink hue of her face. I reach lower into her waistband. Desire flickers in my stomach.

"You promised you'd behave," she breathes into my chest. I'm not sure she means it. Her hips lift to allow my downward progress. Her little whimper spurs me on, assuring me she's enjoying this as much as I am. We don't care about the lady to my left or the people behind us that must have quite an eyeful through the gap. I kiss her, and it's not the lips-on-lips thank-you she gave me, it's a let-me-taste-you-because-I can't-wait-till-we're-alone-again maneuver. The heat in my body spikes.

"Are both of your seatbelts fastened?" The flight attendant's voice interrupts before we leave PG-13 territory.

I jerk my hand out of Sarah's pants and tug on her seatbelt. "Yes, ma'am."

Sarah clears her throat. "Of course."

"Please, stow your laptop for take off."

We giggle as the attendant moves to check the rest of the passengers. Sarah tugs on my seatbelt. I still her wrist before it repeats the maneuver. I might not be a teenager any longer, but controlling myself around her is not getting easier, no matter how many times she's touched me. I want her now. Always. I resist the temptation, kiss the soft heel of her palm, and return her hand to her lap. I use the remains of my willpower to calm my raging blood and not ask Sarah to join the mile-high club.

If we were in first class, or on a private jet, I'd have that option. One day that dream will come true. I have Sarah, and with her, life is one shining possibility after another. My heart swells. She's my shield of invincibility. My love for Sarah brightens every second of every day. "Love you," I whisper into her hair.

She sits up, stretches her neck, and seals my declaration of love with her lips. The plane takes off, and I'm soaring.

Being tall has its privileges, I won't argue that, but when you're six-four and stuck in the middle seat of economy class, you'd wish you were Sarah's size.

Her knees aren't bumping against the tray like mine are. I scrub the palm of my left hand over my eyes and yawn. Sarah's head rests on my shoulder. A contraption I've never seen before encircles her neck. She put up a good fight but two hours into the flight, with the cabin lights low and the gentle buzz of the engines, even the extra cup of coffee wasn't enough to keep her awake.

The numbers on my screen blur and I try to stifle another jaw-breaking yawn. If I don't finish at least one of these deliverables, I'll need to stay awake all night at the Connors' place to plow through my homework. I want to be fully present this weekend to make a good first impression.

The module we're covering in Econ is about the GDP of world countries, and I'm supposed to compare the population pyramids of three countries and explain how they reflect on the socioeconomic position of them in the world. I chose Greece, because of my Greek heritage, Canada, because of Sarah, and Japan, because it's on my to-visit list. Today I'll check Canada off it. I am inputting the numbers for Canada into the spreadsheet to build the final pyramid when the cabin lights come on.

Sarah stirs. "What time is it?"

"My watch says two-thirty."

"Guess we're landing soon. We're supposed to land in Toronto at six." Her yawn rivals mine.

With the time change we lose three hours. Makes sense. Good thing I stayed up. "Need a coffee?"

"I can wait until Tim's. You know that'll be our first stop." She's been talking about the donut shop as if it's the best place on earth. I don't want to ruin her nostalgic glee about the place, but I suspect it can't compare to the proper espresso machine at Blend that I can now operate in my sleep.

"Tim Horton's first. Got it. Then your dad drops our luggage off at their place and straight to Côté Fraise for a proper breakfast. I'm counting on the best butter tarts in the world and homemade croissants."

Sarah's eyes sparkle at the mention of her grandmother's bakery. "Mom'll make enough food for a family of twenty. Even with you, Grayson, and Taylor competing to see who can eat the most, you'll never eat more than Mom prepares."

"I'm up for the challenge." I've never met a plate of food I couldn't demolish.

The plane lands without a hitch, and Sarah's smile is carefree.

"Guess you were right. Having the real Nick by my side is the good luck charm I needed." She stands, leans over, and kisses me while I'm still shorter than her. Her peck wakes the hunger I've suppressed by pouring over my class notes. Not sure we can continue the PDA in front of her parents, I raise my chin and recapture her lips with mine as if it's been months and not hours since I've tasted them. One kiss morphs into two or three and then I lose count, cramming every extra kiss in now.

We go through separate customs lines, but she waits for me on the other side of the security kiosks. We weave through the corridor into the open space packed with eyes scanning the people around us, looking for the ones they are here to pick up. I've seen pictures of Ian, Sarah's dad, but I'm unable to locate him in this sea of faces.

Sarah grabs my arm. Her expression is back to the panic she started the flight with. "What's wrong?"

She shifts away from me, but I tug her close.

"Grayson is here." Her voice cracks.

There are several guys waiting at the arrival gate, and although Sarah and I video chat with him often, I only find him when I follow the direction of Sarah's gaze. Her brother's lips form a thin line as he spots Sarah.

My shoulders tighten. "Did you have a fight?"

"No. Dad was supposed to pick us up. He's not here." Sarah checks her phone. Her palm presses into mine. "No texts from either of them." She looks up at me. The dread from the airplane that I tickled out of her is back. Stronger. "Something's wrong."

Two

Sarah

"Mom fell." Grayson speeds up the ramp in his vintage Dodge Challenger.

I stretch the collar of my shirt away from my throat, aching for air.

Mom fell.

It sounds so innocent. But adults aren't supposed to fall. Toddlers fall. Leaves fall. My spry lively mom doesn't fall.

"When? Where? Who found her? How did this happen?" The words tumble out to the accelerating beat of my pulse. "Why didn't anyone text me? Did she break something?" I grip my brother's bicep.

"She was moving a bag of flour and tripped on"—he clears his throat— "the corner of a loose tile I tried to fix." Grayson extricates himself from my grasp. "Apparently, superglue isn't that super."

Who fixes a tile with superglue? I want to scream. But I don't. Handyman is not on his resumé.

My brother parks and winds Nick and me through the endless corridors of Toronto General. The last time I was here, Grayson had fractured his foot trying a new trick at his dressage lesson, and we spent the night in the emergency room laughing and crying as he flirted with the nurse stuck on duty.

Today there is no laughing.

We step into an elevator and Grayson jabs the button for the fourth floor, palms his back pocket, and huffs at the ceiling. "Can I borrow your phone again?"

He didn't text me at the airport because his was dead. Again. He's been complaining about his "antique" phone and its useless battery for months. The thing better last a few more weeks, because we've all chipped in to buy him the latest model for Christmas.

"What's the code again?" Grayson lifts one brow.

I roll my eyes. "Mémère's birthday."

"Right." And he's lost to the world of technology.

My brother splits his days between sitting in front of a computer in a lecture hall and volunteering at the stables for extra credit. Assuming he's attending his university classes. He much prefers the company of horses.

My muscles turn into ribbons of steel as the elevator takes forever to climb four measly floors. Nick's pinkie caresses mine. I nestle my hand in his, force myself to relax my jaw, and offer him an "I'm okay" smile.

He tilts his head in what I assume is a silent "How can you be?" Nick brushes his chin against my temple, and I sink into the warmth of him. The prickles of worry dull as I lay my head on his chest. The steady beats of his heart drown out the electric hum of the fluorescent lights and grinding gears of the elevator's motor. The big bad 'what if' isn't as scary with Nick by my side.

"Finally," my brother mutters as the metal doors drag open. His grumble reminds me that he's stressed too.

Being the big sister, I want to tell him it'll be fine, protect him from the pain like I always do for my baby brothers. But I can't. I don't have control over this situation. Air leaves my lungs. My fingers shake. I clutch Nick's shirt like he's a raft and we are lost at sea. I have no idea what we're about to walk into.

Our mother is a pillar of strength, always the first up, the one we turn to in a crisis, the cornerstone of our family. The fact that she's not infallible chips away at the illusion we've lived under.

The nurse's station is empty as we pass by, and the halls are eerily quiet this early in the morning. Visiting hours started ten minutes ago, but Dad stayed with Mom in the ER and is in her room waiting for us.

"Looks like 425 is this way." Grayson gestures to a sign covered in numbers and arrows.

Nick's sneakers squeak on the freshly mopped linoleum as we quietly continue down the corridor. We round a corner, and I spot Taylor leaning against the wall.

"Hey." His hug is tighter than usual.

"How is she?"

My youngest brother's mouth twists. "Cranky."

The word eases the knots in my stomach. "Sounds about right."

Grayson pushes open the extra-wide door and I follow him but Nick tugs on my elbow. "I'm gonna stay out here."

My pulse flies into overdrive. "No, I—"

"You need some time with your mom. I'll be right here." He kisses my forehead. "Go with your brothers."

My lips tremble at Nick's recognition that now is not the time to introduce him to my parents. I need to see Mom, process this on my own. Yet I don't want to leave the comfort of Nick's arms, don't want to shove the role of girlfriend to the background and put on the hat of big sister or oldest child. I bury my nose is his shirt to inhale him one more time.

This whole day was supposed to be different. I groan and grind my teeth. He should be officially meeting my family in the warmth of Côté Fraise, munching on freshly baked strawberry shortcake, not wasting the day in the impersonal hospital hallway.

Nick gently nudges me through the doorway before I have a chance to protest.

Grayson and Taylor stand at the foot of the bed by the window. The room smells of antiseptic. Dad rises from Mom's side. On the planes of his face, deep lines etch the mask of an overstressed spouse. The muddied gray of his skin tells the tale of a sleepless night. I whimper. Dad wraps his arms around me, and I can't hold back my tears any longer.

I stifle a sob in Dad's chest as he strokes my hair. He whispers into my ear like he used to in the movie theater after the main character lands in danger. "She's fine." Dad brushes moisture from my cheek. "Just a little bump is all."

A bump? Why don't I believe him? The tightness in my chest rises to my throat, choking me. My vision blurs. I need to see her. I steady my knees and move around Dad to find Mom lying unconscious on the bed. My stomach drops, and the world falls silent except for the whir in my ears at the sight of the cast wrapped around her right wrist. Her pale skin is almost as white as the bandage covering half her forehead.

"Is she—"

"Alive?" My mother's lashes flutter. Watery blue eyes meet mine, and the sounds of the hospital stream back in. Mom is awake. The vice of dread that's been crushing my heart since I stepped through the gates at the airport releases, and my chest doesn't hurt as much.

"Hey, Mom." I move to the side of the bed, avoiding the arm in the cast and taking her other hand. "How are you feeling?"

She sighs. "Like a silly old woman."

"What?" I muster a smile. "This wasn't your fault."

"I was rushing. Should have waited for Julio to move the flour sack, but the Andersons' wedding party was on my mind." She raises her bandaged hand. "Going to be fun making four hundred cupcakes one-handed."

I suppress the urge to roll my eyes. "Don't fret about that. I'm sure Julio or Sandy can help."

Mom frowns. "We planned on closing the bakery for our anniversary, so I gave them both the weekend off. I was supposed to have the cupcakes baked and delivered before our party tomorrow night." Mom's gaze fly to Dad's. "We need to call our guests, cancel the venue." Her gaze moves to the ceiling. "We won't get our money back."

Dad finds Mom's fingers sticking out from her cast and gives them a pat. "I don't care about the money."

"And you don't worry about the cupcakes." I turn to my brothers, who are both staring at my phone as if waiting in line at Tim Horton's for coffee. Am I the only one worried? I clasp the S of my necklace. The thin gold fails to calm the whirlpool of anxiety in my chest. I glance at the closed hospital room door, wishing for Nick's strength around me, for the surety of him. "Nick and I can make the cupcakes."

"Oh, Sarah." Mom's voice turns sweeter than the sugary glaze she puts on her snowflake cookies. "This is your holiday. You didn't come here to run the bakery for your injured mother."

"No, but I can, and I want to do it. It'll give me a chance to show off Mémère's kitchen to Nick. I've been talking about it for months, and he'll get the immersive experience."

Mom pulls at the covers. "If they let me go now, I can still make them."

Dad and I jump at the same time. We put a hand on one of her shoulders and lower her to the mattress.

"You're not going anywhere," he says.

"Well, I'm not staying here." There's the stubborn streak Mom and I share.

"I'm not sure you have any choice." Dad loosens his grip. "The doctors want to keep you another night to observe that bump. Make sure you don't have a concussion."

"I'm fine." Mom wriggles under our grasp.

"Mom. Nick and I will go and make the cupcakes right now." I step away. "Let us do this." I look at Dad. "Don't cancel. It's your anniversary, and we are celebrating. Connor style."

"Yeah, Sarah's right." Grayson hands my phone to me. "You deserve a party."

I turn to Mom. "You stay here and rest. We'll take care of everything."

Her face crumples like she's about to cry, but she nods. "Okay, honey. If you're sure you can do this."

"Absolutely." The knots in my stomach strain. I have no freaking idea if I can make four hundred cupcakes in a day, but I'm not letting her worry.

"I'll give you a ride." Grayson jangles the van's keys.

"I'll go with you. I can lick the icing bowl." Taylor grins. He has quite the sweet tooth. Must be from growing up in the bakery.

Nick's scowling at the screen of his phone when we emerge from the hospital room.

His brown eyes dart to mine, and I can't quite read the expression but my gut screams more bad news. "What's up?"

He shoves his phone in his pocket and gets out of the chair.

"Just some school stuff." He waves a hand between us like he's batting the idea away. "How's your mom?"

THREE

NICK

TODAY DECIDED TO DESTROY whatever expectations I had for this mini vacation. Instead of coffee, food, and lounging on the couch looking at Sarah's delighted face, I jam myself into a stiff chair in a hospital waiting room. So far, my impression of Canada consists of colorless airport corridors and gray hospital hallways. This is not how I imagined my introduction to Sarah's parents would go, but at least I'm here to lend a helping hand, shoulder, ear—whatever she needs.

The wooden armrests dig into my elbows, but if I close my eyes, I will doze off. This is not the time nor the place. I unearth my phone and check for messages. It's barely past five in LA, and I don't expect anyone to be awake on the West Coast, but my personal account pings with an email. I rub my eyebrow. A before-dawn message could only be from Ms. Hansley.

"Blaire release is confirmed for Monday at ten a.m. The first cut of the documentary is due to the editor Wednesday night. Plan to be at my office all day Wednesday. Any time after six a.m. works. The earlier we start, the more likely we are to get some sleep."

Finding a sub for my shift on Wednesday will be hard, but I can sweeten the deal by switching for a Friday night closing. Missing my Econ final on Wednesday isn't an option. If I drive Betty from Ms. Hansley's office to campus, take the two-hour exam, and come straight back, I'll be away for at least four hours. My knee bounces so high it bumps the phone out of my hand. I catch it mid-air, cross my feet at the ankles to keep still, and flip to my calendar app. My un-caffeinated, sleep-deprived brain refuses to put the pieces of the puzzle together, unable to see how the combination of events that need to happen on Wednesday is possible.

Sarah, Taylor, and Grayson emerge from the hospital room. Sarah's eyes are pools of sadness. Deep shadows under them and a line between her brows replace the excitement of being with her parents to celebrate their twenty-fifth anniversary.

"What's up?" she asks.

"Just some school stuff." I don't keep things from her anymore, but none of my woes matter right now. Her mom's in the hospital, and that's centerstage. "How's your mom?"

"Mom will stay for observation." Sarah blots her cheek with her sleeve. "Besides the broken wrist, she hit her head hard enough for the doctors to think it might be a concussion."

"Scary." Mike had a concussion after one of his MMA fights last year. He was wonky for a week. "Is she awake?"

Sarah rolls her eyes. "And ready to bake four hundred cupcakes that are due to be delivered tomorrow."

"Sucks. I'm sure her customers will understand."

That look of determination I know so well crosses her face. "We are not letting anyone down."

I love when she says we, but how are we and cupcakes related? "We?"

"The four of us should be able to do what Mom was planning to accomplish by herself."

Behind Sarah, Grayson and Taylor give each other a look I can only interpret as, "We're in trouble."

"I'll drive." Grayson tosses the keys up.

Sarah snatches them mid-air "I'll drive. You need to call Sandy and find out what kind of cupcakes the Andersons ordered."

Grayson waves his hands in a series of large X's. "Sandy will bite my head off."

"Better yours than any of ours. She has a sweet spot for you." Sarah ruffles his hair, even though he's a foot taller than her.

We storm out the hospital sliding door like baking Avengers on a mission to save the universe one cupcake at a time. I'd make the joke out loud if it were not for the grim expressions of the Connor clan. I press my lips together to suppress a giggle. Everything has the potential to be funny at this stage of my twenty-six-hour marathon day.

Sarah leads the way, and the three of us race to keep up. I'd love to wrap my arms around her and dampen the negative energy she's buzzing with, but I'm not sure she'd agree to pause her mission.

I add another gray blur—this time of highways—to my vision of Toronto. The road in the residential area is bumpy. Red streetcars glide on rails that crisscross the streets.

The neighborhood is lined with two- and three-story buildings stuck together block after block, shops and businesses at street level and living quarters above. Occasional bulky apartment buildings break up the patchy matrix. I capture some of the storefronts on my camera as Sarah silently drives.

She rounds a corner and turns into a back alley where the concrete road gives way to a rougher gravel parking spot. She parks near a peeling brick wall painted charcoal gray. We pile out of the car. A cinderblock addition in front of us has one door with the logo of Côté Fraise stenciled in white on the glass.

Sarah slides a metal silver key into the round handle of the glass door, and stands to the side to let me in. "Welcome to Côté Fraise."

The smell of baked goods hits me, and my stomach demands food. A corner of her mouth twitches and I expect a grin, but she tucks the snippet of that smile away and is back to the tight-lipped face I saw her use so much during the Starlight competition—her don't-mess-with-me face.

"Bathroom is to the left. Meet me in the kitchen." Her hands flash right and left before she careens into the hallway. Grayson and Taylor follow and throw save-us-please glances my way. I'm not sure there is anyone who can stop Sarah when she is in control mode.

The bathroom is white with strawberries of every possible size and shade on the tile, the cabinets, even the soap dispenser. The small mat under the toilet and cover on the lid of the toilet is a green shag with strawberries on it. The smell I love on Sarah packs a punch in the small space. It's strawberry on steroids, and the fact that the sink is closer to my knees than my waist isn't the most surprising part.

I leave my hands under the running water and admire the commitment to the theme. Even the toilet paper holder is a thick dark-emerald stalk with two red strawberries on each side of the roll. The only reminder that this is a place of work is a commercial-looking paper towel dispenser with a sign in English and French instructing employees to wash their hands before returning to work.

The hallway leads to a large open kitchen space. Sarah stands in the middle of a quiet room with a collection of pages in her hands. I hang my coat and hat on a hook next to several aprons.

"The theme is Autumn." She twirls a strand of hair between her fingers. "Sandy says they wanted pumpkin spice, red velvet, and lemon cupcakes with fondant leaves on top of white icing. That's a piece of cake."

"Four pieces of cupcakes, you mean." Taylor's eyes crinkle with mischief. His brother accompanies with a low he-he-he. Sarah glares at them, and the noise stops.

"Keep your humor for when the task is done. You are on fondant leaves duty." She gives Grayson one sheet of paper. "Remember, this is not for a child's birthday party. Think wedding, elegance, romance."

"Romance." Taylor resumes his chuckles, only to bite his lips shut when Sarah narrows her eyes. "Got it."

"Taylor—you are on liner duty. We'll use the brown parchment ones. Get the tins and start lining them."

"Nick." She swivels her head to the large stainless double-door fridge next to me. "See if you can find three boxes of cream cheese in the fridge."

The kitchen comes alive with four of us measuring, mixing, and not talking about what happened to their mom.

Sarah pins the recipes to the wall, crosses her arms, and stares at them. I haven't baked a cupcake in my life, but growing up in the bakery, she must've done this a million times.

She re-reads the text and presses her hands into her face. I hear a whimper. Her back curves, her body sags, and her shoulders quiver. The stern shell cracks, and the girl who's worried for her mom caves under the stress of the morning.

"Hey." I brush her arm.

Her hands grasp the counter, a sure sign she's attempting to hide her feelings. My heart feels her heart. I hate that she's in pain, and I'd do anything to bring back the sunny Sarah.

"We are on the same team. A partnership." I pry her hands away from the steel surface. "Talk to me. I'm here. I'm really here for you."

She turns her tear-stained face to me. "I can't."

FOUR

NICK

Sarah dabs her tears, as if she can force them back into her tear ducts.

"Talk to me." I catch her hands and wait for her to meet my gaze. "Just say what's on your mind."

"I can't do this." Her lips quiver. "This is impossible. Even baking four batches at a time we need five rounds. The cooling time alone will take two hours. Add on the decorations, it'll be close to four. Or more. How was she planning on finishing this by herself?" She's crying full force now, and the last words slur into a mushy mess.

I slide my arms around Sarah, and she tucks her face into my chest. Her rattling sniffs are damp, and I look around for something to dry her tears. She bunches my polo in her fists, drawing me closer, surrounding herself with my body. The crying isn't because this task might be an overreach, but because her mom's taken on too much.

"I understand where you get your overachiever drive from." I kiss the top of her hair, and the aroma of her strawberry conditioner tickles my nose.

Sarah's sobs are quiet, but my shirt is getting wetter. I rock her and take the weight of her emotions and worries off her tiny shoulders the best I can.

"I'm glad you're here with me," she whispers.

I hug her into me, all mixed up inside: my heart beats too fast, my guts twists. I wish there was something more substantial I could do. I wish her mom didn't need to spend the night at the hospital. I wish my love for her made everything better, always. "I'm glad I'm here with you too. Together we'll figure it out. You don't have to do it alone."

"How's she doing it alone?" Taylor shouts from the middle of the kitchen. Either my whisper was not quiet enough or that boy has better hearing than a bat.

Sarah turns, and the façade is back on. "That's two linings in the corner, not one. Pay attention to what you're doing, instead of eavesdropping on the adults."

"You're not an—"

"Taylor Francis Connor. Today in this kitchen, I'm in charge. And you wouldn't be mouthing off if I were Mémère. Or slacking, for that matter." Her hands fly to her hips "Do your job, and we'll get this order done and delivered before dinner."

My stomach rumbles again, the mention of dinner enough to get it complaining. Day-olds from Blend sound good to me right about now, but I'm not mentioning food.

In my pocket my phone sings *Over the Rainbow.*

"Your mom must be up." Sarah recognizes Mom's ringtone, steps away too fast for my liking, and pushes me to the exit.

"I'll call her back later. You need me here." My feet ignore her attempts to move me.

"I've got it under control. It's your first trip abroad. Go tell her you arrived to the great white plains of Canada safely."

"We're from Chicago," I say. The ringtone repeats. "She's aware I grew up with four months of snow a year."

Sarah pushes on my back. "Go talk to her and say hi. I'm totally stealing that Lemon Potato recipe she served at dinner last night. I can't be on her naughty list."

I catch the side of Sarah's face with my kiss and pull the phone out before the ringing stops.

"Morning."

"So you did land." Mom sounds worried.

I slap my forehead. Fuck. With everything that happened, I forgot to text her. "Yeah. All good."

She hums her disbelief. "You don't sound too good."

"Been a day." I step into the back alley and instantly regret not putting my jacket back on. There's no snow on the ground, but the chilly wind shocks the exposed skin of my neck, and the wet splotches on my shirt transform into ice-cold patches.

"You're three hours ahead. You can't complain at ten in the morning that it's been a day."

"Sarah's mom is in the hospital."

"I'm sorry. I didn't mean it. I—"

"She'll be okay. But we're taking care of a last-minute order at the bakery, and I stayed awake on the flight to catch up with schoolwork. I've never hated making graphs and spreadsheets this much. Why do professors care about them?" All the things I want to tell Sarah pour out of me. "Plus, I'm behind on the documentary Dad and I are working on. No matter how much I don't sleep, I can't seem to catch up—"

"Nicky." She uses her sensible voice. The one that got us through the divorce, the move, my mistakes. Practical and calm. "You're alive and well, and I can't ask for more. I'm sure school will be fine."

That's not like Mom to dismiss my education. She drilled into Mike and me that we need to pave our paths in life with hard work and good grades.

I wait for her to elaborate, to tell me I should keep pushing if I want to reach my dreams. My teeth chatter. I jump in place to keep my blood moving. At this rate, I'll need to go back inside or freeze. A cat crosses the alleyway, stops, looks at me as if to say, "You should have a coat on, dude," and disappears between two houses.

The silence on Mom's end of the line lasts a bit too long, and my already tense muscles cramp. I recognize Mom's silences. She has something else to say but isn't sure it's the right time.

There's a clicking noise on her end. "What is it, Mom?"

"It's good news, I promise."

Why does her voice sound like she's about to ask me to drink the castor oil Yiayia insisted made everyone's gut work better?

"Dad and I talked." An auspicious start of a sentence. I'm not a baby. They're not hiding that they're back in each other's lives but— "We're moving in together."

My feet freeze to the gravel while my heart continues to jump. It's yo-yoing up and down and can't figure out how to stop. Mom lives in Chicago. Dad lives in LA. The logistics of what she's talking about are not exactly evident. "Explain."

"After Mike moved in with Angie over the summer, and you moved to LA, I was alone in the house. It's too big for me. I played with the idea of renting a smaller apartment, but visiting you in September, and now, staying with Theo this week, this feels right. I don't want to be alone anymore."

In the ten years since divorcing Dad, I never once saw her flirt with another man, never mind go out on a date. I always thought it was fear of betrayal that held her back. Maybe it was devotion. I wish we were on a video call so I could see her face.

"You're moving in with Dad?" My voice squeaks on the last word.

"My lease is over in January, so it's perfect timing."

Almost too perfect. I want Mom and Dad to be happy, and I understand where both of them are coming from. I've seen how good they are together. What kid doesn't want their parents to be together? I pull at the numb lobe of my ear. But I also worry. I want her to be happy, not hurt. Just like with Sarah.

"What about your clients?"

"I'll find new clients in LA. A hair stylist with my experience won't go without a job. I always wanted to explore event make-up. LA is the perfect place to try." There's more clicking. Is she typing something on her ancient laptop? "Life isn't over at fifty. I'm starting a new chapter. I hope you're happy for me."

If she and Dad are serious, I'm not going to stand in their way. "I guess Sarah and I can count on coming over for dinner now and then."

"I insist. Every day if I had my way. But how about once a week?"

"It's on the calendar."

"Good. Now, the other reason for my call."

If that was good news, then the next thing must be bad. "What happened?"

"Nothing happened. Stop worrying." The clicking stops. "I was going to ask for your help, but I'm not sure now. With your school and you being behind, I'll figure it out."

If Mom needs my help, she'll get it. "I'll make time."

"Only if you can. I rented a POD that'll be delivered to LA later, but was hoping you'd fly up here and make the trip from

Chicago to LA in the minivan with me. Mike is working, and your father got a last-minute pitch request."

Someone's interested in Dad's screenplay? The warmth her words start in my gut counteracts some of the freezing air around me. Dad deserves another chance in his career.

"I don't feel comfortable driving across the country by myself."

"When?"

"That's why I'm not sure it's a good idea."

"Mom. Stop hedging. When?"

"Next Friday."

How long have Mom and Dad been thinking about moving in together?

"If we leave Friday morning," Mom says, "we should be in LA by Sunday evening or afternoon if we switch and keep pushing through."

Next week is already a mess, with the exam and the final edits on the documentary on Wednesday, work, and classes. I'll be beat, but there is a Film History exam session on Monday I can switch to. That'll free up my Friday. "I'll do it."

"I'll pay for your ticket."

I can't afford to argue with that.

"I'll take care of gas and food. I just need you to share the driving with me."

"A road trip. Like old times." When Mom, Mike, and I drove to Florida to visit my grandparents after they retired. A smile tugs at the corner of my mouth. "I'm in charge of the music."

"It's a deal. I love you, Nicky. Thank you for doing this."

"I love you too, Mom. Anytime."

My fingers are numb when I pry them off my phone. Taylor and Grayson run out the back door and almost stampede over me. I shiver as I watch them unearthing equipment from a small shed. I step back into Côté Fraise, which now smells like cupcakes, and my stomach resumes grumbling.

Five

Sarah

I DUMP THE PALE cubes of cream cheese into the bowl of the mixer, drop the paddle, and twist the dial to the lowest speed. Thank goodness cupcakes are not that hard to make. Not sure what I would have done if the party had requested butter tarts or mini éclairs. My fingers are turning white where they grip the steel counter, and I focus on the whir of the industrial mixer.

I can do this.

It's only four hundred cupcakes.

I press my palm below my ribs and shake my head.

The first two trays of red velvet sit on the cooling rack, and the next two are almost done in the oven. I need to get another two ready to go in when those are out. And make this icing, decorate, and deliver. My hand shakes, and I gulp air to steady it. I've helped Mom and Mémère do this a million times. Bake. Ice. Decorate. Pack.

Shit. The crates and boxes. Do we have enough?

I turn to ask Grayson to check on Mom's van and catch them both chipmunk-faced, empty wrappers crumpled in their hands. I grind my teeth. They give me their couldn't-help-it look, and I swallow my anger. "Every one of those you eat means we stay here that much longer."

Grayson at least has the sense to hang his head. Taylor grins at me as his fingers inch toward the closest cupcake like a spider returning to its web. I slap his hand and point to the back door. "Go. Get the crates from the van to pack the cupcakes."

They both have the wherewithal to follow my request, grab their coats, and hurry out of the room. With my brothers gone, I'm alone in the kitchen.

This is my first time at the bakery since Mémère's death last February, when I came for the funeral. The hole in my heart that was born the day she died doesn't seem capable of closing. Everything looks the same, but it isn't. I search for the missing piece. The tidy rows of baking pans are still on the wire shelves. The jars of spice labels still face out. Mom's stark white apron—with the stitched strawberry dangling off the R in Fraise— still hangs on a hook by the door. Beside it is the strawberry-patterned one Mémère wore. Like a snag on a sweater, the sight of it unravels the yarn of memories.

Mémère putting the picture of her and her favorite customers on the wall above the sinks. Her delight at the strawberry doilies I crocheted in middle school. The tears in her eyes as she told me the story of the enormous teapot she carried wrapped in a towel on her trip to Canada from France. The images of our adventures together saturate and overwhelm me. The gaping emptiness aches.

She is what isn't. Isn't in the bakery. Isn't in our lives.

The bakery is all that's left of her.

The back door opens, and I half expect Mémère to walk through it, white curls poking out from under her latest funky hat. The pang in my heart assures it won't happen. The sight of Nick dulls the pain, and when his brown eyes meet mine, it almost disappears.

"Are you sure it won't snow today?" Nick wipes his boots on the mat and rubs his hands together. "I swear it's below freezing."

"No snow until tomorrow." An unexpected snowstorm today won't help with the cupcake delivery. Can we even pull this off? "Did you see my brothers out there?"

Nick jabs a thumb over his shoulder. "There seems to be a game of pickup hockey happening in the alleyway. Sticks and a net appeared out of nowhere. Grayson's in goal."

I huff. "Of course." I love my brothers, but unless Mémère or Mom are testing a new recipe, they are essentially useless. Today seems to be no different. I slam the door of the overhead cupboards and switch off the mixer. Bowl in hand, I scamper between the prep and cooling tables, avoiding the displaced tile by the oven, and grab the free pans.

"What can I do?" Nick comes to stand beside me, watching me intently.

The oven beeps, an acknowledgment that it's at the correct temperature, as if the device wants to reassure me I'm doing everything correctly. I pour the batter into the cupcake tins I prepared earlier.

"You look like you know what you're doing." Nick appears impressed. My cooking skills in the apartment leave something to be desired, and I never have time to bake the few recipes I'm capable of.

"Mémère used to let me help with the cupcakes. She claimed they were foolproof." The kitchen echoes with her voice whispering, "Even this fool." An image of Mémère's flour-covered finger bopping me on the nose floats before me. The back of my throat stings.

Nick turns the second pan of twenty-four around like I did with the first so I'm not pouring batter across the twelve I've already filled.

"Thanks. Most cupcakes are essentially the same basic recipe with a few different ingredients. Mémère brought her family recipe with her when she immigrated to Canada." I lift the first tray and trek to the oven. "She started selling them at local markets on the weekends as a way to make extra money. After a while, she added her signature strawberry tarts, pies, etc., playing off her maiden name Fraise."

"So that's where the strawberry obsession came from." Nick follows with the second tray.

I pop open the oven, shove the trays in, and gently close the door to prevent too much heat from escaping. "Mom says she'd be sold out before noon, and everyone told her she should open a bakery. So she did." I stretch my arms out. "She bought this place in the '80s and gained a following." I gesture to the pictures on the wall.

Nick leans across the sink and inspects the photos.

"This is Natalie. She comes here every Tuesday morning for a chocolate croissant and a coffee." My stomach whines at the mention of real food. Nick's stomach copies mine with a higher-octane rumble. We haven't eaten anything since the plane. I run my hands through my hair. "You must be starving."

The crooked smile I love spreads across Nick's face. "I could eat."

I poke him in the ribs on the way back to the fridge. "I saw some chicken we can use to make sandwiches. Slice a few of the croissants in the basket over there."

"Does your mom make these as well?"

"Yup." I hunt in the vegetable drawer and find lettuce, cucumbers, and tomatoes to go with the poultry. "But they take forever to make so we only bake them on Tuesdays and Fridays. I was hoping you'd get to try some fresh ones, but they are beyond my abilities."

We're eating the sandwiches as Grayson and Taylor bound in the back door, crates in hand. "Did you make some for us?"

"I forgot you were here." I squint and pretend I don't see them.

"We'd just screw things up if we tried to help." Taylor sets the crates by the wall. "We help by staying out of the kitchen."

"Then make the sandwiches yourselves. And don't forget to go downstairs and put together the boxes." I do some quick math, hoping I get it right. "We'll need at least sixteen to fit four hundred."

"I hate folding cardboard. I always get a paper cut." Grayson tosses a croissant in the air.

"Well, it's that or you try your hand at icing the batch that's cooling."

Grayson looks at Taylor and they both shake their heads.

"I thought so. Be careful with the corners. Don't bend them. Even if the bride and groom never see them, they must be professional. The bakery's reputation is on the line."

The sandwiches disappear before the trays are out of the oven, and we return to the long list of tasks to accomplish before we can drive the cupcakes to the venue. Baking reminds me of bartending, but it's nothing like screenwriting. I move, count, bend, use my hands and arms, stretch, wash, measure, re-measure. The rhythm is no longer familiar, and I need to think about every step, every ingredient, and double-check. Mistakes and starting over is not in our time or budget.

I chase away the ideas Karina and I talked about that my fingers are impatient to write down. I can't let them distract me from the tasks at hand. I lift my chin. I must make Mémère proud.

"To get the consistency right, we make the icing in smaller batches." I hear Mémère's words coming out of my mouth and a sense of déjà vu causes the room to sway. I close my eyes and search for a sense of calm. Nick's fingers find mine, and my eyelids flutter open to catch him staring down at me. "I miss her."

His mouth slants south. "I'm sorry."

"She would have loved you." *Like I do* is what I want to say, but I can't get the words past the lump in my throat.

"If she was anything like you, I would have loved her too." Nick nudges my hand and looks around at the impressive rows of cupcakes.

"I had no idea so much went into these. At Blend, I just pull them out of the box and put them in the display case."

"This is why Mom is awake at four a.m. every day."

Nick props a hip against the counter. "What happens when your mom wants to retire?"

The pride I felt at the collection of perfectly baked cupcakes drains. Nick has touched on the sore spot that keeps reappearing between Mom and me. I bite my cheek. It's always been assumed we'd run the place together, follow in her and Mémère's footsteps.

"Growing up in the bakery, I was supposed to fall in love with the place. Which I did, but not in the way Mom did. When I left for LA, they were considering opening another location, and there was talk of me running it. That ended when Mémère got sick. My brothers stated long ago they weren't interested."

"I'm sure if you put your mind to it, you could do anything."

"Thanks for the vote of confidence." I look for the icing sugar container. "But I'm pretty sure you should be able to bake to own a bakery. And that gene skipped a generation."

Nick looks over at the cupcakes. "You could've fooled me."

"We're not done yet." The icing sugar container is on one of the higher shelves, and I stand on my tippy toes, my fingers barely brushing the corners. Nick comes to the rescue, plucking the jar out like it's full of feathers and swinging it over me. "Thanks. But to answer your question, Mom's years away from retirement."

"My mom talks about retirement all the time. Like it's a vacation she's been planning for years."

Nick settles the canister on the counter beside the mixer.

"Won't that change now? I mean, she and your dad are . . . well they seemed like a couple yesterday." We celebrated American Thanksgiving with his parents, and it was super obvious they were back together.

Nick's index finger runs along his chin. "Seems it's official. She's moving in with Dad."

"That's great. When?"

"She asked me to fly to Chicago and help drive her stuff to LA next weekend."

"That soon? How d'you feel about it?"

"Good, I guess?" He scans the floor. "Would be great to have Mom nearby again. And her food."

My lips curve in a smile. His mom uses food as a love language, just like Mémère did, just like my mom does. I felt more at home at Theo's apartment when she was there than on my previous visits.

I scoop a cup of icing sugar and dump it into the mixer. Clouds of white powder billow up, coating my face and hair. I completely forgot the fine sugar has to be added slowly and carefully. I stomp my foot. The sweet dust gets caught in my throat, and I break into a coughing fit.

Nick jumps. "I'll get you some water."

I struggle to catch my breath.

He drags me to the stool in the corner and hand me the glass.

I down the cool liquid and clear my throat. "I'm okay."

"Is it safe to inhale that stuff?" Concern is etched in his gaze.

I grin. "It's just sugar." I run my tongue over my lips, licking the delicious substance. "Tastes good."

He leans in and kisses my forehead. "Mmm. It does." He peppers soft kisses across my skin, along my cheekbone, and the tip of my nose. "Didn't think you could get any sweeter." He nips at my neck. Tingles spread to my navel. If he keeps doing this, the cupcakes will never be finished.

The oven has a different plan and beeps, indicating the next batch is ready to come out.

Over the next half hour, we twirl billowy white icing in thick ribbons onto the tops of the cupcakes, sprinkle them with red sugar crystals, and nestle perfectly into place the few decent fondant leaves Grayson managed to make.

I stand back and survey the forty-eight completed cupcakes ready to be boxed up. Mémère would be proud.

Only three hundred and fifty-two more to go.

Six

NICK

THE ROOM AHHHS IN unison as the final kiss of Rudo and Isabel ends, and El's voice croons in the background. I can recount minute-by-minute what happens in *Indigo*, so I do my favorite thing: watch others watch my creation.

Our creation.

Mrs. Connor runs a tissue under her eyes, and Mr. Connor raises his wife's hand that's not in a cast and kisses it. They gaze at each other, and although their physical appearance has nothing to do with our characters on the screen, the love they share is the same the actors brilliantly captured on film. I rub the tender spot under the lapels of my suit. Love that endured through distance and time. Twenty-five years of marriage hasn't dimmed their affection.

"And will there be part two?" Mrs. Connor asks Sarah over her husband's head. "Or is showing what happens after you get married not a worthy subject?"

"Lots of movies talk about marriages. I'll add it to my list of scripts to write." Sarah actually pulls out her phone and starts typing. I've seen her notes file labeled "IDEAS," and it has a dozen in there already.

"We'll be happy to tell you what love is like when you live together 24/7 with jobs, kids, and schedules." Mrs. Connor's words do not match their touches, glances, even the way they finish each other's sentences. I've seen them anticipate their partner's needs and silently move in unison. With a pad of my thumb, I draw a circle on my girlfriend's wrist. Do Sarah and I look like that?

Grayson flips on the lights and switches off the big-screen TV attached to the wall at the far end of the private room they rented at Essie's, their favorite restaurant. First it was home movies, then a showing of *Indigo*. The guests turn back to their plates and drinks, and the silence during the film erupts into the roar of a party in full swing.

"Time for another round of champagne to celebrate Annelise's and Ian's twenty-five-year journey." A man with a shock of white hair that Sarah introduced as Mr. Connor's boss pops another bottle of champagne and passes it around. I stare at the couple we are celebrating tonight. They are the postcard of love, and that's what I want for Sarah and me.

"Would you like some champagne?" Sarah passes the bottle my way after she refills her glass.

"Funny. Not twenty-one, remember?"

Her eyes sparkle in the candlelight illuminating the room. "I'm serious. You're in Canada. The legal drinking age is nineteen. One of the many great things about living here. If you'd like a beer, they have a tasting menu from local breweries and my favorite West Coast IPA or"—Sarah leans in and whispers —"let me dust off my place behind the bar. This is where I learned my bartending skills. I can go ask my friend, Ivy, who still works here to let me mix you an Old Fashioned."

Goosebumps run down my neck. Still not a fan of Old Fashioneds, even though the cocktail was the reason I met her, but the promise of something else is in her voice, and I definitely want that.

I swallow the bite of steak I was chewing. "Beer would work. An IPA?"

"Be right back." Sarah disappears through the double doors into the main dining room of Essie's.

"Thank you for making us the stars of your movie." Mr. Connor bows in my direction. I should thank them for having such an interesting love story. Helps me pretend I know more than most kids in my film classes. I've used some of the tricks I learned while shooting *Indigo* for the prison documentary. He kneads my shoulder. "I can't imagine a better present for our twenty-fifth than the love of my life immortalized on-screen."

"That was Sarah. The words and the story are hers. I just made sure they came together."

"Just. That is a huge undertaking." Mr. Connor raises his glass. "To love and movies."

Many glasses around the table join his. With his drink in hand, he follows Grayson to the next clump of guests.

Taylor plops beside me. "Can you believe this spread?"

"Your parents have lots of friends." My family wouldn't be able to fill a table, never mind the giant private room of Essie's Bar and Grill. My phone vibrates in my jacket pocket, and I pull it out.

Sarah: We'll have to pay a fine. They switched the drinking age to twenty-one. You're in violation.

The hair rises on the back of my neck and my throat goes dry. I glance at Sarah's empty seat and show the text to Taylor beside me. "Did you know about this?"

He looks up, grins, and points his index fingers at me. "Gotcha."

"Sorry?"

He puts a hand on my shoulder. "It's all good. Grayson has Sarah's phone again."

Punching Sarah's brother in front of their mother is not a good idea, so I call up old Nicky and force a smile. "Funny."

"Can you blame us? After she told us how you two met, we were dying to throw it in your face. Your reaction was priceless, by the way."

The phone beeps and a grainy photo of my scrunched eyebrows, half-open mouth, and squinting eyes might be the least flattering photo anyone has ever taken of me.

Sarah: Perfect for my home screen.

I find Grayson's retreating figure but decide to stay put and not chase him. The tablecloth hides my clenched fists. I see it for what it is. They're testing me. Watching for my reaction. I twist in my seat away from them and offer a smile to Sarah's mother instead.

"Could I have a word with you?" Mrs. Connor points to Sarah's empty chair between us. Because of the boot on her right leg and the cast on her left wrist, Sarah ordered her mom to not even think of moving and inch.

"Sure." I pull on the sleeves of my button-down shirt and suit jacket as I check the doors for Sarah's return. No sign of her, so time to face the music.

"I think you know what this is about." Mrs. Connor's tone is cool, and its iciness coats my skin. I have no freaking clue what this could possibly be about. "Sarah is not a girl you can play with."

"I—"

Mrs. Connor lifts her palm to prevent me from talking. "Hear me out. I'm not the enemy here, but I can't watch my daughter get hurt when she could do so much better."

Much better than me? My pulse beats in my temples. How much has Sarah told her about my past? I exhale slowly. That's not me anymore. I keep my words behind my clenched teeth.

"You can't derail her."

Why would I ever want that? Sarah deserves to reach the goals she set for herself.

"I don't want her to be glued to you because she wants to be near you." Mrs. Connor's tone has the same bossy quality Sarah has when she's determined. Times ten. "My daughter will make her own choices, and I want you to promise me you won't stand in her way."

I have no idea where this is coming from, because I'm the biggest advocate of Sarah's pursuits. "I—" I try again.

"One more thing." She crumples the tissue in her hand. "Your movie is romantic and about choosing love over a career, but if Sarah has to, I hope she chooses herself." Mrs. Connor stares at her husband laughing, surrounded by a group of Sarah's friends. "You don't want to go through life watching the person you love quit on their dreams. It's a lot less romantic than the movies make it out to be."

The base of my skull prickles. There's a story there, and I'm not sure it's the one Sarah is aware of, because from every sentence she's written or told me about her parents, they are the happiest pair living the life they've always wanted.

"My plan is to give her both. I've imagined us getting old together, making movies together" —making kids together is the other dream of mine I'm not ready to voice yet—"one step at a time."

The getting old part isn't as enticing. The balding head, dad bod, and stooped shoulders of Sarah's dad are a big change from the shock of blond hair and slender build I saw in the pictures around their house. Ian Connor at thirty-three beamed at the camera with his arms around Annelise's waist, baby Sarah on his lap. Ian Connor at fifty-seven has earned the wrinkles on his face, yet the calm but powerful glow still shines in his eyes when he watches his wife and kids bicker or laugh.

A shadow crosses Sarah's mother's face. "Life rarely lets you have it all. You will have to make choices. One of you might need to walk away."

How can she ask this of me? My heart cracks at the mere thought of it. Walking away from Sarah is not a promise I can make. Changing my life to make sure hers prospers—yes, putting her career first—I can see that, but not having Sarah in my life? That is not an option. Not ever. I square my shoulders. "I love your daughter, Mrs. Connor."

She places her uninjured hand on my arm. "At this point, you better call me Annelise."

"Annelise, I love your daughter more than I have ever thought possible to love someone. What I can promise you is that I will always put Sarah first."

She raises an eyebrow, and it reminds me of Sarah when I say something she doesn't believe I really mean. "Even if that puts you last?"

"Even if I sell cameras or sling coffee for the rest of my life."

"I don't want you to do that either. You're someone's child too. And I'm sure your mother would not be happy to hear this." She shakes her head. "You need to understand that you are both too young to make a lasting decision about a romantic partner. It may feel like I don't know what I'm talking about, but trust me, I do. With the experience of my fifty-five years on this earth, I'm telling you the honeymoon period doesn't last. You need to each be your own person before you can be a true couple together."

"I disagree." Did I just say that to Sarah's mom, the woman I'm desperate to impress? "We can become what we want supporting each other, side by side."

The sad look in her eyes burns through me. "That's not how life works."

"It's how our life will work." Determination sets in my veins. Annelise needs to understand I'm serious. "We are not you. We are different people, and if you don't believe in us, I do."

"I just don't want you to rip my daughter's heart into pieces." She slams her fist on the table, and her empty champagne glass clinks against her water glass. The room falls silent, and eyes train on us.

"Mom, you okay?" Sarah sits on my chair and places a tall pint by my plate.

Annelise sips water from her glass. "Is it time for the next dose of my pain meds?"

Mr. Connor reappears by our side. "Another thirty minutes." He glares at me as if I were drowning puppies. "But I can give you an ibuprofen to tie you over." He places his hand around his wife's shoulder.

"Please." She closes her eyes. "It's time to go home."

Sarah squirms beside me. "But there's cake."

Annelise's eyes open. "I'll eat a slice tomorrow morning. I don't think I can stomach anything else."

"I'll go home with you." Sarah stands and helps her mother out of her chair.

"You stay." Annelise's gaze sweeps my way. "Have fun."

Their family is nothing like my family, and a tiny corner of me wishes my parents were like this: together throughout my childhood. A dad who's warm and welcoming. A shadow flits across my heart. But I am who I am because of the way my life took me through the hard shit.

SEVEN

NICK

"YOU TAKE THE BED." Sarah slips from under my arm and elbows me onto the Maple Leafs comforter.

"No way." I snatch Sarah's wrist and drag her between my thighs. "It's yours tonight."

Last night, after we delivered the four hundred cupcakes and visited Annelise at the hospital, I passed out on Sarah's twin bed only to wake up to her alarm blaring in my ear.

"I don't mind. I'm smaller." She fiddles with the picture of her jumping in front of Essie's, a bartender certificate in her hands.

I take the picture and set it on the bedside table. "I mind." I sit her on one of my knees and snuggle her into my chest. There's no way my girl is sleeping one more night on the camp cot her parents crammed into her room. The thing looks like it was built for a child and can not be comfortable.

"Well . . ." There's a look in her eyes that sends a hot spike down my torso. I'm going to love the next words out of her mouth. "I'm sure we could find a way to both sleep in my bed." She tugs on my shirt. "Or not sleep."

This is the best idea ever. She undoes my top button, but I'm faster, pulling the material over my head and tossing it. My elbow slams against the pale blue wall. Pain jolts up my bicep. "Fuck."

Her hand clamps on my mouth. "My parents are just down the hall."

I lick her palm.

She releases me. "Hey."

"Sorry," I say.

Her fingers leisurely slip down and unzip my pants. "I'm not."

Two can play at this.

My lips find hers and my pulse skitters. I've kissed her hundreds of times but the sensation of her mouth on mine sends my heart speeding faster than a double ristretto. As if on fast-forward, Sarah shimmies out of her dress. Unable to tear my hands from her face, I bound to my feet and kick off my shoes. Her greedy fingers get rid of my slacks. Every new point of skin-to-skin contact ignites better than kindling. Sarah wriggles, and the friction skyrockets my temperature. Heat spreads across my body like a wildfire. Her rapid breaths fan the flames beneath my ribs. Wrapped in each other, we fall onto her tiny single bed.

She straddles me and I like the new position: her on top, confident hands on my chest. Everything turns slow and steady. We both find what we are after in this pleasurable pace. Our mutually beneficial groove. She leans forward and kisses the spot over my heart, and the organ responds by galloping. Her pushing me to the edge is my favorite game. Those pouty lips of hers trail across my skin, making their way south. Her exploring my body is a gift and a curse. She's a goddess and I'm her sacrifice. I stuff my knuckles into my mouth to muffle my moan.

Sarah looks up. Her eyes are full of love as mine must be. The tendons in my neck strain. Unable to hold in my response any longer, I gasp, turn us over, and wrap her legs around my waist.

She's mine. And I'm hers. We're one again.

Her gasp matches mine. Her body reacts to mine. Her heart screams to mine.

I hear what she is not saying and whisper the words for both of us: "I love you."

Sunlight streams through the window. Sarah's golden hair spills across my chest. She breathes in and I breathe out. Our languid pulses delay the start of the day. One more second. One more minute before we part. I still. She's clinging to me like I'm her life raft in the middle of the ocean. Even though my left side is numb, I revel in the weight of her, the bliss of supporting her as she sleeps.

As if she senses I'm awake, Sarah stirs. "Morning." Her voice is husky.

I stroke her arm with my free hand. "No alarms for us today."

She rubs her nose into my neck. "I like waking up this way."

"Me too." Tingles of warmth radiate across my skin, a pleasant contrast to my numb arm. "This twin-bed scenario isn't that bad."

She slides her thigh off my hip, relieving some of the pressure on my left side. I flex my fingers, trying to alleviate the pins and needles as blood rushes to my extremities.

"Not complaining." She wriggles again, and parts of my body wake much faster than my brain. "But I'd choose our bed at home if I could."

I close my eyes. *Vampire Club* is on hiatus. With what's happening with her mom and the bakery, I can feel the divide in her heart: come home with me or stay here to do what's needed. The pins and needles charge from my arm into my heart. I'm not ready for us to be away from each other.

To delay the conversation, I pull her tighter to me and find her lips for a good-morning kiss. Our little ritual before one or both of us goes to work. My good morning 'I love you' to her.

She bites my lip. The sweet kiss turns into a desperate tangle of tongues and teeth. When we break apart, she's as breathless as I am. Her glossy eyes search mine. "Nick."

It's not time yet.

The flight home is hours away.

I tuck a flyaway hair behind her ear, memorizing the feel of the silky strand. She's here right now, and that's what matters. "One more kiss."

Her fingers glide across my skin and find the base of my neck. She grants me the kiss.

Deep. Frenzied. Breathtaking. Sad.

I can taste the 'I love you' she never says, her lips speaking louder than her words.

A light rap on the bedroom door interrupts us. Her mouth retreats, but her forehead stays pressed to mine, hot puffs fanning my cheek.

"Honey," her mom says through the door. "Dad's starting the coffee. Do you and Nick want crepes?"

Sarah creates a tiny gap between us and whispers, "You must try my dad's crepes. They're amazing."

"Everything your family makes is amazing." Including her.

"Sounds good. Thanks, Mom. We'll be down soon," she shouts toward the door.

"No rush. There's plenty of time."

Except there isn't. There's never enough time. And my time with Sarah is dwindling.

Beside me she shifts and avoids my eyes. I save her from this agony and say the words she can't get out. "You're not coming home with me today, are you?"

Her nails dig into my skin, like I might fly away. "I . . . I need to stay here."

"Hey." I find her gaze and show her I understand. "I get it. I'd do the same if it were my mom. Or anyone I care about." I skim her cheek with my finger. "You need to be here right now. Your mom needs you."

"Just for a week. Until she gets the boot off, and we hire a new shift manager." Her fingers find mine. "Interviews with several candidates are already set up, and once we hire more staff, she'll have enough people helping take care of the bakery. Even with her broken wrist." Sarah winces with the last words.

I stare at her. "Take the time you need. I'm sure Siobhan and Ryan can cover at The Diamond Club."

Her head bobs, but the glassy stare is back. "I only have the weekend shift. I'll call them after breakfast." Her eyes search mine again. "Are you sure you're okay with this?"

"Okay? I'll never be okay without you." I nuzzle her nose with mine to lighten my words. "But you should do this, and somehow I'll survive. Will you be okay here? Working with your mother?"

She snickers. "Not sure. We'll likely be at each other's throats by the end of the week, and she'll probably try to kick me out of the house, but we'll manage. It's only temporary."

Eight

NICK

Instead of inhaling hotdogs or pies during eating competitions, they should try crepes. Every filling Sarah's dad offers tastes like triangles of heaven. I thought the ham-and-cheese was my favorite, but the Nutella and banana version was the bomb. Both are coma and euphoria inducing.

This one with homemade strawberry jam reminds me of Sarah: the smell, the flavor, the tenderness. I should not be comparing my girlfriend to food, but I would eat both every day if I could. I pick another strawberry-jam-infused crepe and pop a piece into my mouth. Summer in one bite. Yes, this is the winner.

"You must have been starving." Annelise places a third strawberry-jam-filled crepe on my plate.

"I'm always starving," I want to say, but between yesterday's feast at their twenty-fifth anniversary and today's breakfast extravaganza with every flavor of crepe known to man, I haven't been hungry for a second. In LA, my neglect of the gym was manifesting as fewer muscles and more of my ribs showing. If I lived in this household, it would be back to how life was with Mom and her Greek versions of delicious foods. If Annelise and Mom got together and combined the Greek and the French recipes . . . they'd create something great. Or terrible.

"Have you decided whether you're coming back for Christmas?" Mr. Connor asks me.

Sarah turns our way. She must've heard the question, but she's on the phone with Air Canada, switching her flight from tonight to next Sunday.

"The idea was to spend Christmas in LA and take the red-eye to be here for Boxing Day," I say. I couldn't refuse Mom's request to spend Christmas with her and Dad. And Sarah assured me Boxing Day is just as important and fun with her family. "Sarah promised I can play hockey on the lake."

"That can be arranged." Mr. Connor places a piping hot crepe on the platter in the middle of the table, and Annelise slathers it with Nutella and places bananas in neat circles over the chocolate spread before she folds it. My eyes want to eat that one, but my stomach swirls, begging, "No more." With a plane to catch, I might be better off stopping with the crepe that's already on my plate.

Taylor snatches the Nutella crepe, shoves half of it into his mouth, and starts talking. "I don't hold back." He bends his arm to show off his budging bicep. He's broader than I ever was, and although he's barely taller than my shoulder, for a seventeen-year-old, he's stronger than I was at his age.

"No need to go easy on me." I sip my orange juice. "I'll bring my skates."

"You can borrow my championship stick." Grayson bites the maple syrup crepe I haven't tried yet.

"I can bring my own as well." Did Mom already pack it in the POD?

"You're the first person Grayson has ever offered to lend his hockey stick to." Mr. Connor says it as if I won a gold medal.

"He's the first person Sarah brought home to meet the fam." Taylor snatches the crepe Annelise just finished covering with jam.

That's news to me. My gaze flies to the room my girlfriend is pacing in.

"Hmm." My mouth is busy chewing the last bite. I'm aware of her boyfriends in LA before we got together. She must've had others in Toronto. I didn't realize how significant Sarah's invitation to meet her parents was. My chest expands. I do feel like I won a gold medal.

"The food. The real hockey. You'll see how awesome life here is and come visit more." Grayson winks.

"Or move here." Annelise taps the jam-smeared knife against her plate. "Seeing Sarah more than twice a year—"

"Maybe we can go visit them in LA." Mr. Connor places a hand on his wife's shoulder.

"In July, Taylor goes to Western for university, and then we'll be empty nesters. I'm not sure I'm ready to see my children only on major holidays."

"I'm still in Toronto, Mom." Grayson points to himself.

"And at the rate I see you, you might as well be in a different country as well."

Sarah comes into the kitchen brandishing a piece of paper. "Done. I'm flying back next Sunday. Karina and I are moving our writing sessions online for this week." With the adjustments Annelise's fall triggered, Sarah hasn't been writing nearly as much as she normally does. "Ryan's paying back the money I loaned him for the rent, that'll cover my share for the month. And seven days should give Nick enough time to miss me"—she tugs on my shirt and plants a kiss on my cheek—"and for Mom to get tired of me and send me home instead of complaining how she doesn't see me enough."

"Toronto will always be your home, no matter where you choose to live," says Annelise. She and Sarah exchange a series of glances and lip shapes that tell me they've had this conversation many times before.

Sarah hugs her mom and dad and play-punches her brothers. "Let's go, or I can't guarantee you'll make it to the flight on time." She drags me out of my seat. "Then you'll come back and be lured to stay here forever. But for now, you have stuff to do in LA."

I have more stuff to do than she knows. Between the four hundred cupcakes, helping Sarah set up for the anniversary, the quickest trip to the CN Tower and the drive by the Scotiabank arena to say, "I saw some of Toronto," and my body deciding it needed eight uninterrupted hours of sleep two nights in a row, my plans to complete the Econ report or do anything for the documentary went bust. I have six hours on the plane, and without Sarah on the flight, I should get a good chunk of work done. But a good chunk is not enough. The crepes sit heavy in my stomach. Might be an all-nighter again tonight.

In the airport I hold Sarah as long as I can, inhaling her strawberry scent like I can intake enough to survive the week without her. I'm not sure I can, but she can't leave her mom now. I squeeze my teeth. I'll find a way to make it until 8:29 p.m. next Sunday when her flight lands in LA.

"You have to go." Her words slice our cocoon.

I let go of Sarah enough to find her lips. There isn't time for a long slow kiss, the kind I could share with her for a lifetime. Instead, I cram a week's worth of passion into the sixty-some seconds I figure I have before I miss my flight.

I consider missing my flight.

Blend can open without me. They'll find a way. I kiss Sarah.

I can find someone to get the notes from the classes I'll miss. I kiss Sarah.

Dad can find someone to hold the camera for Blaire's release Monday morning. I stop kissing Sarah.

Her eyes sparkle, and her chest is rising and falling rapidly. She looks beautiful.

Fuck. I hate this. I do not want to leave her. "I love you."

She presses her forehead into my chest in what I now consider her silent "I love you," as she seems to repeat it after I say the three words. Her hands press against my hips, and she steps away. My chest caves in. This feels like we're living the scene from *Indigo* where Rudo leaves Isabel.

But it's not. Because Sarah will be back in my arms next Sunday.

The report I submit on Monday is shoddy work. My Econ professor will know it too. Which means without a perfect score for the exam on Wednesday, my GPA will drop below 3.5, and the scholarship I've been relying on to cover my tuition and books will be in jeopardy. I slam the pastry case shut.

That cannot happen.

After Wil and El skipped town, the new afternoon shift barista I hired makes my work life miserable. Vito takes thirty seconds to butter toast, when it's a five-second thing max. Sloths would do a faster job. He's excellent at chatting up the customers, and some of them love it, but that slows the process even more, and the morning lines have been getting so long, customers who are regulars are opening the door, seeing the wait, and leaving. I shove the croissant in the bag. I'll have a conversation with Vito, but not today.

"Taking a break," he tells me like clockwork even though I haven't had a break all shift. The line is still to the door. I grit my teeth. His break is his right. I can't make him skip it, even though I want to.

"Next," I shout.

"A large latte and the ham-and-cheese sandwich." Professor Takamado points to the display and meets my eyes. "Nick? That's why you smell like coffee during my classes. How come I've never seen you here before? I eat lunch here every Tuesday."

"I usually open the place but had to film the end of my documentary this morning, so I switched." I pack the scoop with coffee and start the espresso.

"You're filming a documentary? What class is it for, and how come it's the first time I'm hearing about it?"

"It's not for school. It's a job." I pour the milk into the frother and shout over the noise of two machines. "I'm filming inmates before they're about to get out of prison, then on their release day, and we'll do more footage early next year, when they've been out for a while."

He nods. "That sound fascinating. Care to show me what you've got?"

"I'm not done yet, but I'll be putting together a version tomorrow." I create a leaf design in the foam of his coffee.

"Listen, I'll be honest." He takes the cup I slide across the counter. "Have you heard of the Silver Screen Showcase?" Heard of it. It's on my list of things to apply for next year. There's a scholarship attached to winning that would cover most of my tuition. "None of my second years are showing any promise. I saw what you did with the Starlight Foundation but that's not eligible. If your documentary is any good—"

"Oh, it's good." Did I just say that?

He raises an eyebrow. "I'll be the judge of that."

"But isn't Silver Screen only for sophomores?"

"There are exceptions. For outstanding talent."

He thinks I'm outstanding talent? I'm glad I'm done with the foam design because my hands shake. "I'll run it by Ms. Hansley."

"Ms. Hansley and I go way back." Sandwich and coffee in hand, he heads for the exit. "Get it to me by end of class Thursday."

At three a.m. my head hits my pillow. Two hours of sleep is better than zero, and no amount of caffeine was keeping my eyes open. I scroll through the photos Sarah sent me of pastries from Côté Fraise I don't get to eat. I text her an update on my day and five star emojis pop onto my screen when I mention the showcase.

My yawn nearly breaks my jaw, and I turn on my side, wishing Sarah was here. The bed is too large and too cold without her.

Me: Love you.

I close my eyes and dream of the day when she's back, and my life is sunny and full of lazy mornings.

NINE

Sarah

MY CHILDHOOD ROOM IS dark, and the house is quiet. The clickety-clack of Karina's keyboard is the only sound that messes with the somber night outside. My fingers hover over the letters, and I stare at the cursor blinking in the middle of the paragraph. The first draft of the screenplay we are co-writing should be done. Instead, we're behind. Or I should say, I'm behind. I got the characters into the gondola of the Pacific Wheel on Santa Monica Pier but seem unable to find the harsh, gut-punching words that will break their fragile love. Writing it feels wrong. It makes me miss Nick too much. I want to reach for my phone and scroll through his latest photos, but I'm on deadline. Two days without him shouldn't be that big of a deal, but my mind is only interested in happy endings.

The timer on Karina's end beeps.

"Five-minute break. Let's count the words." Karina's face is backlit by the floor lamp in her bedroom. Writing together when we are on opposite sides of the continent has proven more of a challenge than either of us expected. Midnight to three in the morning in LA, three to six a.m. for me, is what we ended up with. We wrap up in time for me to start baking and for her to go to bed. I would much rather be on Karina's end of this deal, but when I'm done at four in the afternoon, it's still the middle of the workday for Karina. By the time she's home from her temp job at six p.m., it's nine here and the only thing I'm capable of is brushing my teeth and crawling into bed.

"Nothing to count here," I say. "But I might have an idea for what the final scene could be."

She lifts her glasses. "You were supposed to be writing the breakup scene."

"You might have to do it. I'm more in a happy ending mood."

"But a breakup in the Ferris Wheel was your concept. So they are stuck there and finish the ride together even after they're officially over."

I chose the ride because it reminded me of the night Nick and I went dancing down at the pier. When I had time for dancing with my boyfriend. His hands on my hips. His stubble against my forehead. The steady thumps of Nick's heart beating like the waves.

I shake my head. Focus, Sarah. "I still think it's a great concept, but I can't break them up right now."

"Fine. Write whatever you want." Karina takes a sip of her water. "Skip to the end and focus on the reunion. You need an extra dose of happy right now."

But we also need to finish the screenplay if we want to start pitching in January, because if *Vampire Club* starts, we won't have any time to focus on *our* stuff. My plans to block hours off for writing last weekend didn't materialize. If it's slow at the bakery this week, I can hammer out a few extra pages.

The timer beeps again. I crack my knuckles. The breaks always seem too short, and the writing time lingers too long these days. I do need a happy ending where Mom is well, I'm back in LA with Nick, the show is back on, and everything is as it was.

Two sprints later, what comes out on the page isn't the happy ending we planned for our couple, but it's the best happy ending for them. I say good night to Karina, pull on comfy clothes that my apron will mostly cover, and leave the house before Mom wakes up and asks to tag along. Julio, the assistant manager of Côté Fraise, opened the bakery this morning, but I'm due to prep the sandwiches and cover the lunch rush.

I place the croissant in front of Natalie. "It's on me today."

"No, no." Her broach of the day twinkles in the weak morning light, the tarnished silver matching her pinned hair. "I'm on a fixed income but I still have the money to support my favorite bakery." She snaps open the clasp of her brocade bag that looks like something from another era, retrieves a small change purse, and counts out a few dollar coins. "Keep the change. You've been doing so well while your mom's recovering. Tell her they finally fixed my radiator."

I ring up the cost of the croissant and slip the cents that remain into the tip jar. With the morning rush out of the way, I can get back to restocking. In the kitchen, I avoid the still-loose tile and slice a cardboard box open. I stand and the bag of coffee cups teeters in front of my face.

"Sarah." Julio glances behind me. "Annelise's here."

"What?" I set the bag on the counter. For once, Mom was not in the kitchen at home when I left. I thought she finally managed to sleep in. A knot forms in my chest. "Where is she?"

"I poured her some tea and forced her to take a seat in the office." Julio pushes his glasses up his nose.

"Can you finish these lattes?" I jut my chin to the empty cups. "The order was for eight large ones, to go. They'll be picking up in ten."

Julio nods, and I head into the office, texting Dad and the boys.

Me: Mom's at the bakery. Can someone come pick her up?
Dad: What?
Grayson: How????
Dad: Stepping into a lunch meeting. Be there by 2.
Grayson: On my way.

I cross the short hall and step into the cluttered room to find Mom, her face pale, staring into the teacup on the saucer in front of her.

"Well, this is a surprise." I lean on the corner of the desk, careful not to disturb the stacks of papers. "Aren't you supposed to be home resting?"

"I signed all the anniversary party thank you cards," says Mom.

"Not what I asked."

Her watery eyes meet mine. "I can't do it. For twenty-five years this bakery has been my life. I don't know what to do with myself."

"Mom, it's only temporary." I crack open the stapler that didn't work this morning and dig out the mangled metal clogging the mouth. "You'll be back on your feet before you know it. But you need time to heal."

"I'm still useful." She tries to cross her arms, but with the cast, the best she manages is to clank her wrist on the desk. "I can fill the tarts with one hand while sitting."

"No one's saying you're not useful." I swirl my hand around. "The bakery needs you, believe me. Sandy has been giving me a cold shoulder, as if I'm the one who's keeping you away from the place and not the doctor's orders."

"Doctor's orders." She twists her lips. "What does the doctor know about what's good for me? Serving my customers, seeing the smile on their faces, that's my life."

"And your customers will still be here. Natalie wanted you to know she got her heat issue fixed. She's eager to talk to you again." This brings a little smile to Mom's face, and the knot in my chest loosens. "We'll get the new manager settled, get you the help you need, and all will be well."

"Unless something else goes wrong." Grayson leans against the doorframe, a blue-and-white cap covering his sandy blond hair.

I glare at my brother. We used to be best friends. Now that I've been gone for two years, he's changed. Not just broader shoulders and bigger biceps, or the fact he's graduated from high school to university. There's a new seriousness to him that his evergreen smile hides. "Nothing else will go wrong."

"Did Mom tell you about the insurance rate hike?" I shake my head. Grayson points to Mom, who busies herself with the cup. "After the break-in—"

"There was a break-in?" I ask.

"On Halloween. Some kids smashed a few windows." Mom waves her hand. "Nothing serious."

Grayson stuffs his hands into the pockets of his varsity jacket. "The insurance company didn't agree. They increased our rates because we don't have any surveillance cameras or security system. All things B&B said they'd install."

The acronym is familiar but doesn't fit the conversation we're having.

"Boulangerie and Baguette?" I unscramble my memories and picture a green sign with swirly lettering in gold.

Our vacations as kids always included visiting local bakeries to contrast and compare their goods to ours, to find ways to improve the store or learn the latest trends. Being a small local chain in Quebec, they were the ideal Mémère looked to for Côté Fraise to follow if she franchised. Their Montreal location was a wonder to visit, almost as good as stepping into a café in Lyon, according to Mémère. Every care package mom sends to LA includes a canister of their hot cocoa.

I narrow my eyes at my brother. "What do they have to do with it?"

"They offered—"

"Grayson." My mother's tone is warning, and the hair on the back of my neck rises.

I look at Mom. "What's going on?"

He crosses one foot over the other. "She has a right to know."

Mom sighs. "B&B made an offer to buy the bakery. They want to move into Ontario. Have for a while now." She sips her tea. "A few months ago, they approached me about buying Côté Fraise."

A few months? The shock lodges between my ribs like a puck in a goalie's net.

"I told them no," says Mom.

"It was a good offer." Grayson wrenches himself off the doorframe. "Even split four ways according to Mémère's will, it could make a huge difference in our lives."

Nick's and my dream of a home of our own: a little bungalow, close to the beach. A big bed. He'd be so happy. I'd be so happy. A thrill climbs my vertebrae. Just the two of us.

My gut twists. No luxury bed is worth taking the only life Mom has ever known away from her. How could my mind even go there? The ghost of Mémère stands in the corner, her arms crossed. Mémère built this business for us, not for some soulless conglomerate to destroy.

"You can't sell Mémère's dream." My voice is loud, but not enough to dampen the "no-no-no" hammering on repeat in my skull.

"Even if it's killing our mother?" Like a slap, Grayson's words burn.

"Grayson." Mom's gaze begs him to stop.

"I'm tired of keeping quiet. Sarah is part of the family. She needs to be part of the solution." My brother's normally jovial eyes are like unyielding stones, the seriousness I detected earlier on full display. "Mom's not been giving you the whole story. The bakery is struggling. That's why the tiles haven't been replaced. I tried to fix them, but I'm not a handyman," Grayson yells, like when he couldn't stop falling while he learned how to skate.

Mom leans on the desk, reaching for the crutches, but Grayson gets to her first. "You're not supposed to be walking."

Mom wraps her arms around him. "It's not your fault, honey. I wasn't paying attention."

Grayson separates Mom from his chest and sets her in the chair. He takes her teacup. "I'll put this in the dishwasher and we can leave."

As our gazes meet, the guilt on Grayson's face slices my heart. What else has this family been keeping from me?

TEN

Sarah

Waking up at four a.m. for the fourth day in a row should've gotten my body used to the new routine, but it's one a.m. in LA and I'm usually falling into bed, curling up with Nick. I yawn. My eyes refuse to open no matter how many times the crystal alarm tone on my phone rings. It's getting louder, and if I don't turn it off soon, the noise will wake Mom. I fumble for the phone, tap snooze, and give myself two more minutes to wallow in the memory of what it's like to wake up in Nick's arms.

A metallic buzz shatters the quiet. I bolt out of bed to silence Mémère's old-timey mechanical clock that's rattling the dresser. That did the trick, Mémère. I'm awake now.

I pick up my phone and scroll through Discord, catching up on the lives of my friends on the other side of the continent while I try to make my left eye crack open. I see the green dot beside Nick's name. Why is he awake?

Me: Are you still up?

The little dots appear immediately.

Nick: Getting ready for bed.

My finger hits the call button before my brain has a chance to think and after half a ring, my boyfriend's handsome face fills the screen. At least the shadow of him.

"Good morning." Nick's image is pixelated and too gray, but I recognize the outline of the Starlight Foundation Best Director award over his shoulder. I uncurl my fingers. He made it back to our bedroom.

"Morning." I lift the phone above me and sink back into the warmth of my pillow. "But I'm not agreeing to the good part." I rub my left eye and force it to open.

"You look like you could use more sleep." His voice is gravely, but not in the cute I-just-woke-up way I love so much. It's more in the I'm-exhausted way.

"Feel that way too." I blink and can finally focus with both eyes. "But it's worth it to see you."

I get a little smile and my heart leaps. I'd get up at three a.m. to make him smile. I miss our moments in bed together like this, before the craziness of the day sets in. Or at the end of one.

"How's your day been?" I ask.

His day was packed, and we'd planned on talking later this morning when he's up, but my desperate fingers couldn't wait that long.

"I'm too exhausted to make any pronouncements, but we did the best we could with the documentary footage." He puts his arm behind his head and gives me a flash of his bicep I'd love to have wrapped around me, not watch from two thousand miles away via a flat lifeless screen. "I have a list of things I could've improved upon if I had another week to work on it, but with the time we had . . ."

"I bet it's amazing." Because everything Nick creates is amazing. His talent is undeniable, and people just need to give him a chance, see his work, and they'll be as in love with him as I am.

"You sound like Ms. Hansley. She's sure the editor won't have a lot to change."

"Because you are brilliant." If I were next to him, I'd put my hands on his chin and raise it to meet my eyes.

He leans back and stares at the ceiling. "You're my girlfriend. You're supposed to say that."

"I wouldn't if I didn't mean it." I put confidence in my voice, so he knows I'm serious. "She thinks you have a chance at the Silver Screen Showcase?" I roll onto my stomach and try to decipher Nick's facial expression.

"She thinks I'm the best. You two sound like you've been sourcing your praises from the same script." His grin is infectious, and my lips stretch as well. "You'll have to tell me the truth when you see it."

"When do I get to see it?"

"Sunday night. I'll stash two bags of popcorn, we'll lock ourselves in our room, and I'll give you a private showing." He bites his knuckle as if saying his wish out loud could jinx the whole thing.

"Two private showings?"

"Wait until you see it once, you might not want another one."

"Not what I meant." I roll my eyes because I'm not thinking about his movie right now.

"Oh." Understanding shines in his eyes. "I can definitely promise you many of those as well. We'll be inseparable all evening. And night."

"And morning?"

"And morning." He smiles.

I wish today was that morning. "I can't wait."

Neither of us speaks but I know we are on the same page, lost in the possibilities of our future. The one that has us together in the same country, city, apartment, and bed. Where the finger he's rubbing against his chin draws letters on my skin.

"Fu-u-u-ck." Nick's sigh of frustration wakes me up for good. He scrapes his free hand across his face and peeks at the screen. "How's your mom? How are you dealing with everything?"

"I'd rather keep talking about being in your arms."

"Sarah." Nick says my name slowly, drawing out the A's.

Even after what we went through on Halloween and my promises to open up, it's still awkward. Not as hard, 'cause I actually want to talk to him. Have for two days now since Mom told me about the offer. Part of me wants to write this down first and then send to him, but I'll feel better knowing his perspective. I rub my eyebrows.

We're partners.

"Mom's worse." I take my filters off and tell him the truth. "Her twisted ankle is swollen, because instead of rest, ice/heat combo, and anti-inflammatories, she took a taxi to the bakery yesterday. It's like she can't sit still."

"Hmm." His non-committal hum might as well be Nick-speak for "Sounds like someone I know."

"Yes, yes. I get it." I roll my eyes at him. "But she needs to heal. She refuses to use the crutches. How does she not get that she's delaying her recovery?" I bury my head in my hand. "I don't understand."

"What does your dad say about her?" Nick's voice is low and gentle.

I roll onto my side. "I love the man, but he totally caves into anything she wants. While I'm not sure she's been making the best decisions."

"What do you mean?" Nick blinks rapidly.

Am I freaking him out? I stretch my lips into a reassuring grin.

"I wanted to tell you yesterday, but with you cramming for the Econ exam, it isn't a text kind of a conversation." I'm concerned about *him* too. "How did the exam go?"

"Don't change the subject." He furrows his brows. "I'll tell you about the exam after you tell me about what happened between you and your mom."

I need to tell him everything. "Mom and Grayson have been keeping things from me. The bakery is in a lot more financial trouble than I thought. There was even an offer from a competitor that Mom declined."

"Really?" Nick's forehead wrinkles.

My jaw relaxes. He gets it. Nick understands, and it means the world.

"Really." I squeeze the phone with so much force the case creaks. "Grayson sounded like he was ready to sell. How could they have not told me about it?" I blurt out to Nick what I've been holding in since my conversation with them. "Or about the break-in."

"There was a break-in?" Nick leans into the camera.

"And an insurance rate hike. It's like if I'm not in Toronto, I'm not part of the family. I don't get the right to know these things." My shoulders ache with the burden of their betrayal. "Grayson might think he's in charge, but I'm here too." I jab my thumb at my chest.

"Breathe." Nick's tone is gentle. "We can figure this out." The word *we* is like a balm on my frayed nerves.

"I can't talk about this anymore. I don't want to be the rare medical case who has a stroke at twenty-three. Period. Tell me about your Econ exam."

Nick's gaze shift to the left. "That. Right." He scratches his stubbled chin and looks right. "I finished it."

I wait for more, for him to paint the picture he usually does. He raises the lid of his laptop.

"Well, that's a given," I say. "How did you do?"

"Won't know for a while."

I sit up in bed, unable to lounge around anymore. "But how do you think you did? Anything surprise you or you weren't prepared for?"

"Maybe. The last five questions didn't make sense."

"Five out of?"

"Twenty." He rakes his fingers through his hair.

"Okay. If you got the others perfect, that's still 75 percent."

"Not sure I got those perfect either. And I need an 80 percent to keep my scholarship."

"Shit." Words of comfort elude me. I chew on my lip as a whirlwind of worry starts inside me. I'd kiss away his fears, if I were there. But I'm not. I'm a six-hour plane ride away. I probe for another way to help. "It's one test. I'm sure you did better than you think. You're just tired."

"Says you." His tone is dull, lifeless, nothing like Nick.

"I wish I could wrap you in my arms and kiss every part of you and give you the energy you need."

"I'd give it right back to you." The bags under his eyes are the same color as his irises. Might just be the bad camera on his phone and the fact that it's night in LA, but he doesn't look like he can stay awake any longer.

"You need to go to sleep, and I need to get dressed, find Mom's spare keys, and drive to the bakery before Mom decides she wants to come too."

"You're a criminal mastermind of bakeries."

I smile, and the whirlwind in my chest calms. I have three more days to hire a new manager and get back to Nick. "More like a superhero. Let's hope my plans work and one of the candidates is exactly the person who'll help make Côté Fraise what it used to be."

"You can do anything you set your mind to."

"You keep telling me that." I fluff the blanket around my waist.

"I love you, Sarah."

"You keep telling me that, too."

Nick's lips curve. "Can't wait to see you Sunday."

"Me too."

I hang up and plop onto my back. My eyes threaten to close but I can't let them. I get out of bed and start the day.

This is what Mémère would've done.

I will make her proud.

Eleven

Sarah

"A BLUEBERRY MUFFIN AND a pain au chocolat." The woman in a sunny yellow dress covered in a lemon pattern hovers her finger over the display. "What would you say is your signature pastry?"

"Tarte aux fraise, but we don't have any left." Or baked. I won't mention how I went to make the strawberry filling this morning and discovered the five quarts of fresh berries in the fridge had turned to rotten clumps. My molars slam together harder than when I shut the door of Côté Fraise van every time it refuses to close. I might not be eating anything strawberry for a while. Julio tossed the moldy cartons while casting a disappointed glance my way, because the strawberries I bought at the market were from the wrong vendor. I school my face into a pleasant expression.

"I had my heart set on strawberries." She hums her disappointment. "What would you recommend I try then?" The woman clamps her folded coat under her arm and smiles, oblivious to the turmoil her question sent me into.

I get her point. It's in the name of the bakery, but things happen. I take in her matching lemon-shaped purse. "Our lemon tart is popular. It's not too sweet." At least Julio approved the lemons.

"Sold. Add a lemon tart and a café au lait, please."

I ring up the order and expect her to join the trio at the table in the back, but she sits by herself by the front window. That's my favorite spot for people watching. Like the area, Queen Street is a cornucopia of personalities. But I have no time for character inspiration today.

The bakery has had a steady line almost to the door since we opened at six this morning. The customers come and go faster than at The Diamond Club. I like being busy, but the tips suck. When I was a kid, customers would drop their extra change into the tip bowl. I wipe down the counter around the mostly empty bowl and take deep breaths. With everything done by tap now, there's no extra money that way. The customers who do stay tend to hang out for an hour and leave an extra dollar or two.

I'm beginning to see the struggles Mom's been dealing with. Even with Julio and Sandy making, baking, and serving the goodies Mémère declared as daily staples, the menu eats up our time.

"Make sure you order Demerara." Julio points at the empty shelf as he drops off a fresh batch of croissants.

"I'm on it," I lie. Who has time to find the supplier's number, never mind ordering the fancy sugar?

I scribble 'sugar' on a sticky note and slap it on the bottom of the register to deal with after I close. I never thought much about where the supplies at the bar come from. Mrs. Marino has a whole back-office team including a purchaser whose sole job is to keep the resort in good working order.

"Do you have strawberry turnovers?" A woman in a fuchsia parka points to the display case where Sandy is replenishing the pastry trays with freshly baked cinnamon rolls.

Sandy, currently our main and only baker, has barely looked at me this week, and that's my fault. We used to gossip like schoolgirls when I worked here, but we're so short-staffed, I haven't had a moment to say more than commands and instructions.

Sandy keeps stacking, so I step in.

"Sorry, we're out." I grip the tongs tighter. The strawberry debacle from this morning haunts me.

"Didn't you go back to LA?"

The voice registers and my cheeks flame. "Ivy, I didn't recognize you without your Essie's T-shirt." Before I left for LA, Ivy and I spent endless weekends together bartending. Another person I should have kept in touch with more, besides occasional messages in our Canuck group chat.

Ivy removes her coat. "Do I look more like myself now?" She's wearing a white T-shirt with the harp and scythe logo of the bar. I wore an identical one for years. "I'm working an engagement party. Hopefully I'll have one myself in my near future."

"That's great." I try to look happy for her. How did I not know she was at that stage with her boyfriend? What was his name?

The next customer in line clears his throat.

I steal a glance at Sandy pleading for help, but she's ignoring me, hyper-focused on rearranging the muffins, making space for the pumpkin spice ones currently baking. The back of my neck heats. Something's off. She's been efficient and polite this morning, but not her usual self.

"Are you staying in Toronto?" Ivy surveys the pastry display.

"Just until Mom is back."

Ivy purses her lips and gives me a commiserating stare. "Right."

That's the last thing I need this morning. I redirect her gaze to the display. "Apple fritters are just out of the oven."

"Apple fritter it is." Ivy counts out quarters.

Sandy closes the display case and disappears back into the kitchen. I select the largest apple pastry, place it in a bag, and ring up the order.

The next customer taps his fingers on the counter. "Where's Annelise?"

When I left this morning, Mom was sitting at the kitchen table drinking tea. "Old habits are hard to break," she said when I asked why she wasn't sleeping in. "I've been getting up at four a.m. most of my life."

"She's taking a little vacation." I smile at him. People don't need the details of Mom's business.

"She never takes time off." He crosses his arms.

After another two hours of disappointing regulars who were looking for a chat or a smile from Mom and serving what feels like half of the Beaches, the line slows and eventually peters out. I step from behind the counter for the first time this morning and wipe the strawberry-patterned tablecloths on the bistro tables.

When I return to the kitchen, Julio, with his arms crossed, scowls at Sandy, who's staring holes through the fridge in the kitchen.

"Everything okay?" I lift my eyebrows.

Sandy glances at Julio then glues her gaze to the floor. "Julio thinks I should rip off the Band-Aid."

This is not how one starts a conversation about good news. "Usually the best approach." I tuck the rag I used to wipe the tables in the belt of my apron. Did she find out about the offer? "Did Grayson say something to you?"

"Grayson? No. He has nothing to do with it." She looks at Julio and jerks her chin up. "I got another offer."

Offer? "Did Mom talk to you?"

"I haven't talked to Annelise yet. I was hoping she'd be in today so I could tell her." Sandy wrings her hands like she's kneading dough. "We've worked together for so long, I don't want her to think I'm betraying her."

Betraying Mom? Sounds like we are having two separate conversations.

"But I can't wait." Sandy slides her hand into the pocket of her apron, takes out an envelope, and hands it to me. "This is my notice."

"Notice of—"

She waves her arms in the air. "Let me finish before I start crying."

My chest tightens. Sandy can't leave. The air in the room grows heavy. If Mom were here, she'd know how to talk Sandy out of this.

"I had an interview and last weekend I worked a shift at the restaurant. I'll be their pâtissier. I love your grandma's recipes, but I'm ready to do things on my own. I want to experiment, develop, and test new desserts." She glances at Julio. "And they pay almost double the salary I earn here."

"No." I shake my head, because we can't manage the load as it is. Without Sandy we are doomed. Julio and I can't do this on our own. "I'll talk to Mom. Maybe you can introduce some new desserts. I can't promise to double the salary, but I'm sure we can figure something out. We need you. Côté Fraise needs you." As I say the words, I can almost see Mémère sitting in the corner watching me. The back of my throat burns. She built this business for her family, and we will keep it alive.

"I can stay till the end of the year."

I don't want to lose Sandy. She's like family. "Is it because Mom and Mémère aren't here?" The ghost of Mémère shakes her head. I stave off my tears and step forward. "Or is this really what you want?"

"This is the best move for my career." Sandy's gaze meets mine. "I'll never forget what your grandmother did for me. She was the one who suggested I start looking for my next step. She said I was ready."

Sandy might be ready, but I'm not. I dab the corner of my eye with my knuckle. "If you stay till the end of the year, that'll help a lot." I take the envelope. "I'm happy for you." I force out the words.

I am. Even though my body is fluctuating between zaps of panic and waves of nausea, I'm happy for her. Mémère hired her right out of culinary school and bragged about Sandy's potential.

"Côté Fraise will always be the place I call home. Your grandmother treated me like her own. I'll miss my family."

I end our awkward standoff by wrapping my arms around her shoulders. Her sigh of relief clears some of the agitation coursing through me. "We'll work this out."

I give Sandy's sturdy frame one last squeeze and release her.

She sniffs and digs for something in her apron. "I'll help with the training."

Julio takes my place and wraps Sandy in a bear hug.

Tears makes my vision swim. I take the rag from my waistband and wipe the chalkboard that will have our lunch menu. Focus on what needs to be done, Sarah. "What's the lunch special today?" I ask him.

"Smoked salmon on rye."

Mémère's favorite. She loved all things seafood. On sunny afternoons, we'd go to the beach for picnics with these sandwiches, pretending Lake Ontario was really the ocean. Just the two of us on an adventure, dreaming of distant shores, and planning trips to exotic locations. Vacations we never had a chance to take. The memory stings. I regard the corner, but the shadow of Mémère has faded.

"I'll go get the cream cheese from the storeroom." Sandy disappears downstairs.

In my pocket my phone buzzes, and I pull it out expecting to find my "Good Morning" message from Nick. Instead, it's a message from Karina.

Karina: When are you coming back to LA?

My stomach twists. With *Vampire Club* on hiatus and her temp job going bust, our screenplay has become the new shiny thing she obsesses about.

Me: Might be here longer than expected.

Karina: Will you still be in Toronto next week?

Karina: I'm totally bored and have always wanted to see Niagara Falls.

Karina: Thought I might come up.

Karina: If that's okay?

Karina in Toronto? I breathe easier. With her here, she'll make me sit and do daily sprints to finish our screenplay. I can switch rooms with Taylor and share the bunk beds with her. Make it our private writing camp. The thought calms my churning mind. If I can't have Nick or Siobhan by my side, Karina is the next best option.

Am I planning to extend my stay in Toronto? In my head, I'm still here next week, while the ticket in my desk says I'm flying out this Sunday. My heart ticks like a stopwatch. My breath matches the beat. I won't see Nick this week, because there's no way I'm leaving Côté Fraise like this. Julio must be freaking out. We need to hire two people. Dad's back to work. I can't. I hear my pulse in my ears.

I scroll through Karina's texts again, then re-read the ones from Nick about seeing me soon in LA. There's no indecision on my part, only remorse. I want to be back in Nick's arms, but my desires need to go on the back burner, just this once. I clutch the phone tighter. Family first.

Me: We need to talk.

Nick: Let me get into the hallway.

The bakery is not the place to talk about this. Too many ears. I open the door onto the street and walk along the row of buildings. I can ask him to take a week off and hang here. Could be like a vacation for him. He needs to rest. Nick's ringtone battles with the drumbeat in my ears.

"Is it your mom?" Nick sounds like he ran a mile.

"No. Mom's the same. It's about me."

"Did you get hurt?"

"No. But things are not better here. They are worse. Now I need to find someone to replace Sandy."

"The baker I didn't get to meet?"

"Yes." My throat works against me, but I swallow the bad taste in my mouth. "I need to stay another week. Or until we hire her replacement and the new shift manager."

"Which one is it?" The hesitation in his voice pierces me.

"I don't know. My heart is torn." Shit. I hate doing this to him. It's Halloween all over again. Regret chokes me. I'm deciding things without him. "I'm so sorry, but I don't feel I can leave. I'm torn between you and Mom. But I don't have anything going on in LA right now, and Mom needs me. How about I stay here till my birthday, and you fly in for a long weekend? We celebrate here, and go home together?" My voice wobbles.

"Hey, hey." His tone softens, and the heartache that splits me in two abates. "It's okay. I understand. There's a reason why I'm flying to Chicago to drive with Mom to LA. Family is family."

"You are my family too." I massage my temples.

"But with parents, it's not the same. We can work this out." Nick's face is so close on the screen, but I want it to be this close in person. "I'll look for tickets to Toronto to spend your birthday there. It'll make your mom happy too."

He thinks he got off on the wrong foot with Mom somehow, and no matter what I tell him, he won't believe she likes him.

Caesar, the local cat, scampers across the alleyway, back to his owner's home after his afternoon prowl. I'm envious of the cat. He gets to go home. "Prepare to spend every minute by my side, because it's killing me not to kiss you good morning before I get out of bed."

"It's killing me not to be kissed." His voice has dropped low, and his deep rumble reroutes blood straight to my core. I lean against the brick. The chilly air I suck in does nothing to dampen my desire to have Nick right here, right now. "In another week, I won't be able to stop touching you when I get the chance. Make up for lost time."

"Try and keep me away." Nick chuckles. "I'll be glued to you the moment you land."

"I'd love that." I press my forehead against the freezing wall.

"Me too."

We hang up and I proceed with a new plan.

Me: I will be in Toronto till my birthday. Come. You can stay at my parents' place.

Karina: Booking my ticket now.

TWELVE

NICK

THE DOOR CREAKS AS I sneak back into the classroom. My already fast heartrate from the conversation with Sarah shoots higher as Professor Takamado squints at me. I slide into my seat in the front row. The problem with being the teacher's pet is that it's much harder to hide a call when you're six feet from the lecturer.

Not that I'm complaining about being his favorite student. Hours upon hours of watching movies and reading about directors after Valentine's Day while I was sick with pneumonia paid off. I get his references, raise my hand, and give extended answers, and this is one class I'm confident I'm getting an A in, even if I'm half asleep at the exam. Maybe I can compensate for my Econ grade. Maybe my answers weren't as bad as I thought.

"Fun fact. The wallet here"— Professor Takamado stretches his hand to the screen with the frozen image of Samuel L.

Jackson's character Jules in *Pulp Fiction* —"really belonged to Quentin Tarantino. Often directors, screenwriters, and other production folks will add personal items to create a more authentic story."

Sarah does this with her screenplays. She changed Wesley's drink from Rum and Coke to an Old Fashioned after meeting me last Christmas. In *Indigo,* Isabel and Rudo were her parents. What will she put in the screenplay she's working on with Karina?

Sarah, who I won't see for ten more days. I tap the back of my pencil against my notebook. The news of her staying in Toronto obliterated any hope for a good week. The pain in her voice from being torn between her need to help her mother and her wish to come home was worse. I had to say I was okay with her staying. With a crack, the pencil splits into two. I let go of the jagged wood. I get it.

The screen goes dark. "This is it for today." Professor Takamado looks my way. "Nick, please stay after class."

Is this good or bad news? I stuff my backpack and tap my heel against the floor while some of my classmates finish their questions.

After the last student files out, Professor Takamado sits at the desk opposite mine. "You asked to take your exam on Monday instead of tomorrow?"

I roll my fingers into a fist. I hate asking for favors. "Yeah, I'll be out of town. The office said it was okay."

"Wish you asked me first, but there is no harm in you switching." He adjusts his wire-frame glasses. "Does it mean you won't have time to finish your documentary?"

"It was uploading to the server when I left for class." I take the thumb drive out of my pocket. "I also brought this as a backup." I was in Ms. Hansley's office until after seven, then added final touches until two in the morning. Not sure about brilliant, but I hope Sarah is right and the people will see what I was aiming for.

His gaze meets mine. "I know what I'll be watching this weekend."

Dad's Toyota is in the parking lot where he promised. The smell of burgers and fries punches me in the face when I open the door.

"Got some for me?" I ask, buckling my seat belt.

I doubt it. Him giving me a ride to the airport instead of practicing the pitch for his screenplay that he is giving tomorrow is Dad's way to contribute at least something to help Mom move.

"Your favorite double cheeseburger with fries. No pickles." He pushes a white bag with grease stains my way then points to the drink holder. "And a Coke."

The thrill of him knowing my go-to food order shoots through me and manifests as a smile. "Thanks."

"Is the backpack the only thing you're bringing?" He eyes the bag at my feet.

"Toothbrush, underwear, and a T-shirt. What else do I need?"

"A warm jacket?"

"Left them in Chicago." I shrug. "Mike will bring one to the airport when he picks me up."

Dad's silent for a little too long. Like with Sarah, I'm learning to read the signs, and I think he's struggling to say something. I set my hand on his shoulder. "Dad?"

He shrugs it off. "How's Mike doing?"

Mike is still not talking to Dad. He has his own issues, and I'm not getting into that mess. My big brother can figure his own shit out. I wipe ketchup from the corner of my mouth. "In love. Bossy as ever. His martials arts academy is blowing up. Mom doesn't give you the play-by-play?"

"Too busy packing." Dad goes silent again. He signals a lane change; the measured tick of the indicator fills the interior cabin. Dad clears his throat. "He still won't answer my texts."

Guess I am getting into their shit. "You can't rush Mike. Took you and me almost a year, and we're in the same city. He'll get there." I stuff the last of the burger into my mouth and wash it down with a swig of Coke.

He pulls onto the freeway. "Would you talk to him for me?"

I sigh. I really don't want to disappoint Dad. "I tried. But I'll try again. Mike's stubborn when he makes up his mind."

"He must realize I love him just as much as I love you and your mom."

The fry sticks in my throat. This is the first time Dad has said the phrase out loud to me. I've seen it in his handwriting, in the letter he gave me for my birthday, but this is different.

"Love you too." The explosion beneath my ribs hurts but soothes at the same time. Our words are true. The bond I've created with Dad is priceless. I've craved it for so long, I don't remember not wanting his love. But my heart aches. Not for Dad. It aches for Sarah. She loves me. I see it in her eyes, feel it in her touch, but I can't wait to hear the words.

I won't hurry her. I'm sure of her feelings for me. I crumple the paper bag on my knees. Me saying that I love her doesn't mean she has to say it back. Hearing the words is a treat. My ear hits the headrest and I stare at a stalled car on the side of the road. I rub my chest and acknowledge the longing pinching my heart. My soul craves them from Sarah just as much as it did from Dad. Possibly more.

Dad takes the exit to the airport. "I'll see you and Mom at my place on Sunday. Don't speed. If you're tired, stay another night at the hotel. I want you both to drive safe."

"You know Mom. I doubt I'll have any say in what we do when." I take another sip of my drink. "She has every minute of the trip planned. Wouldn't be surprised if she has a folder with the itinerary, places we're staying, eating, visiting, and a spreadsheet of how much we can spend at each stop."

The crinkles around Dad's eyes multiply, and we both laugh. "Take care of her. I should've been the one driving her here."

"Trust me. I'm capable of getting her to you in one piece. My ears and emotions may take a beating spending three days on the road with Mom, but don't worry about her. Focus on the pitch. If this works, you'll have a much better job."

His hands grip the steering wheel, and the crinkles disappear. "A lot more money to support her while she figures out what she's doing."

I put on Sarah's present, my black-and-red Chicago hat. "Still can't believe sometimes that you and Mom are back together."

"Me neither. I pinch myself. But I won't let her down again." His expression softens. "I've learned my lesson, and we lost so many years we could've been together because I screwed up."

"We're both happy to have you back."

Dad scoots into the empty spot right in front of the doors. "You sure you don't want me to go into the terminal with you?"

"Not worth the cost of the airport parking."

Dad takes off his seatbelt, leans over the console, and hugs me. First his I love you, now a hug. I might float to Chicago. Is this something I should be getting used to or is this a special occasion?

The red eye isn't leaving for three hours, which gives me time to memorize the names of the directors who won the Oscars over the last fifty years for Professor Takamado's Film history exam on Monday. I find an empty seat and settle in. I'll try for some sleep on the flight this time.

I follow Mike along the rows of cars in the O'Hare parking garage, looking for Mom's minivan. I try not to think about the last time he collected me from this airport. If only I'd been more aware and recognized Sarah, months of heartache could've been avoided. But I'm with her now. That's what counts.

The brake lights flicker on a forest-green SUV and the back door opens. "Throw your backpack in there and grab your parka." Mike veers to the driver's side of the car.

"Whoa." The plates on the vehicle are still the temporary ones the dealership issues. "You got a new car?"

"Angie and I did. With Mom taking the minivan to LA, I had to purchase something more appropriate to haul stuff."

"What about Beauty? I can't believe you sold your bike." Mike lived for his motorcycle. "Mom didn't say anything?"

"No, or she'd be celebrating. Beauty's not going anywhere, but me and this new car are doing well."

I nudge Mike's elbow. "Do I get to name this one too?" One of the rare moments we openly acted like we liked each other was when Mike brought the bike home and we went for a ride. I suggested the name "Beauty," as in Beauty and the Beast, because no matter how big the bike was, Mike was bigger.

The car door dings and he says over his shoulder, "Aren't we a bit old for naming cars?"

Mike is only a couple years older than Sarah, and she named her car Betty. "No such thing. I dub thee Shrek." I touch the panel of the car in front of me with my index finger, pretending it's Excalibur.

"Shrek? Really? I was thinking Rhaegal, after the green dragon in Game of Thrones." Mike squishes into the driver's side. The pilot seat that would swallow Sarah suits him, conforming to his bulky muscles.

"No, we are sticking with cartoons. It's green and big." I open my door, and the smell of new car fills my nostrils. "And gooey inside for the right person. Shrek."

Is that a hint of a smile on my big brother's face?

"Why am I feeling like you're giving me a new nickname and not my car?" Mike pushes the start engine button.

"Think what you will. But expect a Shrek key chain and air freshener as your Christmas gift." I shift in my seat. "You're still coming to LA, right?"

He nods. "Angie will be there for work. Her parents said they'd drive to LA as well. It works. Helps to keep the Stavros family tradition of spending Christmas together, no matter what."

"Dad will be happy to see you."

Mike presses the gas, and the car peels out of the parking spot. "I didn't say I'll be visiting him."

The seatbelt presses against my sternum. My chest is tight inside and out. "Mom and Dad are moving in together."

"Don't rub salt into the wound."

I twist to direct my words at the big oaf. "You can't avoid him much longer."

"I'm two time zones away. Shouldn't be hard." He rolls his shoulders. "He managed to avoid me for ten years, I think I can return the favor. In ten years, we'll talk."

I would've punched him if he were not driving. The truthteller in me wants to tell Mike to give Dad a break or explain why Dad stayed away, but I can tell by the way he's speeding down the 79A that today is not the day. I steel my nerves. We'll work on him at Christmas, as a family.

Mike nears the house and parks on the street because there is a POD container and Mom's stuffed-to-the-brim minivan in front of the garage. "Ready to say goodbye to your room?"

"I guess." When I left for California, I couldn't wait to get away from Chicago, this house, this neighborhood that was stifling me. But I knew my room was there for me, waiting to take me back if I needed shelter and help. The warmth the safety this place provided, that Mom provided, wraps around me. I was not alone. Mom's move makes everything more permanent. The fact sits heavy in my gut. My childhood is officially cut off. No return.

I snap a picture of the house and text it to Sarah.

Mike punches my arm. "You can always stay with Angie and me. Her office doubles as a guest bedroom."

"Thanks."

The walls of the house are bare. There are some pieces of furniture here and there. I toe the battered side table that held our hats, mittens, and scarves. "Are you donating these?"

"Angie is trying to sell them, but if no one buys them before the move-out date, dumpster it is. If there's anything you want that's still out, pack it into the POD, or never see it again."

Upstairs, my door still has my "DO NOT ENTER" sign with a skull I put on it the first week we moved into this place. I was so mad at Mom for taking me away from my friends. Before me stands the naked bunkbed we moved from our downtown Chicago apartment. Mike and I used to sleep on the rackety thing before he got his own room. My desk is stripped of the knickknacks I didn't have space for in my bag when I moved to LA.

"It's the end of an era," Mom says behind me.

I take in the tiny space. A snowball of emotions larger than the room crushes me. I slump onto on the bottom bunk. "How long did we live here?"

"Seven years. Feels like a lifetime." Her almost-black eyes meet mine. The finality of today grips my throat and paralyzes me. Mom indicates the two boxes by the open and empty closet. "I put your stuff in there. Go through them. Take out anything you don't need, and Mike will deal with it. We're leaving in an hour. I'm packing snacks and a cooler."

One box is my clothes. My hockey jersey. Mom packed my championship ring, the only one we managed to win and were so proud of, and my trophy as well. I take them out. I stare at the golden cup on the large pedestal, heavy in my hand.

Could be worth taking it to LA, showing them to Sarah. Put it next to my Best Director one from the Starlight Foundation.

I return the award to the keep box.

Most of the clothes she packed I get rid of, but keep the Kodak 35 and my photo development set. I could always convert the bathroom into a dark room when I need it. Taking pictures of Sarah and watching her image emerge on paper in front of my eyes would be gratifying.

With everything I'm keeping consolidated into one box, I run to the first floor.

"No running on the stairs," Mom shouts, then laughs. "I had to give that one last go. Won't be able to shout that at you anymore."

Another thing to say goodbye to. I squeeze the box.

"No stairs in Dad's apartment." I set the box on the floor and wrap my arms around her.

"Group hug." Mike puts his hand on my and Mom's shoulders. "The last time the three of us are in this house together."

I catch my breath and store the old memories, freeing space for the new ones. With a shaking hand, I take out my phone and capture our smiling faces and sad eyes. I try to smile on the inside too. The end of an era indeed.

Thirteen

NICK

My left butt cheek is numb. I wiggle my foot to bring it to life and sit up in the driver's seat.

"Time for a break?" Mom places a hand on my elbow. She notices everything.

We've been driving for four and a half hours with one quick stop for gas. Mom's minivan guzzles the stuff, but I've just about worked out the optimal speed where the needle doesn't drop drastically. I want to go further, but my stomach demands food. The croissant sandwiches from Morkes we snagged on the way out of town are long gone, and I've already had half a dozen of the cookies Mom made for our road trip snacks.

"Good idea." I suppress a yawn.

"The GPS takes us to a park in Des Moines. We'll stop for lunch and stretch our legs."

Besides stocking the little cooler with sandwiches, Coke, water, and her Melomakarona cookies, she also planned the route we're taking to LA, including booking motels and lunch and dinner breaks. Me? My only plan was to show up and drive.

I blow a breath through my nose. I've missed Mom.

My independence and living in LA for the past six months has been great. But I missed the way she makes everything magically appear. I glance at Mom's profile. I now appreciate what she did for me: meals that required no cooking when I got home, laundry that got washed, folded, and put away without me lifting a finger, sheets that magically changed to fresh ones, even the availability of snacks, the doctor's appointments, and arranging travel plans.

Mom is a miracle, and being away from her, I was able to see the complete picture. As if before, the light in my life was flickering and I only caught some of what she did. Now it's fully lit, and I understand the extent of her care. And that's on top of her overtime with her clients.

But it's more than that. With everything we went through because of Dad's incarceration, Mike became the protector, and I became Mom's friend and confidant. With so much distance between us, I've missed knowing what's going on in her life and the newfound ability to see her anytime I want sends my happiness into overdrive.

My stomach's happy even when I think about home-cooked dinners at Mom and Dad's place. Or maybe it's my hunger talking.

"Take this exit." Mom indicates the two lanes exiting the highway.

I follow her instructions. After a few turns we find ourselves at the Pappajohn Sculpture Park. Parking brake on, I almost fall out of the van when my leg refuses to bear weight. I hobble around the front, trying to not make it obvious.

Mom tugs the cooler out of the van and points to the path between two modern art sculptures. "Walk it off while I set up the food."

Yep. Mom notices everything.

I circle the statues, and the further I walk, the more feeling I get in my leg. I slip my phone out of my pocket and take a picture of what looks like two huge chess pieces and text it to Sarah.

Me: First pit stop of the day.

The three little dots start dancing.

Sarah: I stopped there when I drove Betty to LA.

Her immediate response makes me smile. Was she waiting for my text? There's no way she misses me half as much as I miss her, but it makes my heart sing knowing she's thinking about me.

Sarah: They have good coffee at Horizon Line on the corner of the park.

It's like she can read my mind. I suppress yet another yawn. I barely slept last night on the plane.

Me: I'd much rather be driving Betty. Mom's minivan is like a block of cheese on wheels.

Sarah: Tell me about it. The bakery's van is no fun either. I miss Betty.

Sarah: I miss you more.

The words balloon in my chest. Warmth and lightness drive out the monotony of being on the road. When she types these things, they're more than platitudes. These are her I love yous. Someday she'll say or type it back to me. I can't wait.

Me: I miss you too. I love you.

One of the balloons in my chest pops when Sarah's response is a smiley face. Then I remember it will mean so much more if she says it to me in person for the first time. It will be worth the wait.

"Incoming call from Theo," Mom's phone announces through the speakers.

"You're on speaker," Mom says before Dad has a chance to utter a hello. Did she think he'll embarrass her?

"Where are you?" Even though his voice is tinny through the cheap speakers in Mom's van, I can sense the excitement in his question. Is it because he's talking to Mom? Or about her moving in with him? Or something else?

"We just crossed into Nebraska"—Mom looks at the GPS in front of her—"and are trying to get to Utah before we stop for the night."

"You're making good progress," he says.

"Yes, well, Nicky drove like a bat out of hell at first. I'm driving now, so it's the speed limit till we get there."

I pull a Sarah and roll my eyes at Mom's tease.

"Drive safe." Dad's said that so many times I roll my eyes again. "They loved the pitch, Nick." I like how Dad uses my name. Mom is the only person who gets to call me Nicky since I left Chicago. He calls me Nick, and I call him Dad. I grin. It feels right.

"Really?" I close my *Short History of the Movies* textbook. Nothing I was reading was getting absorbed anyhow. Why did I think I could study while Mom drove?

"Ate it up like it was candy. The thing that got them was the scene that Nazir's leaving prison reminded me of. The one you rushed to film. Life imitating art."

Like I could ever forget that day. I fold my hands on my lap and let my gaze skim across the dashboard. The day I got my dad back, standing in front of the prison that tore us apart. Nazir was released early, and I scrambled to record the touching moment. It took a few edits to get what I filmed to sync into a story.

"I swear they got teary-eyed talking about the touching re-union between my MC and her long-lost twin sister."

"Have I read this one?" Mom asks.

"I only showed you my current work, this is the one I wrote two years ago." The familiar clanking of Dad's coffee mug echoes in the van. "The big dinner we had last Christmas Eve was when I met the producer."

I slip the textbook into the back seat. There's no way I'll be able to even fake studying after this news. I can feel the high of Dad's success coursing through my veins. They liked his screenplay. This is a game changer for his income, his career, for the life he and Mom can build together.

"I'll email it to you both. You're going to love it, Chrissy." Pride shines through Dad's voice. "The filming won't start for another year, but I'll see if Nick can get in on it."

I know him better now, but I also trust him more. I trust that he is feeling what he is saying, and that there's no secret plan or reason for these words. My dad thinks highly of me, and that is no longer a fantastical thought.

"I still got it. My words can still make people feel." Dad's glee bleeds through.

The late afternoon sun cuts across half of Mom's face, accentuating the huge grin I rarely get to see. "Well, I could've told you that." She catches my stare, and the creases at the corners of her eyes make them appear brighter.

I like seeing Mom happy.

"But now the world is going to see it," he says.

I rub my two-day stubble and lose myself in the giddy enthusiasm of the moment. I've longed for Dad to get back to his old self. No, to be a better version of his old self, confident but not desperate to keep up with the Joneses anymore. Dad sharing his work with me is better than any stamp of approval. I treasure his choice to let me see what he came up with before anyone else. And him accepting my feedback is as open and vulnerable as most people in creative jobs get. The work-in-progress screenplay he gave Sarah and me to read made me want to pick up a camera and start shooting. Sarah took notes on the way he captured the atmosphere for the scenes.

Dad is talented, but it doesn't mean the professionals in the industry will agree with me.

"What's next, Dad?"

"The studio is considering two other scripts next week, but Colleen says it's perfunctory. They want my script, but they are obligated to look at more than one. If she's right and they go for mine, I'll need to storyboard and fix any scenes they want changes to. Also see if they want to read any of my other stuff, but only after we get deeper into the project first."

Mom nods like she's part of the team. Which I guess she is now.

"Colleen and I thought Sarah might want to join and shadow, see how the process works." Dad's words run faster than my driving. "We can negotiate some form of a payment or a credit for her too. Good learning experience, and extra cash wouldn't hurt."

My fingernail traces the hard edge of my phone. I want to call Sarah and share the good news right now, but the what-ifs of Sarah staying in Toronto till Christmas muddle the satisfaction. She'll probably be able to quit The Diamond Club, and our schedules would align more. This could be a job for her. A boost for her career. My cheeks heat and my pulse rams against my ribs. I gulp. My imagination sputters, as if it ran out of fuel processing the potential of what could be.

"But let's cross that bridge when we get there. Concentrate on getting back to LA safely." I hear the squeak of his kitchen chair. "How much longer until you stop for the night?"

"A few more hours." Mom slows to let a sedan pass. "I'll text when we check in at the motel."

"Sounds good. I love you." The words roll off Dad's tongue. Not sure how I feel about Dad openly declaring his love for Mom in front of me. "Both of you." That I can get used to.

"Love you too." Mom responds for both of us.

And it's that easy.

Fourteen

Sarah

"The timer should've gone off by now." Karina stretches her arms over her head in a sitting yoga pose.

I look at my phone. "Oops. I forgot to hit start. We've been at it for forty minutes."

"Goofball." She pinches my elbow.

I massage it like I'm in pain, and we both start to giggle. Me, because I'm in a weird third-wind mix of tired and giddy. Tired because of a week of getting up at four a.m., baking and serving customers, and giddy because my friend is here, injecting new life into my Toronto existence.

"Ten pages and two decent scenes written today. I say we deserve to celebrate." Karina wiggles her eyebrows.

"Oh yeah? What do you have in mind?"

She looks out Taylor's bedroom window. "I wanna see some of this city. It's Saturday night. What do you do for fun around here?"

Before I went to LA, I was on the list of the hottest clubs in town. Now we'd wait in line with the regulars. It's too cold for that. It hasn't started snowing yet, but the temperature dropped today, and if we're dancing, I'm not lugging my coat.

"Did you bring club clothes in that trunk of yours?" I point at the oversized luggage and additional carry-on Karina walked out of the airport with.

"You bet I did. A few options." She pops out of her seat and opens the case. "You like?" The cream dress would be floor-length on me but on her it hits mid-calf. "I was thinking this for your birthday."

I glide my hand over the soft silk. "I approve."

"As for tonight . . ." She eyes her clothes. "Tell me about the place, and I'll decide."

"Let's keep it local for your first night in town. We can Uber over to Essie's," I say. Ivy will hook us up with discount drinks. "The crowd is not as posh as downtown, but we can show a girl a good time out here in the Beaches."

Karina's short curls move as she nods. "I like it. As long as they make a decent martini, I'm good to go."

An hour and a half and two outfit changes later, we walk into Essie's, and it's like stepping back in time. Nothing has changed in the two years since I left.

The U-shaped bar still has its polished brass rail, colorful tap handles for the local brews, and red leather stools. Square tables, each surrounded by black lacquered chairs, match the dark stained floor. The lighting is low, except by the small dance floor where spotlights are swirling.

Out from behind the bar comes Ivy, her red hair piled into a knot.

We hug and I introduce Karina. "She just flew in from LA, so of course we came here first."

"Happy to meet you." Ivy hugs Karina. I forgot to inform my LA friend that Ivy is a hugger. But Karina takes it in stride and hugs her back.

We plant ourselves on stools in the back corner so Karina can survey potential targets.

"How's your mom?" Ivy's question punctures the lightness of catching up.

"I think she's finally enjoying her forced vacation." This morning she was still in her pajamas when I got home from the bakery. "Yesterday she spent the whole day binging cooking shows and called me to bring home avocados and uruchimai because she decided to make sushi for dinner. I had to go to the Japanese market."

"Same thing happened with my mom when she first retired." Ivy pours clear liquid from a shaker into two wide-rimmed glasses. "Except it was pottery, not cooking. She made the most awful mugs. I tried to break a few but they are sturdy."

Ivy moves down the bar to serve another customer, and Karina leans over to chat up the fine-looking guy sitting beside her.

I sip my drink. Everything's the same, but different. Like my favorite mug but in a different color. Nick would appreciate the atmosphere. If we lived in Toronto, we could spend evenings after work here, sharing a bottle of wine or a few beers. Or I could take him downtown and finally get to dance the night away with my boyfriend in a club.

Nick isn't going to live here. I shake my head. His life is in LA. Especially now, when he's starting to get the attention he deserves. The love and excitement for him in my mind overflows. This is just the beginning for him.

Nick needs to stay in LA. That's for sure.

"Who's here?" I bolt at the high-pitched scream and whack my forehead against the ceiling. That's what I get for sleeping in the top bunk in Taylor's room. We put him on the twin in my former room that now serves as a guestroom so Karina and I could share.

"What the fuck?" Doesn't sound like Karina.

"What the fuck, indeed." Now, that sounds like Karina.

I fumble for my phone and turn on the flashlight. Lying on the floor in the fetal position is my brother, Grayson, cradling his private parts. Karina is standing over him, her foot aimed at his nose.

"Stop," I shout. "That's my brother."

"Don't care if he's the King of Morocco. The creep tried to get into my bed."

"It's my bed." Grayson sounds like when he was ten and I held his favorite Transformer hostage until he agreed to share with Taylor.

My mind swims through the fog of too many martinis and not enough sleep. I giggle. I can't help it. The laughter starts in my chest, bubbles out, and leaves me gasping.

Two sets of eyes stare at me. One pair, brown and soft, looks at me like I've lost it. The other blue and bloodshot pair tries to focus on me, the laughing hyena in the room. From my vantage point on the top bunk, it's like I'm in the balcony seat at a comedy of errors.

My brother is drunk and must have come home instead of back to his dorm. I gulp air and try to stop laughing as I slip down the ladder to the floor. Karina is leaning against the dresser, arms crossed, eyeing Grayson as if he might attack at any moment. My brother is still moaning on the floor.

How many times have I come home tipsy and crawled into our bed in LA where Nick welcomed me with open arms? My chest pangs with something I don't want to name. The Nick-sized hole in my heart throbs. We've texted incessantly today, but I miss him. I need to hear his voice and the way he says my name, the slow A's he elongates in Sarah as his tone drops, evaporating my will to do anything but fly back to him.

I place my hand on the V of my PJ top as if I can close the gap. "Grayson, you're in the wrong room."

"Horsies," Grayson slurs.

"I think you mean horse shit," Karina says.

"No." I point to the wallpaper. "When he was eleven, Grayson wanted to be a cowboy. Mom decorated the room with a horse motif. I used to joke it was his My Little Pony phase."

I lean down and touch my brother's shoulder. "Yes, Grayson, the horses are here. But we moved in. Remember? I told you I was playing camp getaway with my friend."

Grayson's eyes meet mine, and I think he understands.

"Ride 'em cowboy?"

Or not.

"Okay, cowboy." I put my arms under his armpits and hoist him up. "Let's find you another bed to sleep in."

His head swivels. "I want that one."

"This cowgirl owns it." Karina takes the other side of a now-standing Grayson and helps shuffle him out the door.

He's pitching from side to side, too drunk to walk a straight line. As we turn the corner in the hall, he drapes himself across Karina. "You smell nice."

She snorts. "You smell like a barroom floor."

We lug him down the hall and into my old bedroom. I shove the wannabe cowboy into the bed, and Karina drapes a blanket over him.

"Sleep it off." I twist to the door. I look back at Karina, who's staring down at my passed-out brother. "You coming?"

Karina jumps as if I've shocked her. "Right behind you."

Back in our room, I try to get some sleep, but it's no use. The uneasiness in my chest returns. I switch on my phone and scroll backward through the texts between me and Nick from the last few days, as if they could be the balm to abate the effects of Nick-withdrawal.

Fifteen

NICK

Saturday was another day of twelve hours of driving and no studying. Mom and I made it to Utah, and I got some awesome shots of the sun setting over the rock formations in Arches National Park I sent to Sarah. I would much rather be in Toronto with her. At least Karina is there helping complete their screenplay.

My textbook wavers on my knee, and I try to make the letters stop dancing. I blame the harsh light of the motel bathroom. It's six a.m. on a Sunday and could count as sleeping in during my normal schedule. I rub sleep out of my eyes and pick up my phone. Having a pre-arranged time to chat means Sarah and I don't have to shout over the noise of the road on my end or the chatter of the customers on hers. And there's privacy. I'm grateful for the thin door separating me from Mom. Privacy has been lacking with Mom listening to every word, even though she was pretending she wasn't.

Mom's a good driver, but no matter how good you are at the wheel, six hours at it would tire anyone out. She didn't stir when I crept into the bathroom to study an hour ago, still asleep like a baby.

I scroll past the pictures Sarah sent of Karina and her holding martinis last night and read through her barrage of texts.

Sarah: We're planning my birthday. Can't wait to see you here.

Sarah: A cowboy-themed party.

Sarah: Would you ride a pony?

Sarah: Or are you too tall for that?

Sarah: A giraffe could be another option. They have them at the Zoo.

Will have to ask her how many martinis it took to get to the giraffe stage.

Me: Never dreamt of riding a giraffe, but before meeting you I didn't dream of much.

My email has a message from Professor Takamado.

"Color me impressed. I watched the cut you sent of your documentary three times last night, and I think I'm going to show it to the dean. Do you have more footage? This could be a great showpiece for the department. I can't wait to see what else you've got."

Show it to the dean? I thought he'd be nice and throw some perfunctory praise at best, or at the worst offer feedback I might not want to use. But show my work to the dean? That is awesome.

My phone vibrates, and the picture I took of Sarah on the night of my birthday fills my screen. Five a.m. on the dot. I accept the call and the real-life version replaces the static. The tiredness of two days on the road drops at the sight of my girl.

"Hey," I whisper.

"I had to search the house for my phone. Found it under Grayson's pillow," she whispers back. I spot a strawberry-patterned towel behind her.

"Still planning to hire giraffes for your party?"

"What giraffes?"

"From your texts?"

"What texts?"

"I got five texts from you stamped 4 a.m. your time last night."

Sarah's eyes narrow. "I never sent you any texts. Karina and I were asleep." She groans and slaps her forehead. "Grayson. My phone was on the charger in my room, where drunk Grayson crashed. He must've sent them."

"Tell your brother to stop sending me texts."

"I'll do you one better. I'll change my password." One side of her mouth wrinkles in an evil grin. "Now I don't feel bad about Karina kicking him in the balls last night."

"Ouch." I writhe on the edge of the tub.

"He deserved it." She glances to her left. "Guess where I'm hiding?"

"Under the stairs?"

She moves the phone away. "In the bathroom."

I bark out a laugh.

"What?" Her face is so cute. I'm desperate to kiss it. "It's the only quiet place in this busy house. Karina is still asleep."

I snicker and pull my phone away to show her the white tiles of the motel bathroom I'm sitting in. "Mom's still asleep. We're sharing a room."

When I turn the screen back to me, Sarah has her hand over her mouth, and her eyes are sparkling. "What have our lives become?"

"It feels very Stanley Kubrick."

"We should be in the same bathroom together." The sparkle deepens as her pupils dilate, and my heartrate speeds into overdrive. "Preferably in the shower. Doing something a lot hotter than sitting."

Heat wells inside my chest. "Like what?"

"Remember that thing you did?" Her eyes dart away from the camera.

"I did a lot of things with you in the shower." I bite the inside of my cheek. "Be more specific."

Her head jerks to the side. "Sometimes I have a feeling Grayson has an ear to the door, listening in on me. He used to when he was a kid."

"We are not talking about Grayson. We are talking about you and me in a shower."

"I get hot and bothered just thinking about it." She licks her lips, and my body lets me know I'm fully awake.

"Welcome to the club. There's been too much thinking and not enough doing."

The devilish smile I love appears. "I like our doing."

I groan and shift to the edge of the bathtub, trying to relieve some pressure. "What shower thing?"

"When you slide your fingers—"

The door to the bathroom opens. "Here you are. I thought you might've decided to go for a coffee run. And I told you yesterday, I have a perfect coffee and breakfast stop planned for us."

Mom's eyes fall on the phone in my hand and then lower to my lap. I was not lying to Sarah when I said there was not enough doing.

"Hi, Chrissy," Sarah shouts from her end of the continent. She isn't seeing what Mom is seeing.

"Hi, dear." Mom keeps her eyes firmly on the wall to my left. "I'll go get dressed. Don't leave the bathroom without knocking first, okay, Nicky?" She's shouting as if I'm not right in front of her.

"What was that about?" Sarah asks.

I tilt the camera so she can see my lap too.

"Oh. Your mom saw that?"

"Yep." My situation does not diminish. It's been too long. "In 3D. And we have ten more hours on the road today."

Sarah giggles, and the sound brightens my morning. "We are adults, and I'm sure her and your dad are doing—"

"No way. No." I wave my hands. "I do not need to hear about that." The words rectify my below-the-belt situation.

"I guess I'll be the one having the birds-and-the-bees conversation with our kids when the time comes. If I leave it to you, they might think storks bring kids, or they find them in cabbage patches."

I've imagined walking down the aisle with Sarah. Women are supposed to be planning their weddings, and until I met her, I wouldn't have believed anyone who'd say that I'd be imagining mine. But with Sarah, I am. Kids though? The thought is not sending me into panic mode.

There are a lot of years between now and us having children. But it's more about time than fear.

"Mom never had that conversation with me, and I turned out all right."

Sarah twirls the end of her ponytail. "I'm not complaining. But when it's our turn, we can do better."

"I'll do anything for you."

"Me too."

A cold, lonely shower later, I knock on the door to exit the bathroom and hope Mom doesn't decide to have the birds-and-the-bees conversation with me at this point in my life.

I should've learned by now that when I drive to LA and think I'm almost home, I'm at least two hours away from setting my foot inside my place. LA traffic is not an exaggeration.

"Sarah and you." Over three days on the road, Mom and I have gone over every conceivable safe topic of conversation. "How serious is it?"

Maybe it's because of what she saw in the bathroom this morning, or because she thinks I don't need to concentrate on driving quite as hard when we are moving five miles per hour, but she goes for it.

"Very." I'm not planning my proposal yet, if that's what she's worried about, but my life is tethered to Sarah's. We're an item.

Mom takes a sip from her steel water bottle. "She's lovely. Hard not to love someone so positive and hard-working. Seems like you are compatible in other areas as well."

"Mom. Let's not talk about that." I keep my eyes firmly on the road.

"I'm not trying to stick my nose into your relationship, but now that I'm practically your neighbor, I was hoping I'd get to see you more. With Sarah in Toronto this week, you could stay on the couch. Help me unpack?" She screws the lid back on. "I'll test my pots and pans in Theo's kitchen and make you two some of your favorites? The recipe book with Yiayia's creations is in the back. Might be a good way for us to catch up on family time?"

"You won't see me much. I have work, and school, and exams." Plus, I'd be forced to resort to whispering in their bathroom when I want to talk to Sarah.

My stomach misses Mom's food. And I miss Mom's care. The freedom of LA is starting to lose some of its shine when I haul laundry to the laundromat down the street and negotiate who's buying groceries and paying for gas. Escaping from Siobhan might be a relief as well. "A dinner would be nice though."

Mom perks up. "Tomorrow?"

"I have my film history exam."

"Tuesday?"

"Can't." I tap on the brakes and we come to a standstill. "Have an evening shift and we close at nine, to compensate for the Friday and Saturday I took off to help with the move."

"Wednesday?"

I shake my head. "Double shift again."

"Thursday?"

My mental calendar does not immediately deliver anything for Thursday night. "Can I bring my laundry with me?"

"Theo's washer and dryer are at your disposal. You can come every week. Laundry and dinner night? Two birds with one stone?"

Mom's always been practical. She knows my weak spots too well. "Thursday it is. How's six?"

She rubs her hands together like a villain hatching a plan. "This will be great. The three of us together this week. My table will be a tight fit in Theo's kitchen nook. It sits four, so when Sarah is back, I'll . . ."

I tune Mom out to take the ramp to Dad's street. We're less than ten miles away from the neighborhood I was born in, but it might as well be a different universe.

Do I wish Dad never got into trouble and we still lived in the mansion with a pool and a basketball court in the back yard? I'd be lying if I said I didn't. And I'm done with lying. Having my family together, even though we had to go through crap, is more proof that love conquers all.

Sarah's parents' twenty-five years of marriage after spending five years on different continents and my parents' reunion after ten years apart are very different stories. But both are confirmations that you can't run away from love.

Same story with Sarah and me. Despite what kept us apart, I found her. No matter what, I'm never making that stupid mistake again.

Sixteen

Sarah

THE OFFICE AT THE bakery is becoming my sanctuary. The only place I can be myself and by myself. Inviting Karina into it changes the vibe of the room. No longer full of memories of Mémère, the space is filled to the brim with Karina's energy and efficiency. We could've stayed in the boys' bedroom at the house and written there, but we tried that during our last few sessions and my word count failed to cover one page in two hours. Not even a good page. The dialogue would send the cast and crew into a coma.

I swig my coffee and squint at the desk Karina cleared for our laptops and notebooks. Without the folders, and the rolodex, and the inbox container with receipts, the surface looks nothing like Mémère's workspace anymore.

Karina moves her cup of coffee away from her and yawns. "If I'm here at this hour, we better be writing and not daydreaming."

"It's six a.m." I finished the prep, and Julio and Sandy promised they have it under control until seven when the real rush begins.

"Entirely too early for anything that involves my brain, but I'm here for you. Let's make the best of these sprints." She interlaces her fingers and stretches them back and forth as if she's an athlete.

Karina attacks her laptop. Her eyes are intent on the screen, and the familiar clatter of her fingers hitting the keys sets the mood. Her working on her typing is paying off, and I hear the speed increase.

I look at the sentences in front of me. Now that I've finished the happy-ending part, the breakup portion is back on my plate. I hunt for words that would hurt, for phrases to scorch my heroine's soul and make the hero regret he ever said them. Instead of synonyms for heartache, my mind serves me the list of the candidates for the shift manager's job.

Barry sounded best on paper. He has just the right amount of experience and comes from a similar style bakery that was taken over by a bigger chain. He's probably looking for the same family feel I want to keep here at Côté Fraise.

Regina might be too young for the position and doesn't have any viennoiserie experience, but if she's willing to roll up her sleeves and learn, I'm sure Mom will be able to teach her the techniques.

The last candidate I'll be interviewing today is Fran. She checks all the boxes, but she's from Montreal. When will she be able to start? I don't have a month for someone to relocate to the area.

I need a Mary Poppins employee who can hold this place together while Mom is resting. Because I plan to get back to LA. Back to my life. Back to Nick. I have five days to find that magical creature.

The timer buzzes to indicate the end of our first sprint. My screen displays five questions for the interviews and nothing for the screenplay. "Perhaps we need to take a pause on the screenplay until the bakery business is settled?"

"Or we keep going and write." Karina's inquisitive eyes meet mine. "Even two hundred words a day gets us to a thousand words each week. Four thousand words a month. It all adds up."

"Maybe *Indigo* was the last screenplay I had the creativity for." I switch back to the screenplay on my screen, and it sparks no joy in me like it did when we started the project.

"Or you're tired and stressed, and your brain is operating on minimal resources."

"Maybe." I want Karina to be right, to believe that the light at the end of the tunnel is a complete screenplay. I've done it three times already, and while my first screenplay might never see the light of day, Holly and Wesley got me into the Starlight competition. *Indigo* got me the *Vampire Club* job. I lay my forearms on the desk and rest on head on them. I've completed those three. Why does it seem like finishing the fourth one is a much more challenging task?

"Remember to let go of the daily stuff. That's what the sprints are for. Start typing. Start feeling with our characters. Even if it's a couple of sentences. We'll get there." She leans forward in her chair. "I'm not giving up on you."

"Bakery and writing"—I bury my face in my hands—"it's not how I imagined creating this screenplay would be."

She huffs. "When is life how we imagine?" Her voice has the confidence I can't seem to find these days. "You can do both. I know you can. We'll get to the end of this project, and you'll be so happy when we do."

Feeling happy would be an interesting change. The first step to get me there is to put the words on the screen, and for one of the interviews for the shift managers today to result in a hire. I cross my fingers and toes. I need help.

During the next sprint I manage to hack through my mental block and slap phrases and sentences together. It's all description, but it's words. Karina barricades herself in the office as I greet today's customers. Christmas carols play in the background as we hand out hot coffee and warm pastries.

The breakfast crowd thins, and we have at least an hour before lunch starts. I eye the door every time it opens, hoping one of the people will be the shift manager I've been manifesting.

A cascade of bells Mémère insisted sounded like the ones from her childhood in Lyon drives my gaze to the entrance.

In walks a woman in a bright pink knit dress and matching overcoat with a bag shaped like kissing lips in a similar color. She doesn't walk to the register but swivels and waves when she sees me. "You must be Sarah."

My name is on my badge, but it's unlikely she could see it from this distance. The pile of papers next to me together with my apron and name badge are good clues for her to assume I'm the person who's waiting to interview her. "And you are Ms. Valois?"

"Fran. Yes. That's me." Her dark bob shimmers as she nods.

"Great. Take a seat." I point to the table by the window. "Can I get you a coffee? A pastry too? You should try what you'll be selling."

She clutches a binder in her arms. "Do you have tarte aux fraise today?"

Might be a tactic, but I appreciate the effort. Julio sourced hot-house organic strawberries, and even though they were three times the cost of the generic ones I picked up, they are worth it. Mémère would approve.

The weak December sun offers little heat as we sip our coffees. Fran puts her folder in the clear space on the opposite side of the table, pulls out her résumé, and slides it in front of me. She must be younger than Mom, but guessing a woman's age when they are between forty and fifty is not a skill I possess. "This place is just lovely. The authenticity. The flare. The smell. Like a little piece of France in the middle of Toronto."

"Are you French?" Her name sounds French.

"My parents were. I speak French and lived there for a few years. Graduated from La Cuisine Paris." She points at the line of her résumé that indicates her education in the culinary world. "You follow the classical recipes here, no?"

"We do. My grandmother was the founder. Born and raised in France. She came to Canada when she met my grandfather. She prided herself on keeping the food artisanal, small batch, and as close to the original ingredients as possible."

"My kind of mentality. I fell in love with this place the first time I took a bite of your pain au chocolat. You could taste the real cocoa. Not that fake waxy stuff the blockbuster places use."

"You've been here before?"

"Yes. A couple of times. Gobbled the lemon tart when I was here on Thursday."

"Oh." The lady in the lemon dress. "Your outfit. I remember."

"Yes. My dresses are bold. I've always been a fan of color. I'm not afraid of my personality. Each of us is unique. Why not show it off?"

My smile catches me by surprise. This doesn't feel like an interview, but rather a conversation with a friend. I can see working alongside her. And Julio and Sandy will love her sunny personality. They need a bit of happy energy around here. "You caught my attention."

"I hope it's in the best of ways. I'm a serious person though. I've worked at several high-profile places before and ran a family bakery." She keeps moving her finger to the lines on the résumé.

"And I can follow whatever system you have. I'm a quick learner."

She sounds too good to be true. "Why do you think working at Côté Fraise would be a good fit for you?"

"I recently moved to Toronto and my goal here is to serve authentic French patisserie and viennoiserie to this area. Bring France to the people, add to the culture of this magnificent city. Everything I've seen and tasted here tells me this is the perfect place."

Perfect. This is why Mom didn't need to consider B&B's offer. Côté Fraise is perfect. A big corporation would destroy its charm and authenticity.

The questions I had evaporate. My heart leaps into my throat. The déjà vu sensation sweeps over me. This moment is familiar. I swear, I can smell strawberries around our table. The aroma isn't coming from the half-eaten tart on her plate.

Goosebumps rush across my forearms. I've been seeing Mémère everywhere, but this feels different. The acute ache beneath my ribs is sweet. Fran is the personification of the Mary Poppins I needed. Mémère heard me, and she delivered this person exactly to my specifications. Côté Fraise will be fine. Mom will rest and recover with this woman at the helm. I will have a trustworthy person to leave the ordering, and the baking, and the smiling to the customers to. "When can you start?"

She lowers her gaze. Shit. If she says in a month, I'm screwed. "Anytime, actually. I don't want to sound too eager, but I'm by myself in Toronto. Although exploring the city has been fun, living at a hotel has me itching to get my hands into some flour. I've been bakery hopping and sampling the goodies every morning, but I might be running out of places to do it at." She leans in. "And I might be in love with The Beaches Cinema. That building is beautiful."

Another Mémère moment. We snuck away on cold winter afternoons to watch the double matinee at the old theater. This is a sign.

"Actually, one of the reasons we're looking for a manager is"—should I tell her the truth about Mom? If Fran starts working here, she'll find out no matter what, might as well be honest—"Mom had a fall and can't do the workload"—work overload more like it—"so if you can start—"

"How about tomorrow?" She places her hand over mine. "Sorry about your mom. Must be tough handling it by yourself."

Her touch is nothing like Mémère's, but my reaction to it is the same. I want to hug her. I want to let the tears of tiredness out. I want to tell her my worries and sorrows, but Fran is not Mémère. She is a stranger, and I'm just exhausted and need a week's worth of ten-hour nights dedicated to slumber. I'll get them when I'm back to LA. After I spend a couple of nights devouring Nick.

I remove my hand from under Fran's. "Would you like to see the premises? The kitchen? I can give you a tour now, and then we can sign the papers."

"Does this mean I'm hired?"

"Côté Fraise has a three-week probationary period to make sure we are right for each other. That guarantees that you stay with us for the next three weeks and gives us a chance to find a replacement if this doesn't work out." I offer her a smile. "It also gives you a chance to leave without any hard feelings at the end of the three weeks. If you find another place that suits you—"

"I'm sure Côté Fraise is the right place for me. I can feel it in the air. Can't you?" She looks around at the walls Mémère picked the color for. The display Julio is restocking with Bredele cookies which Mémère guaranteed is the best recipe from Alsace. At the café tables with petite pitchers of milk, bowls of sugar, and the signature Côté Fraise sign on the window.

I feel it too. "Let's hope."

Mémère, is this the person you want to work here? The scent of strawberries I thought I smelled earlier intensifies as Fran joins me on the walk to the kitchen area. It's her. Fran. She smells like strawberries. "You smell lovely. Is it a perfume?"

"Oh, no. It's this artisanal conditioner I bought at Kensington market on one of my early morning escapades. Strawberries and cream. Isn't it divine?"

Divine. My hair rises on the back of my neck. I'm afraid to ask, but I do. "Is it Strawberry Fields by Kasha?"

"Yes. You're familiar with the brand?" Her eyes shine.

The brand Mémère and I found on one of our adventures. Goosebumps cover my entire body. "I've been using them for several years."

"What a coincidence." She claps her hands. "My hair is extra silky, and I just fell in love with that smell. Just like I did with Côté Fraise. Toronto has woven its magic. I can't imagine living anywhere else."

A lightness washes over me. Mom will love Fran.

Seventeen

NICK

Without Sarah to look after, the red-eye from LA to Toronto seems to take twice as long. The flight was delayed in LA, and we circled Pearson International Airport in Toronto for half an hour as the pilot waited for a runway to clear. My spine is taught and tense as I walk out of the plane. Is the universe trying to keep me from her again? It can try, but it will fail. Sarah is my girl, and nothing will keep me from her.

I did manage to get a few hours of sleep on the plane. Thanks to Mom's care packages of food and the new hire at Blend who actually seems competent, I had the luxury of extra pockets of time to catch up on my exam prep, so this weekend can be all about Sarah.

The doors to the arrivals area open. Clusters of people wait for their friends and loved ones. I scan for Sarah, hoping she's close but not getting crushed by this crowd. No golden hair in sight. I follow the ramp down, swiveling, desperate to see her.

"Mr. Old Fashioned."

My heart lurches at the sound of her voice. Not the crappy audio from my phone, the full-bodied, brimming-with-emotion voice of the girl I love. I turn to my left, and there she is, beaming at me. I drink her in: her Maple Leafs' hat, pink parka, dark jeans, and tall black winter boots. I can't wait to get those clothes off her, kiss every spot my lips have been craving for weeks.

For right now, I'll have to be content with her mouth. She runs to me and I lift her in my arms, her legs wrapping around me. My lips find hers and I'm home. My worries forgotten, I absorb her. Time slows, and I feel every millisecond of us together.

I smell, taste, touch, hear, and see her. She's my focus, and the airport around us blurs. The camera of my soul is trained on her and captures every minute detail of Sarah on the film of my memory. Loving someone so much surprises me time and time again. I want to keep it this way. I tremble with the intensity of feeling she rouses in my body, my mind, my soul. I crush her harder into myself.

She presses her forehead against mine. "I missed you."

I want to tell her that I missed her too, that I love her, but my throat is thick with the barrage of emotions, words, and desires. I'm afraid if I try to speak, I won't be able to. So I kiss her again, letting my lips do the talking. She gets my message, and her nails dig into the back of my neck. I groan, and she embraces me tighter.

We need to get out of this airport, or we're going to be in trouble.

She takes her lips off mine. "We need to get out of here."

I love how we are on the same page.

I settle her to the floor, but she keeps a tight hold on my waist, tucking into me. I certainly don't mind and can't resist kissing the top of her head. We manage a weird three-legged race to the bakery's van.

Intoxicated by each other, we don't speak. Within eyesight. Within a breath. Within touch. We feel.

She opens the back doors of the van and climbs in.

"Is something wrong with the—"

She tugs me by the jacket and I tumble into the empty cargo bay of the van, landing on my back. I barely gather my knees as she slams the doors shut. With only small, tinted windows in this portion of the van, the daylight dims to murky grays, but the light in her eyes is undeniable.

"Nick."

The cells in my body are on high alert at the way she says my name. They go into attack mode as she straddles me and her fingers claw at my sweater. I shiver when her cold hands press against my stomach.

"I need you."

My zipper comes undone.

"Now."

Her mouth returns to mine, and I'm not complaining. I help in my undressing, but she has entirely too many clothes on, so I switch to remedying that fact. Is it possible her skin got softer in the two weeks since I last touched her?

I investigate every inch I can reach, while her lips start at my happy trail and dip lower. I thought I remembered what I was missing, but my imagination didn't some close to this scene in the back of a van in an airport parking lot. I sink my teeth into my bottom lip, as I watch Sarah's hair cascade over one shoulder. A perfect shot to add to the reel of my favorite Sarah moments. Blood rushes from my brain. If she continues, I won't last. I drag Sarah's face up and kiss the girl who made my life into a romance movie. I want to linger and cherish her, but it's been too long, and I give in to her frenzied need.

We are arms and legs, hearts and souls as we come together. We are fast and furious, racing to the finish line where Sarah shudders and collapses on top of me.

I whisper, "I love you."

"Hmm," she sighs.

Somewhere in the distance a car's horn blares. We are in a parking lot at the airport. The van floor against my shoulder blades is freezing. Sarah's back is cold to my touch. This is not LA, and the last thing I need is for her to catch a chill the day before her birthday.

"Hey." I kiss her forehead. "I think we should go."

She moans, and her shoulders hitch as she clings to me. I caress her and try to roll over, to at least use my body warmth to warm her, but she refuses to move. I find her discarded jacket with one hand and drape it over her.

She must realize I've abandoned my plan of moving because her muscles relax. I draw hearts on her skin and her breathing regulates. I'm not entirely sure what's happening here.

"Everything okay?" I ask.

She nods into my chest. This is weird. My hands find her cheeks and her face tilts toward me, wet with tears. They drive my pulse to the rate I'd rather reserve for what we just finished doing. "No, no. Don't cry." My thumb works to erase the tracks of her tears.

She hiccups. I wait patiently. It's hard for her to express her emotions out loud.

This is it. She's going to say the three words I've wanted her to say to me for weeks. No, months. No. Since the moment I met her. The wait was worth it. Right now is the perfect time to tell me.

Eighteen

Sarah

Nick's I love yous might be my favorite thing in the world.

I store each one in my heart, stockpile them for the day when I'm down on myself, or am too sad, and then open the treasure trove of Nick's I love yous and use the love and affection to prop myself up. This one, today, hurts, because I'm not numb or unfeeling. He wants to hear the words back. And I want to be ready to say them, because Nick is everything to me. I've never felt like this, and this sounds cheesy even to me, but I'm certain I'll be able to say the words.

If Nick's the one who likes to take it slow when we are in bed, I'm the one who needs to, must, take it slow when it comes to my heart. I clutch at his shirt. I might be pragmatic, like Mom, but when it comes to love, I'm a romantic. I promised myself I'd wait and have the person I say I love you to be the one and only, the person who I'll spend the rest of my life with. To be the only one who hears those words from me, until death do us part.

The more I'm around Nick, the more I discover him, I can see Nick being that person. I want more than anything for Nick to be that person. Because I love him. I love him so much it scares me. I understand the poets and bards who wax on about overpowering love making them weak, making them lose control, lose themselves in the other person. I'd love to do that with Nick, but if anything happens, if my "I love you" is wasted, if what I feel for him is broken, my tears and heartache will take years to get over, if I get over it at all.

I burrow myself deeper into his chest and listen to the frantic beats of his heart. I inhale the familiar scent of his skin and taste the I love you on my togue. It feels natural, right, but . . . this is not the time.

The day I share my final secret with Nick, the day I tell him I love him, will be perfect. Movie-scene perfect. The way I planned everything out for his birthday: the hockey game, the hotel. That's the least he deserves. I need him to understand I'm serious. That we are right together.

The back of Mom's van is nether perfect nor right.

My hand finds its way over his heart, and he lays his over. Blood whooshes into my palm that's sandwiched between my two favorite parts of Nick: his heart and his hands. "I missed you so much." I try to laugh. "Didn't mean to attack you like that."

"No one's complaining over here." His eyes shine, and my heart dances. How did I find such an amazing partner?

I search for my top. "We better go. They'll be wondering if we got stranded in the snow. The storm was getting worse on the way here, and although I don't want to share you with anyone, Mom made moussaka in your honor. We don't want to disappoint her."

"Disappointing someone. We don't want to do that." His voice sounds hollow, or maybe it's the empty van.

I hold his hand on the drive home, and the silence between us is charged with the things we didn't share despite our calls and texts. His presence here should alleviate the heaviness in my chest I've been hiding this week from Mom, from Karina, from everyone.

He's my representation of sunny LA. But his light is not bright enough to get through the clouds of my mind. Nothing feels right. The unsettling feeling in the pit of my stomach is not because I missed lunch again to drive out here and get him. It's because in the back of my head little voices are telling me the bakery is not in the shape it needs to be.

"Are you going to do gifts at the party?" Nick brings my hand to his lips and distracts me from the swirl of regret and hope.

"This is not a kid's birthday party. Mom and Dad gave me cash to fix the alternator on Betty. Grayson gave me a new Maple Leafs Jersey, and Taylor gave me a gift card to Roots. It's a clothing store here. Karina went all out and got me the writing software I've been salivating over, so no bags or big red bows there."

"I have a bag for you. No bows, but I hope you like it."

A flutter of curiosity at what it could be short-circuits my brain. "I thought you buying the ticket to get here was the present."

"That's the present from Mom and Dad. They sponsored the trip. It was either that or me being late on rent this month." Nick rubs his chin, facial hair trimmed, and I see the scar from the puck that got me close to him on the first date at Griffith Park.

"I didn't mean for them to spend money."

"They offered when I went to dinner Thursday night. It's not a gift for you; I was joking." He shifts in his seat, tilting my way. "Mom made me promise we'll go over there next week for a proper homemade cake with candles. Nothing like what your Mom and Grandma could whip up, but food is one of the ways she shows her love. That and hugs. The final step is when she shouts at you to do something around the house—you'll know you're a part of the family."

My lips tug up. I see how Nick and his mom are alike. "Your mom is so warm and caring. She does remind me of Mémère sometimes. In all the good ways."

"The way you describe your grandma, I can see it." Nick lets go of my hand, unzips his backpack, and retrieves a shiny light blue bag, large enough to have taken half of the room in his pack. "And Mom won't take no for an answer."

"I wasn't planning on refusing food." I gawk at the gift bag he places on his knees. "Is that your gift?"

"It is. Focus on driving." He points out the windshield. "We can't do it in the middle of the road."

The bottom of the bag rests on Nick's lap, and the top goes up to his chin. "It's big," I say.

Nick gives me a goofy grin. "You two have been well acquainted at this point. I trust your judgment."

I reach out and poke him in the ribs. "The bag. I meant the bag."

"Did you?" His eye catches mine, and his good mood finally pierces the cloud of my unease about the whole Toronto situation. "Chances are, they're both big."

"Shut up, you goof." I poke him again. "Stop teasing me."

"No can do. I love seeing you get embarrassed and excited at the same time. The combination is irresistible." Nick opens the top of the bag and thoughtfully examines what's inside. "It is definitely big."

"Stop it. I have ten more minutes of driving. We don't want to get into a crash on my birthday."

"We do not."

Finally, I park the van in the driveway. Nick opens the door.

"Wait." I pull on his leather jacket. "The present first."

"You don't want to wait until we are in front of your family to open it?" He sounds serious, but his eyes twinkle. He's well aware of my impatience when I want something.

"With the hints you've been giving me, I'm pretty sure I do not. I might die of embarrassment."

"No one has died of embarrassment to my knowledge, but sure. What is more romantic than opening birthday presents in a bakery van?"

"Having sex in the back of a bakery van?" I grin, but that heaviness from before pushes in.

"Okay. Yes. You win." He thrusts the bag my way.

It looked big on his lap, but his and my proportions are not the same. The easiest way for me to extract whatever it's hiding is to lean the bag sideways.

My hands close around something . . . bowl-shaped? He got me dishes? The dishes we have at the apartment are from garage sales or IKEA, but I was expecting something a bit . . . more after his birthday.

Not that I'm comparing.

I pull on the item, and once a portion of it shows, I see it is definitely not a bowl. It's metal, and heavy, and long. And the shape is very familiar. Some kind of award?

"A trophy?" I give him a puzzled look.

"A trophy. Read the bottom."

I bring the plaque into view. It's an actual plaque, not taped-over words like Ryan made for my fake screenwriter's award after I lost the Starlight Foundation competition. "To the best girlfriend of the world. You made my cup full. With all the love. Nick."

There will be a hospital visit on my birthday, because my heart crashes into my ribcage so hard there might be internal bleeding. The whoosh in my ears is deafening. Nick's lips are moving but I don't comprehend his words. "What?"

"There's more."

"More?" My ability to speak is reduced to single-word utterances. Not good for my professional career.

"There's always more." Nick leans over the console and kisses my nose. "With you."

I dig into the bag and come back with a long velvet box. Too long for a ring.

"I don't have cash, but this is sort of a compromise." His voice drops to that low pitch that radiates in my core. "A promise of something more once I do have the money to spoil you."

"You don't have to."

"But I want to. I plan on spoiling you every chance I get."

He does already. Just by being him.

I lay the trophy on the dashboard and open the box. A pretty silver chain stretches across it and a hockey championship ring lies attached to it on one side. I pick it up.

"Read the inscription." Nick points to the inside of the ring.

I tilt it so the light hits the internal part. "To old-fashioned love, forever."

I can't breathe. He'll need to perform mouth-to-mouth resuscitation along with chest compressions. My heart sputters. I gasp. My hands clutch at the piece of jewelry that means more to me than any priceless diamond.

"I had another plan for your birthday, and I hope we still can do that when you're back in LA, but with the change of location, I had to figure out something else." He's rubbing his chin again. "When I saw my hockey trophy and the ring, it just clicked. I went to the engraver and got these inscriptions. You love words, so I tried to write some for you that'll show you everything you mean to me and—"

"I love your words." I tug on his shirt. He lowers his face, and I kiss him as if I'm claiming him, marking him mine. He does know me. This gift is better than a night at a hotel, better than a fancy party. It's the one-of-a-kind thing that only I will have. "They are perfect. You are perfect." I love him so much. "I—"

A rattle at the driver's side window pulls my attention away from Nick.

"Lovebirds." Grayson taps on the non-existent watch on his wrist. "You can kiss and make out later. I had to drag my ass out here because the battery on my phone is dead again. Mom says the moussaka is getting dry. Come on."

I make eyes at him to go away and leave us alone.

Grayson waves at us to get out, unimpressed. "Chop-chop. Time waits for no one, and we're tired of waiting for you."

With the wrong kind of groan, I pull away from Nick, put his ring around my neck, and climb out of the van. I have all weekend to kiss my boyfriend.

Nineteen

Sarah

Sometimes I think being on the outside of a party is better. Serving people and observing them gives me material for writing. My notes are full of random encounters, real-life stories I overhear, and tidbits no imagination would be daring enough to conjure. I catalog people's looks, mannerisms, and speech patterns to create characters for years' worth of screenplays. Being on the inside of the party used to be fun too. But maybe because I turned twenty-two today, or maybe it's because I want everyone else to have a good time, that I'm . . . not.

The best part of the party is introducing Nick. The look on the parents' faces when he talks about being at UCLA and having a merit-based scholarship says, "Good going, he must be smart." The look on the girls' faces says, "Damn, he's hot." The look on my face better say, "Hands off, he's mine."

He is mine. Body and soul and whatever other plane exits. I realize Nick is 110 percent in, and I'm scared to disappoint him. I love him, and that scares me more and more, because I'm not sure I can keep the words inside for much longer. If Grayson hadn't interrupted us in the van, they would have tumbled out. I tighten my grip on Nick's elbow and snuggle into his shirt. Possibly for the best. That was not the right or the perfect place.

Nick and I don't separate even for a minute. I'm glued to him just like I intended. Through the layers of clothes I absorb every drop of his nearness. The further we're into the party, the more I my shoulders drop and my breaths deepen, even though I have to track how much food and drink is on the table and order more to ensure the guests are fed and hydrated.

"Do you want another drink?" asks Nick.

I shake my head and raise the Old Fashioned I've barely had two sips of.

Ivy slings her arm around my waist pulls me away from my boyfriend. "The girls need you."

"Go," Nick whispers in my ear. "I'll be fine. Don't worry about me."

"You sure?" The desire to stay with him plants my feet in place.

"Sure. I'm not going anywhere." Three beers in, he might be a bit too cheerful, but at least he is having fun.

I comb for any trace of what he calls the Nicky persona he uses to try to fit in, but find genuine, carefree Nick. A calm settles in me. "Okay. Don't let anyone tell you any embarrassing stories while I'm not here to defend myself."

"I'll plug my ears, I swear." He laughs, kisses my temple, and nudges me into Ivy's arms.

The table Ivy sits me at is full. It's great to see my high school and college friends again, but we've been out of touch for two years, and the conversation falters past the basics. I don't seem to have much in common with them anymore. Karina joins us just as Ivy asks, "Have you met anyone famous?"

I lean one elbow on the wooden surface. "El Vella sang the song for the movie Nick and I shot."

"Who's that?" Ivy draws her brows together.

"Her debut song *Don't Give Me Comfort* just went viral."

Ivy's eyes sparkle with recognition. "I loved the music video. The kiss at the end was so hot, I believed they were a couple."

I bite my lip to keep El's secret. "That's the one."

"And"—Karina winds her arm through mine—"don't forget Kyle Bardot."

Ivy's mouth drops open and the other women sit up, now paying close attention. "From *Vampire Club*?"

He's"—Ivy fans herself—"hot."

"He is pretty dreamy." I glance at Nick, who's talking with Grayson and Taylor on the other side of the bar. Kyle has nothing on Nick.

"The very same." Karina swirls the tiny red stick in her drink like she's brewing a good story. "Sarah and I write for the show."

Ivy's eyes swivel between us as if we've revealed we spent last summer at Shawn Mendes's summer villa in Spain. "Get out. Do you know what happens?" She's bouncing. "That cliffhanger was killer. I can't wait for next season."

Neither can I. Rod will find out any day if we get picked up.

Karina leans into the girls and nearly spills her drink, the red liquid sloshing over the rim of the martini glass. "Remember the car chase before the bar scene?" The girls nod, enraptured. "Guess who was in the car with Kyle?" Karina raises her hand above me and points downward. "This girl."

If I were writing a screenplay of this moment, I'd use the word swoon to describe the look on my friends' faces. I refuse to think about what happened after I met Kyle that day. There's a moment of panic. I search for Nick but can't find him in the crowd. He's here. Not gone like that night.

Ivy's pulling on the sleeve of my dress. "Tell us about it. Don't leave out a minute."

Karina doesn't give me a chance. "Our girl saved the day." She weaves the tale of how I taught him to drive a six-speed, like the great storyteller she is.

"Do you know Shonda Rhimes? I have the best idea for a new show." I half-listen to Ivy's proposal, nodding in the appropriate places before making my excuses and leaving Karina to tell more stories. The need to hold Nick's hand is overpowering.

"Have you seen your mother?" Dad catches my arm on my way to the bar.

I haven't paid too much attention to her, apart from making sure she rested and wasn't trying to take over the hostess duties. I don't see her by the bar. "Not sure. What's up?"

"I have her meds. The alarm went off for her next dose." The concern in his eyes is adorable. Dad would do anything for Mom.

My gaze snags on Nick talking with Taylor. Gone is the strain I've seen in his face during our video chats and the tense shoulders from a day trying to please my family. My boyfriend is happy. The party fades away and warmth permeates my chest. Being apart sucked, but it's over now. We're going home tomorrow.

Dad's elbow hits mine and the noise of the bar floods back in. Along with the reason I'm not kissing Nick right now. I tilt my head to the back of the room. "Let's try the patio."

I glide between the people and chairs, round the corners, and get us to the exit in record time. If there were a sport of get-your-father-through-the-maze-of-a-bar I'd be winning it. I open the door to the patio.

"... I can't ruin her birthday." Mom's panicked tone and the icy wind breach my mellow warmth, and a snowstorm warning flashes in my mind.

"This isn't only about her." There's something harsh in Grayson's voice. My head snaps back. Since his bar-hopping fiasco last weekend he's been shying away from alcohol so I know he's not drunk.

Mom rubs his arm. "But this is her day. If you must, we'll tell her tomorrow."

"Tell me what?" I step onto the stones and watch my mother and brother exchange miserable glances.

"Not in the middle of your birthday party. People are waiting for you." Mom always wants to avoid a scene. Right place, right time. I learned that from her. "They drove to spend tonight with you. We'll sort it tomorrow. Not like anything is going to change."

"Mom, I cannot go and pretend I'm cheery and cordial if I think there's a big secret you're hiding. Is it your arm? Your leg? I thought both were getting better." I scan her body for any sign of pain. The worst-case scenario leaps into my had. Mémère had it. What if it's something genetic, something Mom also has? "Do you have cancer like Mémère?"

Her face crumples. "No, honey. I promise, my health is fine." Mom shuffles over my way. She puts her hands on my cheeks and meets my eye. "I'm healing well."

"Then what is it?" The feeling of dread curling in my stomach has not dissipated. The way she's stroking my skin, like it's the last time she'll ever get to touch me, intensifies my storm watch.

"It's the bakery." Grayson steps out from behind a heat lamp.

My gaze slips to Grayson, whose arms are crossed, then back to Mom. That dread lingers, waiting to pounce. "What about it?"

"Remember the offer B&B gave us last summer?" he says.

"Yes." I pull out of Mom's embrace like I can distance myself from what comes next. Whatever it is, the scowl on Grayson's face means I won't like it. "The one you refused."

"The one Mom refused. I reached out to see if they're still interested."

I stare at my brother. "Why?"

"Because a lot has happened since last summer, and it's time."

His betrayal sets the kettle of my anger to simmer. "You what?"

Has my brother been scheming behind our backs? No. Grayson isn't capable. He's too busy chasing girls, horsing around at the stables, and barely attending classes at university.

As if he reads my mind, he stands tall. "I knew this day would come. When the bakery would be too much for Mom. We need to think logically and not with our hearts."

"But the bakery is part of our family." Mom nods in agreement. I glare at my brother. "I can't let go of it and pretend it's a good decision."

His confidence from before transforms into hesitation as his gaze flickers to the floor. "I'm not questioning how important the business was for Mémère, for all of us. But sometimes we outgrow things, or they outgrow us. The bakery would be in better hands with B&B." When he looks at me again, his resolve is back. "I've thought about it, and I want to sell."

Rage comes to a boil, and I advance on him. "It's Mom's decision to make, not yours."

"It's mine as well." He taps his chest. "I own 20 percent of the bakery. So does Taylor. So do you. The decision belongs to each of us. We get a say in the running of the business. Besides, I've been here, know the real picture with facts and numbers to support me."

His accusation jabs me.

"The only choice is to keep the bakery in the family. It's Mémère's legacy." Why does Grayson not see this? She was his grandmother too.

"Kids. Enough." Dad's usually quiet voice blankets our rising voices. "This is not the time or the place for it. We need an honest conversation. As a family. Look at all the options. Discuss what selling might mean."

The thought of not having the bakery wars against a flash of what life could be like with my portion of the money.

Nick's smiling face from moments ago cements in my mind. He wouldn't have to work long hours at the coffee shop, could concentrate on school. His teachers, his dad, Ms. Hansley—they all see the talent he has. What could he do if he wasn't tired all the time?

No more shifts at The Diamond Club would mean weekends with Nick. The thought of spending a lazy Saturday afternoon in Nick's arms is tantalizing.

But not at the cost of everything Mémère worked her life for. "My vote is no." I jerk at the loudness of my voice.

"You're only one vote. We decide as a family." Grayson's gaze turns to Mom over my shoulder.

I follow and meet her eyes.

"I think we should talk." Mom leans on Dad, who wraps one hand around her waist.

"You want to talk?" I squeeze my hands into fists. "Fine. Let's do a family meeting." I spin and run inside before I start screaming like a kettle on high boil. I can't go back to the bar now. The smiling people, the incessant questions, I can't handle any of it. I need to let my thoughts settle into some semblance of cohesiveness before I show my face again.

Or I'll just walk to the bakery and let them have the fun I'm not having anyhow.

I turn to the front exit and run outside. The snow that the roof of the covered patio was protecting us from swirls in the air and lands on my head, not quite cooling the fury inside but reminding me I will get through this too.

This is not the end.

Grayson thinks he'll persuade me with his cold-blooded logic if we talk, but I'm good with words. I'll write a list of the arguments for keeping Côté Fraise part of our family as it's always been. I'll persuade him to see Mom and I are right. I shove my freezing hands into my armpits. I just need to get my facts straight. I'll turn his weapon against him and make a freaking spreadsheet of pros and cons that Grayson cannot refute.

Time. I shiver. I only need a bit more time.

Twenty

NICK

The music switches from modern rap to old-school rock-n-roll as I exit the bathroom. Several hours into the party, the guests have picked up a dozen decibels and show no sighs of slowing down. I'd usually be asleep by now, but today is not about me. It's Sarah's day. I scan the room for her blue dress. I'll stay up as late as she needs me. I wave at Ivy and Sarah's other friends. Karina's laugher rings over the bar. Grayson's slamming the bar top like he just told the best joke.

I make a slow three-sixty but Sarah is nowhere to be seen. I stalk to Karina and Grayson.

"So you actually can make a horse kneel on command?" Karina's stares at Grayson like he's a magician.

"I started with dressage when I was a pre-teen. Now I'm teaching pre-teens." Sarah's brother leans closer to Karina. "But the best part is when I get to come up with a new trick and train the horses to do what they've never done before." He has that look Sarah gets when she's explaining beats and character arcs, like it's their lifeblood.

Karina smiles and Grayson steps forward. His lips are awfully close to Karina's ear but I can still hear him. "I usually prefer horses to people, but—"

"Where's Sarah?" I ask.

Karina's hand halts on Grayson's bicep. He jerks away from her and points to the door. "Outside. She needed a minute."

My neck muscles tighten at his tone. Somethings not right. Her coat is still on the hanger. This is not the weather to go outside in a tiny thin dress. I grab her coat and mine and storm out.

The freezing air invades my lungs as soon as I step onto the sidewalk. Down the road, the lights of the streetlamps reflect off Sarah's golden hair.

"Sarah!" I shrug on my jacket and run after her. "Wait."

She stops and raises her face to the sky, her eyelids shut.

I catch up. A current of anxiety ripples through me. "What happened?"

She covers her face with her hands. "Ahhhh," she yells into them.

"Is it your mother?"

Still hiding behind her fingers, she shakes her head. I throw her coat and then my arms over her shoulders, but Sarah pushes me away. The motion hurts, like the rope connecting us tenses and pulls my skin away from my muscles.

"No. My brother. My stupid, stubborn brother." Sarah stomps.

My lungs constrict. Stepping toward her would be my go-to, but I don't want to be rebuffed again. I stuff my freezing hands into the pockets of my coat. Next time my packing list will include gloves, a scarf, and decent boots. I can see my breath in the cold air, trailing toward Sarah. It wants to be with her too. With her coat wide open, and her cocktail dress exposing her tanned skin, she must be freezing.

"Grayson?" I suck in frozen air.

Her bright blue eyes blaze with fire. "I can't believe he's doing this to me. To us." She waves her hand between us and fear licks my neck.

I'm not sure what Grayson can do to us aside from the prank texts he's been sending to my phone.

"What is he doing?" I stand in front of her. "Talk to me."

Rage blazes in her glare. "He's been talking to the business that wants to buy the bakery." The heat of her words melts the cage of her restraint. "Behind our backs." Her hands dance in the air, and her jacket hangs precariously on her tiny frame. "They made another offer, and he wants to sell. Dad suggested we have a family meeting tomorrow. Grayson believes the rest of us are heartless enough to destroy Mémère's work."

My chest constricts. This is about the bakery, Sarah's need to preserve her connection to her grandmother.

Yiayia and I were tight when we moved in with Aunt Valentina in Chicago after Dad's arrest, before my grandparents moved

to their retirement home in Florida. My best memory of Yiayia
as a kid is her food, but I was never that close to her. She's still
one of my favorite people who can't say no to me, but Sarah and
her Mémère are on a different level. This bakery is like Sarah's
lifeline to her dead grandmother.

"He insists Mom isn't up to running Côté Fraise anymore.
That the money we each get will be more useful than keeping Mémère's memory alive." She tightens her fist and almost
growls.

"Have you considered his perspective?"

Sarah glares at me.

I raise my hands. "Don't hate me. I'm trying to figure out
how this works. This week it's hiring a new manager and a
replacement for Sandy. What will it be next week? When does
it end?"

Her mouth gapes. "Never. That's the point. I thought you
understood."

"I do." I run my hands through my hair and regret it. Is my
hair frozen in place? "It's . . . I don't know. Doesn't your whole
family need to make this decision? You can't do this by yourself.
From what I see, your dad only talks about the authors he gets to
discover for his magazine. Grayson's focus is horses, jokes, and
sometimes hockey. Taylor is leaving for university in the fall, and
anyway, what apart from hockey and video games interests him?
Not baking or running a store. And with you in LA . . . I don't
see the long-term plan here."

She steps back as if my words jolt her. "Not you too." Ache pools in her gaze.

The look kills me. We've come this far and it's a punch to the gut that she'd imagine I would not support her.

"You think we should sell?" She grips the S on her necklace.

"It's not that." I inch forward. "There's no doubt in my mind there's a way to keep your grandmother's vision alive. But at what cost?"

"You're on his side." She turns away, hiding her expression.

"That's not fair. I'm always team Sarah." I step in front of her, dip down to ask her to look at me. I try to show my love and support with my eyes. "Always."

A long stream of frozen air hangs between us as she exhales. I pull the open ends of her jacket together in an effort to keep her skin from turning the same color as her blue dress. "Have your meeting tomorrow. Skip the studio tour Karina set up, and then we get on a plane and go home."

Her eyes flicker between me and the sidewalk, then settle on me.

The tightrope in my spine slackens. I hold her gaze. "I'm freaking freezing. Can we go back to the party? Or grab a cab and go home?"

"Home." Determination lights her face. "We have a battle to prepare for."

I mock groan. "Why do I feel a spreadsheet coming up?"

Sarah pulls on my shirt, and I bend down, her lips brushing against mine. "You know me so well."

Twenty-One

Sarah

THE DINING ROOM TABLE is unrecognizable. Instead of festive placeholders, decorative dishes, or the steaming food I'm used to seeing on it, we have papers, a pitcher of water, and five glasses.

No one would confuse this with a boardroom, since we are surrounded by photos of our family: Mom and Dad at their wedding; Mémère and me at the beach building sandcastles; Grayson's bald head bobbing in the tub; Mom, Dad, Mémère, Grandpa, Grayson, and me looking at Taylor smiling as he took his first steps. I see our birthdays, graduations, vacations. This wall is a testimonial of the happy times, and the losses. A perfect backdrop to what is about to happen.

Deep breaths in and out. I'm not afraid. Mom doesn't want the money. Mémère is on our side, and she is the biggest ace. There's nothing new Grayson can throw my way. Deep breaths. I've worked at the bakery. Fran is here to help. Julio is staying.

Sandy will train her replacement. The customers are happy. In and out. We can do it, as a family. The Connors don't run away from problems. We face them straight on. I ball my hands into fists. Together.

"Will there be refreshments?" Taylor adjusts his tie and acts like he's a CEO of a major company. His effort to provide comic relief doesn't work. I didn't even know he owned a tie.

"Look at you, pretending you're interested in the bakery and not only the food it provides." I sound harsher than I intend, and the hurt look on Taylor's face is not what I'm after. I need him on my side. "I have madeleines left over from an order for a confirmation party. Want some?"

"I'm fine." Taylor stretches his lips but there is nothing genuine about his expression. I clench my jaw. I'm shooting myself in the foot before negotiations even begin. Stop it, Sarah. What negotiations? This is just me, Mom, and Grayson. Dad might chime in, but Taylor doesn't care.

My fingers are numb, and I wish Nick were here to warm them. We stayed up until 3 a.m. rehearsing my speech, and he gave me a kiss for good luck this morning before heading out with Karina. They are touring movie studios, and I am fighting for a business I never wanted to be a part of. Evil laughter fills my mind. Life sure throws curveballs.

Mom walks into the dining room. "Where's Grayson? He said he'd be here at ten."

Dad follows with a plate of apple cranberry galette, and Taylor's face comes alive. "The only thing he's on time for are his horses."

The front door slams. "Speak of the devil." Taylor swipes a piece of the galette while everyone watches the hallway.

"We're in the dining room." Mom brushes non-existent crumbs off Dad's shirt.

Grayson rushes in, takes a wedge of the dessert, and mumbles, "What did I miss?" through the food in his mouth.

"Nothing yet." Dad looks around the table.

Mom and Grayson mirror each other from the short sides. Dad and I sit closest to Mom, and Taylor is next to Dad. Intentional or not, it makes it feel like Grayson is the opposition, or the bad guy. I'm the good guy here. I want to preserve things, not rip them apart.

"Thank you everyone for coming," Dad starts. "Grayson got a new offer from B&B to buy Côté Fraise." Dad slides a paper my way. "I consulted with a lawyer, and Grayson is right, it's fair, almost generous."

"I've read it." I fold my arms and lean back in the stiff dining room chair. "The offer is good, if you are in it for the money. But we are not. We're here to preserve Mémère's legacy."

"Who is we?" Grayson's voice is ice compared to my fire.

My gaze rounds the table. "Our family."

"Have you asked our family"—he raises his voice on the last word, as if it has a different meaning from mine—"their opinion?" His tone digs his disagreement into my breastbone.

"I assume we're in agreement." I slap both hands on the table, and water splashes out of my glass.

"Let's not assume." The muscles in Grayson's jaw tick. With anger. I can feel it emanating from him and wafting my way. "We live in a democracy. Let's take a vote."

"Sure." Everyone at this table loved Mémère. That's a fact. I'm certain I'm winning this round.

"Raise your hand if you think we should sell the bakery to B&B." Grayson raises his fingers. Dad pats Mom's hand but he's not raising his. He loves Grayson as much as he loves Taylor and me, but he's on Mom's side.

Taylor's arm creeps up.

"Taylor?" I dig my fingers into my palm. What is his problem? It's not like he even does anything for the bakery.

"I can use the money for my room and board at Western. No crappy dorm living for me. With a car and no need for a job, I can visit Mom and Dad any time. Makes my life easy." He grins at Mom, crumbs falling on his shirt.

"Your life is already easy," I say.

The corners of his mouth fall. "You don't know anything about my life. You barely talk to me. Do you even care what I'll be studying at university?"

"Have you decided on a major?" Last I heard, he was still finding himself.

Taylor sits up straight and puffs out his chest. "Last year. Mémère and I visited the campus. I decided on video game design."

That fits. But how was I not aware Mémère took him? "I'm sure you can manage without the extra money. You would've if Mémère were still alive and running the place."

"Stop it, kids." Mom's lips tremble. "Why are you so set on selling?" She looks at Grayson across the table.

I drill holes through Grayson with my glare. "A burning need for money?"

"No." Grayson doesn't flinch. The two years I've spent in LA transformed him from an overconfident youth to a self-assured adult. Mémère's stubborn streak shines in him too. "Don't try to make me look like the selfish one. Money will be useful for all of us, but it's about more than that. It's about common sense and what's best for our family." Grayson throws my earlier words back at me and has the guts to look humble.

"What's the long-term plan here? I'm not going to take over the bakery." He taps the top button on his polo shirt. "I have career plans that involve horses, not pastry. Dad has his editor job, plus he's not a baker. Taylor has made his plans clear."

Grayson meets my stare only for his gaze to fall to the center of the table. "Mom can't do it alone. When Mémère was around it was different. But between Mémère's sickness and this last year without her, it's taking a toll. She comes home exhausted every night." His eyes flicker to her and land on Dad. "She shouldn't even be thinking about work now. Besides, it could be time for you"—he looks at Mom, the anger replaced by softness—"to take a real break, try something new."

"It's harder to keep the bakery going without your grand-mother." Mom runs a finger under her eye. "No one has tried harder to keep the business going than me. It's a lot of work. This"—she holds up her broken wrist—"has brought to light that I'm not as young as I thought I was."

"But you love working there," I say.

"I wouldn't trade my time with my mother for anything. It was a pleasure to work with her day in and day out. Without her it's . . . not the same." Mom's eyes lose focus.

My breath hitches. It's hard for *me* being in the Côté Fraise kitchen, where shadows of Mémère linger at every corner. I press the heel of my palm into my stomach. What has it been like for Mom living with her ghost week after week? Mémère's apron still hangs on her hook at the bakery. Her handwriting decorates the labels on the spice jars. Every knickknack in the café screams of the loved one no longer with us. Mom has been struggling to keep the business afloat alone for a year.

But she is not alone. I ball the cable-knit design on my sweater in my fist. I'm here. And Julio. And now we have Fran. Fran will take on Mémère's responsibilities at Côté Fraise. Mom will love working with her. The bakery will be a happy place like before. Mom will be happy. The customers will be happy. I release the hold on my sweater.

"What about Mémère's customers?" I ask. "Think of Natalie. If you sell, who will serve her chocolate croissants on Tues-days?"

"I . . ." Mom sighs.

"We can't make decisions based on Natalie." Grayson's palm swipes across the table, like he's brushing away my silly arguments. "We are barely managing to cover the payments on the van, never mind the maintenance. This house needs a new roof, and Mom and Dad keep putting it off."

We all look up like the ceiling might cave in on us. I had no idea the roof needed repairs. Then he stares at me. "And you." He lets the accusation hang in the air.

Me?

The eldest daughter that was supposed to take care of Mom, of Mémère, keep the business alive, the daughter who failed the family by moving to LA.

"You don't know the worst of it." He pulls a folder out of his backpack and slams a spreadsheet printout in the middle of the table. "This is a list of our vendors and costs." He points to a column of dates with percentages beside each year. 2 percent, 3.1 percent, 4.2 percent. "Buying local ingredients has doubled in cost in the last three years alone. Especially in the winter when greenhouse fruit is what we can get."

The carton of moldy strawberries Julio tossed last week because of my purchasing mistake is now covered with flashing dollar signs in my mind. I roll my lips between my teeth. How much money did I waste there?

"A small business like Côté Fraise just doesn't have the profit margin to maintain these costs." He drums his fingers across the lines of numbers like he's adding them up on a calculator.

"We'll charge a little more," I say.

"Sure." He scoffs at me. "The big-box bakery down the road sells six croissants for half the price. Mom can't make them that cheap. If you care about Natalie so much, you should care that she can't afford the increase. She's on a fixed income. Côté Fraise needs new customers with big wallets, but that means losing our old customers."

Natalie's daily coffee. Her little Christmas angel brooch she was sporting last Tuesday. I choke down the spear of anguish. How can I raise prices on her? Tears sting my eyes.

Grayson thinks he can scare me with numbers. He should think again. I came prepared to fight. Fight for what's right. Fight for Mémère. Fight for our family. "Big box stores don't have the same flavors, the same craftsmanship. Patrons pay for artisanal. The people who want a dozen big box cupcakes for their birthday are not the right customers for us. Mom is amazing with customers. They love her."

I turn to Mom for backup and meet a pinched face, her mouth in a straight line. "I can't do it alone."

This is what she's worried about? My body relaxes. Not a problem. "You have Julio, Fran, and me. Once we figure out Sandy's replacement, we'll be fully staffed. We'll find someone great. You don't need to worry, I'll help. I'll stay here until you're rested and ready to go back to work."

The words leave my mouth, coming straight from the grieving hole in my heart. The Nick-shaped portion of my heart screams, "What about me?" I place my hand on my chest, like I can hold the two sides of my heart together. I just made an offer that will change our lives without consulting him. I can't do that to him again.

Yet, I can't let my family down. Mom shouldn't be forced to let Mémère's bakery go. It's all we have left of my grandmother.

"Sarah. Be honest." Grayson's voice blasts through the drum in my ears. "You never wanted this life."

"I didn't. But . . ." I absorb the smiles of my family trapped in the photos across the room, as if they'll give me the right words. Clear blue eyes peer at me from under a wide-brimmed flowered beach hat from the snapshot I took before I left for LA.

Mémère.

"I can't let Mémère's dream disappear."

Grayson crosses his arms. "Two years ago, you left Toronto, wanted to be in LA, following your dreams. You didn't care about the bakery. Or Mémère. If you want to be in LA, be in LA."

"People change." I mirror my brother. "I needed to be in LA two years ago. Today, I need to stay here. Help Mom get the bakery back on its feet. This won't be forever."

Twenty-Two

Sarah

"I thought Grayson was coming." Karina looks expectantly behind me.

The table at Dark Horse Bar and Grill seats four. I promised I'd bring Grayson along, my mind set on him agreeing with Mom and me as the only possible outcome. I stuff my hands into my pockets and play with the keys. This was supposed to be a celebration.

That was before the forces that have been brewing while I lived in my blissful ignorance in LA erupted and put fresh cracks in the foundation of our family. A web of knots tightens my chest. "Grayson and his spreadsheet are not welcome anymore."

"Went that well, huh?" Nick draws me into his side and kisses the top of my head. "You didn't win?"

I sink into his warmth, his strength. "No one won. It's a stay of execution. We reconvene on December 23rd."

Nick leans away and finds my eyes. "You're flying back here and missing Christmas with my family?"

The plan was to spend the winter holidays in LA, enjoy the views of LA from the height of the Griffith Observatory on Christmas Eve, and celebrate the first anniversary of the day Nick and I met.

"Not quite." I wince, and he rubs his chin. Is he waiting for me to break his heart? "I'm staying here till then." I try to read his face and clasp his hand, pleading for him to understand. "I promise I'll be home on the twenty-fourth in plenty of time for our date." Save the bakery in the morning, in Nick's arms by nightfall.

He squeezes my fingers like he doesn't want to let me go. "Two more weeks?"

"Mom and Grayson agreed to give me these two weeks to show a solid plan on how we can turn this situation around. I can beat his measly spreadsheet with my own." I bounce my knee. "I'm a queen of spreadsheets."

"You do love those." Karina hides behind the rim of her glass. "Our screenplay would've been a mess if you didn't organize the beats and characters and chapters." I hope the lines of disappointment around her eyes are because Grayson is in the wrong, not because she's unhappy he's not here.

"What happens on the twenty-third?" Nick's voice is too still, too lifeless.

"I hire Fran full-time, we vote not to sell, and I pack to come home."

The corner of his mouth curves in an almost smile, and one of the thousand knots in my chest loosens. "So you got Grayson on your side?"

The strings pull and the knot cinches. "No. But I don't need him. Mom holds 40 percent and each of us kids has 20 percent. As long as Mom's with me, Grayson and Taylor can't do anything but agree. And I will always agree with Mom's decision."

"What if she decides to sell?" Karina is a straight-shooter, and it's one of the qualities I admire about her, but she doesn't quite get the connection Mom had with Mémère.

"She won't." I wish, just like I do with Nick, that I had a chance to introduce Mémère to her. To see Mémère's approving eyes burst with delight at how well my life in LA is going. "I know Mom. I just need a couple more weeks to get the staffing resolved, straighten out the numbers, and set Côté Fraise up for success. I can do it." The confidence in my voice is part truth, part bravado. A manifestation of the result I want.

"Absolutely." Nick crushes me into him.. "If this is the thing you need to do, you have my support." His hug is like a vise. "I've waited so long for you, waiting until Christmas isn't the worst. As long as we're together, it'll be the best Christmas." Nick's finger grazes my cheek. "Because you'll be my early present."

The pounds of doubt my brother piled on me slide off. Nick's touch, familiar yet not enough, awakens the part of me that needed him the moment he landed in Toronto. I've waited for Nick for a long time too. I was supposed to go home and make up for lost time, but now we'll be separated again.

I want to punch Grayson.

I want to kiss Nick.

I choose pleasure over pain and tug on the lapel of Nick's jacket. The tsunami of love he creates in me stirs and I long to get lost in him, take my fill while I can. He meets me halfway, and I kiss him, letting him experience how strongly I feel. The busy café vanishes, and we give in to the storm within us.

"Well, that's my cue to leave." Karina's chair scrapes the floor.

I tear my lips from Nick's. "No, you need to eat."

"Nick and I inhaled a plate of nachos already." She takes a bill out of her wallet and places it under her empty beer glass.

He gives me a sheepish grin. "What? I was hungry."

"More importantly, I have some flights to change."

A trickle of joy washes away some of the sourness from the family meeting. "You're staying?"

"If that's okay? The studio we visited has some people I'd love to chat with." She loops the purple scarf I lent her around her neck. "This'll give me a chance to do it in person."

If I can't have Nick, Karina is an awesome consolation prize. "You know you're always welcome to stay."

She gathers her bag and coat and stands. "Besides, I might be addicted to those strawberry tarts you keep bringing home." Her gaze ping pongs between us. "See you back at the house?"

My hand clamps onto Nick's thigh and his leg jerks. "In a bit." I can't go back yet.

With Karina gone, Nick hands me a menu. "What are you in the mood for?"

Not food. "Let's grab the check and go."

"Okay." A dent forms between his eyebrows. "Thought you didn't want to go back to your parent's place."

"I don't." I lick my lower lip. It's too cold for another round in the van, but the bakery is warm.

"I have an idea."

With a click, the back door unlocks and we slip into the darkened kitchen of Côté Fraise. I flip the lights and strip off my coat.

"Are we going to bake something?" Nick doesn't remove his leather jacket and rubs his hands together.

I loop my arms around his waist and imprint myself into him. My body heat should warm him. "Remember when I said I was going to stick like glue to you this weekend?"

He nods. "Liked the theory, but kinda hard to execute when you are bunking with Karina and I'm sleeping in the same room as Taylor."

I draw a circle on the small of his back and dark pools form in his eyes. "The bakery isn't ideal, but there's no one here but us."

He raises an eyebrow. "Are you saying . . ." He looks around at the oven, prep area, counters. "Isn't this some kind of health code violation?"

My laughter erupts like a tide that crested too high. The man who offered me a fake ID the night we met is suddenly worried about breaking the law. "There's a couch in the office. Sometimes when we had big orders, Mom or Mémère would pass out on it. It's surprisingly comfy."

Not able to let go of Nick, I guide him through the kitchen toward the small room I'll be living in for the next two weeks. I want it covered in his scent. He doesn't let go of me either, and we bump into the corner of the counter. Frustrated, I move to release him so we can fit through the doorway when gravity wins, and I'm in his arms.

"Glue, remember?" He kisses my cheek, and I encircle his neck. I commit to memory the feel of his strong arms holding me, his hands on my thighs. He's here with me, but I already miss him. The hesitation I shooed away when Grayson mentioned the offer creeps back in. My pulse quickens. It could be so easy: sell, go back to LA, have extra money for a place of our own where we don't have to sneak around and keep quiet. A sanctuary I could share with Nick every day and night.

One of Mémère's hats on the shelf we brush by reminds me why I'm not here to choose the easy way out. Why tomorrow I'll redouble my efforts at the bakery. I can do it.

"Where did you go?" His puppy dog eyes study me.

"Thinking about tomorrow."

"Don't." His voice is thick, like the first night we slept together. "Stay with me. Here. Today."

I push the thoughts of anything but Nick out, plaster myself to him, and feel his body respond: warm, hard, mine. I answer with a kiss, letting my mouth say the things my heart is bursting with.

He sets me on the desk and starts peeling off his jacket.

"Stop," I say. One arm out of his coat, he pauses. "Let me do it."

Nick raises an eyebrow but shrugs it back on.

"This is my favorite coat of yours." I inhale the leather laced with the scent of Nick. "After you left me on Christmas Eve, I went home and slept in it." I meet his curious eyes. "That was the first night I slept with you."

He swallows, and I can't help running my finger down his neck, feeling his rapid heartbeat at his jugular. My pulse quickens. Even after months of being with him, watching his body come to life like this floors me.

"I slept with your jacket for weeks. Dreaming of the man who came into my life and changed it forever." I stare at his parting lips. "Did I tell you the entry that won me a spot in the Starlight Foundation competition was based on our kiss?"

"No." The single word packed with emotion, wonder, reverence, delight. I sway to him.

I trace the small scar on his left cheek. "Right down to this."

The skin is puckered, and I kiss it, like I can remove the imperfection. But I don't want to. That scar is the reason I got to taste his lips for the first time.

"I was never happier to have a hockey injury than that night." His fingers brush the back of my hand, and the tenderness radiates to my heart. He kisses my palm. "It was my desperate excuse to get close to you, a reason to kiss you."

I cup his jaw. "I wanted you to kiss me from the moment you told me it was impossible to choose one favorite song of all time." By the end of our first night, he rivaled with the rainbow cake I asked Mémère to make for my birthday every year. Over the months we've spent together, *he* became one of my favorite things. My mouth waters, hungry for more than his words. I slip my hand under his jacket, the cold of the metal zipper scraping against my wrist. The material slides, my fingers relishing every curve of his biceps.

"Sarah."

I close my eyes at the way he says my name, sweet and scorching like a shot of liquid chocolate, as if I'm the only Sarah in the world.

Nick leans forward and captures my mouth with his. The layers of love and desire combine to create a fusion stronger than I thought possible. He's the flint that sparks against me. His heat advances, starting the blaze that spreads up my spine. My need to turn us on high, speed this up, flickers in me. But I ignore it and force myself to slow down. Nick's tongue has a different idea, dancing in my mouth, pushing for more, stoking my flames.

"I love you so much," he whispers into my smile. Yet I detect an inkling of pain in his husky voice that reverberates through the love-filled chambers of my heart.

I bracket his face and pull back. "I love how you love me."

The gap between us cools my skin. Today I don't want a fiery passion that burns faster than a pair of matches. I'm after the smoldering embers that'll prolong this feast. I kiss his nose, his forehead, one eyebrow, then the other, collecting bits of his light to hoard and treasure. My lips graze his eyelids, temples, cheeks, pausing again on the scar that makes him perfect. I brush past his lips for another taste but don't let them absorb me. There's so much more to taste, to touch, to memorize.

I re-explore his earlobes, lick his neck. Savor him like a perfect cake, layer by layer. Jacket gone, my hands find the buttons of his shirt and undo each one, placing my lips on the newly exposed hollow of his throat. A groan rumbles through his chest and it's music to my ears. Nick's fingers dig into my waist and propel me forward, his hard chest meeting mine.

My plans of taking things slow evaporate. The fire takes its rightful place, consuming us in a blaze neither of us can control. His shirt is off in seconds, and I'm working on his belt buckle, my fingers desperate to get to the prize inside. No longer a surprise, I will never stop wanting to see him fall apart because of me. Lust melts me, my heart turning to liquid. My mouth, a red-hot iron, brands every familiar freckle, every taut muscle, every bone and ridge. His palm runs along my thigh, lifting it off the desk, hooking my leg over his hip.

We switch. I'm the cake with a rainbow middle. He's the one expertly cutting me open. I arch into him giving myself over to his exploration, letting go as he traces kisses under my chin, along my neck. He nuzzles the spot over my heart as his greedy hands create more pressure, pushing me higher and higher. I'm the one who explodes into a waterfall of colorful sprinkles. Nick is kissing my heart, and I never want him to stop.

We take turns. I consume him. He devours me as if I'm the most delicious thing in this bakery. His nearness pushes away the fear of losing the last piece of Mémère, because at this moment I don't grieve for my grandmother. I'm not angry at my brother. I'm too busy committing every caress, every sound, every breath to memory, to sustain me for the long, lonely nights ahead.

Twenty-Three

NICK

Mike and I barely fit in the apartment. Mom moved some of her furniture in, and the sparse space I remember from when I crashed on Dad's couch is now stuffed with family photos, mementos, and the familiar lemony smell of home.

"Should I make extra, just in case Angie gets out of the studio early?" Mom shouts from the kitchen.

Mike hits mute on the TV. "No, Mom. She hasn't been home before midnight once this week, and I doubt tonight will be any different."

Sounds like our girlfriends have a lot in common. When Sarah was working on *Vampire Club*, she'd crawl into bed at two a.m. Does Angie go out for drinks with the band after their sessions as well?

"I'll put more skewers in the oven, just in case." Mom's dominating the stove, insisting she wants to cook for her boys. It took the lure of her homemade chicken souvlaki to get Mike here. He insisted he'd never set foot in Dad's apartment and still refuses to talk to him.

Dad texted that his meeting with the studio execs is running late. They had more questions. He assured me it's a good sign.

"Shoot." Mom's banging cupboard doors. "We seem to be out of oregano for the salad dressing." She wipes her palms on her apron. "Could you boys run down to the corner store and grab some?"

Mike unfolds himself from the couch. "Sure Mom." He turns off the TV. "You coming?"

The last twenty minutes felt like the first time I've sat down, aside from falling exhausted into bed. The couch is comfy and I don't want to move. But Big Bro has other plans, and since I'm playing nice in the hopes that he'll at least talk to Dad before Christmas, I shuffle my feet.

Unlike chilly Toronto, we don't need a coat for the short trip. The store is busy with after-work customers, and we walk to the end of the aisle to find the tail of the line. I'm not getting back to that couch any time soon.

"Are you coming to see the prison documentary in the Showcase next Friday?" I asked Mike as soon as I found out, but he hasn't replied to my texts.

Mike peeks over the heads of the people in front of us, as if he can make the cashier check people out faster. "Depends on Angie's schedule."

What he means is it depends on if Dad's there.

"Sarah won't be in LA, and I could use all the support I can get."

He bounces on his heels and shoves both hands into his pockets. "Are you sure Sarah will be here for Christmas?"

The question brings back the ire I felt as a child when he'd interrogate my excuses as to why my homework wasn't finished. I scowl. "Yes."

He raises his hands. "Just asking. No need to get pissy."

"I'm not." I'm more than pissy when anyone mentions Sarah these days. Not at her—at the lack of her. When Siobhan cleaned the bathroom over the weekend she removed Sarah's strawberry conditioner from the shower and hid it under the sink.

"It's not like she's using it," Siobhan said.

I wouldn't admit that I pop the lid and inhale the scent when I'm taking a shower. The sheets in our room have stopped smelling like her. The whole room, actually. It's like she's disappearing from my life molecule by molecule. I just have to hold out another two weeks.

". . . for sure." Mike studies me like he just revealed the secret combination to his safe, and I'm not duly impressed.

"What?"

"I said, do you know for sure?" Mike yanks on his ear. "Owning a business is a lot like having a kid. Unpredictable. Last week I had to get up in the middle of the night and go to my taekwondo academy because the alarm went off. Turned out some kids were using the parking lot at night as their skate park and one of the skateboards flew through the window. Spent the night between calls to the insurance company, the window replacement company, and filing out the police report."

"Sucks. But Sarah has it covered. She's training the new manager, Fran. Her mom lives there. They'll handle that stuff, so Sarah is free to come back here." To me.

"I have my co-owner, Ben, and no one is more reliable than him. Still, I had to close the dojo for the holidays. If it wasn't for Angie asking me to come, I wouldn't be here."

"But you are."

"I'd follow that girl anywhere."

"Me too."

"Really?" Mike raises an eyebrow. "Are you considering moving?"

"Moving? Sarah's life is in LA."

"I'm not trying to rain on your parade." He puts his hand on my shoulder. "But face the reality. Making it in LA is one shot in a million. If she has to stay in Toronto"—his words kick me—"do you have a plan B?"

"Like move there and sling coffee for a living?" I just got back to LA, and I like it here. Although we left LA when I was nine, in some ways it feels more like home than Chicago ever did. I shove away the memories of our first years in the Windy City. I didn't fit in there.

"I guess that's an option." He crosses his arms, and the girl browsing the candy display ogles his bulging muscles. If not for Mike's full head of hair, he and The Rock could be brothers.

"But what about attending school there? Transfer your credits to the University of Canada. I'm sure there's a useful degree there."

"That's the country. She lives in Toronto."

Mike inches forward. "The University of Toronto then, smartass. The point is, go to school there." He turns and glares at me. "Whatever you do, don't quit."

I take a step back. Over the years, Mike has ordered me about a lot. A lot, a lot. My knee-jerk reaction is to drop out just to spite him. But I love film, and I won't give up. "Not planning on it."

"Good." He looks over the heads of the customers again, and I follow his gaze. The lonely cashier is arguing with an older gentleman, and I don't think this line is moving anytime soon. "'Cause you've got good taste." I'm not sure if he's saying this to me or the lady in front of us holding an expensive-looking bottle of Tequila and a box of fancy chocolates.

I hold my hand to my ear. "Sorry. Did you say something?"

His arm shoots out, and before I can blink, he has me in a chokehold and is mussing my hair. "You heard me."

My heart twinkles. I push him off me and inspect the candy rack, hiding my giant smile.

The apartment smells of roasted chicken and spices when we enter, and my mouth waters.

"We're back," I yell into the empty living room.

Hushed voices echo down the hall from my parents' bedroom.

"Fuck." Mike is halfway out the door before I catch his arm. I lean with all my might and drag him back in. "Get off me." He's stronger, but I have desperation on my side. This will happen sooner or later, and right now seems ideal, when it's just the four of us.

"Do this for Mom. You can't avoid Dad forever. She's happy." I push the door shut and block Mike's exit. "Let her be happy."

"Fuckety fuck." Mike paces. "I . . ."

"Did you get the oregano?" Mom's voice is chipper. A little too chipper.

"Here." Mike juts the brown paper bag in her direction.

Mom takes his offering and continues forward, wrapping him in a hug. She whispers something in his ear only he can hear. Mike's eyes close, and his shoulders drop. He whispers back, and it's safe to move away from the door. He's not going anywhere.

Mom releases him. "Theo," she calls over her shoulder. "The boys are back."

Dad creeps into the room like he's walking on eggshells. He tries to meet Mike's gaze, but Mike resumes his position on the couch and stares at the dark screen of the TV.

"I've got great news." Dad turns to me. "They love my screenplay. Best that they've read, they said."

My brain buzzes. I slap Dad on the back. "No way!"

"This could really happen." The hope in his voice releases butterflies in my chest. "Might need to go to a few more meetings, shake a few more hands, but once the signatures are on paper, I'm back to being an employed screenwriter."

Mom claps her hands together, reminding me of her cheering when my hockey team scored a goal. Her shining eyes might be the best part.

Mike's staring into space. No congratulations. No smile.

Dad and I exchange a look. Our grins fade.

Twenty-Four

Sarah

I'm no fan of Monday mornings. Between not seeing Nick for a week, burning the butter tarts on Friday, and avoiding Grayson and his cold iceberg of animosity all weekend when he showed up at the house, I'm dead on my feet. What's worse, Karina is leaving, proving I'm right — Mondays suck.

"Thanks for driving me." She yawns. "I can't believe you volunteered to take me to the airport this early in the morning."

"I hate to admit it, but I might be getting used to getting up before dawn." We fly down the road, streetlights dotting the sky. The dark highway reminds me of our late-night *Vampire Club* sessions.

"I might miss this town of yours." She watches the lake shore wiz by.

"The town or a certain someone whose name starts with G?" Grayson spent entirely too much time at Mom's house instead of his dorm ever since Karina kicked him her first night in Toronto.

She sets her ankle-boot on her knee. "I still can't believe you're not coming back with me." Way to change the subject. She might not want to talk about Grayson, but I want to talk about not returning to LA even less. Especially after Rod's call to announce the next season of *Vampire Club* is officially a go.

"You can dive back into the show. Our first draft needs edits, but it's complete. Screenplay bootcamp worked." After cramming in a final writing session last night, we're both exhausted. Our celebratory sip of wine to christen the complete script turned into finishing off a bottle.

"After sharing a bed with you—"

"A bunk bed." I roll my eyes. "Don't be so dramatic."

"I'll miss you even more."

I'll miss her too. My heart is heavy. Not as much as I miss Nick, but missing more than one person doesn't make the sentiment for each of them any smaller.

"You'll be fine." I follow the signs for the 427.

"Working on *Vampire Club* won't be the same without you."

"It's temporary. Rod agreed I can join in January. With the skeleton crew of four, you'll be able to manage your coffee runs without assistant number two."

"I'll DM you the juicy bits. By the time I hit send you'll be getting up and reading them first thing."

The time difference between Toronto and LA might be a good thing for once. "Ready to get back to the night owl regime?"

Karina's vigorous nods compete with the best bobbleheads. "I hate mornings."

Perhaps it's because we are overtired, or it's our way of coping with the separation, we giggle, then we laugh, then we cry, then we're back to giggling.

Julio's ringtone interrupts. I hit the answer button on the steering wheel. "Julio?"

"Thank goodness." The light joy evaporates at the panic in the bakery assistant manager's voice as it echoes in the van. "We have a problem."

Karina gives me her 'what now' eye roll. At the bakery our writing sprints were interrupted way too many times with Julio desperately knocking on the office door. It's like he can't make a move without me. I arranged to come in late this morning to hug my friend goodbye at the airport. I straighten my shoulders and ignore the headache brewing.

"What happened?" My eye roll matches my friend's.

"I opened the fridge to get the crème for the éclairs, and everything's gone."

"What? Have we been robbed?"

"No," Julio says. "Everything is spoiled. There's mold on the fruit, the milk is sour, the smoked salmon has this film on it, and the stench. It smells like the fridge has been without power for at least a day."

Shit. My stomach drops, and the headache takes hold. The fridge. It's been wonky, but I didn't think it was serious.

"I need to get the first rise started on the milk bread, but the dairy spoiled. What are we going to do?"

I scan the horizon for inspiration. The 427 highway isn't much help until I see the sign for Weston's Bakery. Muffins. He can do muffins with mostly dry ingredients.

"Check the butter. Is it still okay?" It's kept in an airtight container so it shouldn't reek of mold or curdling milk.

The clang of the fridge door opening and low dings crackle through the speakerphone. "Yeah, it smells okay."

"Good. New special today. We're making muffins. There's a recipe in the book." I imagine leafing through Mémère's hand-written notes. Her basic muffin recipe is a miracle in a bowl, and we can make multiple flavors by splitting it into batches. "Near the back. For Strawberry Muffins."

"Yeah, we made them in the summer." I hear Julio flip through pages. "They were good. But they need fresh fruit and ours is all—"

"Add chocolate chips to the first batch. I'll figure something else out by the time I get back." Nausea hits me at the idea of having nothing to sell. I throw the van into park at the airport curb. Karina unbuckles her seatbelt. "Sorry, but you'll have to go alone from here," I say.

"I get it." She's already out of the van.

I can't let her go like this. My throat constricts. I don't know when I'll see her again. I sprint around the van and engulf her in a hug. "Thanks for coming. Thank you for the writing support and for the life support. Thank you."

She crushes me to her, and I'm doubly grateful for the hug. I reluctantly let go. Our eyes meet.

"I'll see you in LA." She pulls away. I nod. "Soon." She holds my gaze. I nod again, unable to trust my voice. "Good. Now go make muffins." She winks and scampers through the airport doors.

I can't take a full breath as I navigate the van back to the bakery. Traffic is still light on the highway. No one else wants to be awake at this dark, dreary hour. I search for a grocery store or fruit market I can stop at and buy some strawberries, but no luck. Julio is a mess when I enter the kitchen. This is the reason he can't be the bakery manager. He can't handle the stress, and we both realize it.

"Two batches are done. But we need other flavors for the muffins. We can't just do chocolate." He squints at the clock on the wall, his glasses perched on the tip of his nose. "We open in ten minutes."

I wrap my hands around his biceps. "It'll be okay. Have you started the coffee?" He shakes his head. "Let's get that brewing. I'll deal with the muffins."

The whir of the mixer usually calms me, but today it grates on my nerves. My second round of creative solutions is not so inspiring, but it'll have to do. I unearth two jars of jam Mom experimented with. It won't be Mémère's usual "all fresh ingredients," but it's fruit.

My heart pangs as I plop the preserves into the batter. It's like I'm betraying Mémère, adapting her recipe. "I'm sorry," I say to her shadow, always lurking at the back of the kitchen.

TWENTY-FIVE

Sarah

BY THE MID-MORNING LULL Fran is late, the guy Mémère has listed for fridge repair in the old rolodex in the office has left for Christmas break, and I'm out of tricks for the "Chopped" bakery edition I have on my hands.

"The customers loved the new muffins." Julio's smile is back. A complete 180 from his frazzled state this morning. The state I'm fully immersed in now.

I desperately want to call Nick, hear his voice telling me everything will be okay, but I can't lay any more bad news on him. He took the Grayson betrayal like a champ, but me being a continent away is weighing on him. I can feel the distance between us. I don't know what he had for breakfast, or even if he's eating at all. When he gets stressed, he tends to not eat.

I shoot a text to my roommates.

Me: Is Nick eating?

Siobhan: Us out of house and home.

Me: No, seriously. I'm worried he's not taking care of himself.

Ryan: His mom drops off care packages daily. I'm in love with her.

The tumult of the morning that threatened to spill over and destroy every good thing I have retreats. Of course his mom visits, now that they live in the same city. She'll look after her son. I guess that's good. I don't need to worry about Nick quite so much.

Why do I feel worse? Like Nick not needing me is another crack in the bond holding us together.

"I'm so sorry, I'm late." Fran bursts in the front door, her teal kitty-cat hat askew. "The streetcar broke down. I've been running for blocks." She unwinds her matching scarf with cat paws at the end.

The tension I've stored in my shoulders since a minute before her shift was supposed to start dissipates. I exhale. With the way the day has been, Fran quitting on me without notice would've been in line with the general stink. Transit delays I understand.

"I really need to find a house or apartment to rent near here." She grabs her Côté Fraise apron from the hook on the wall. She added cute pins to it, and even when she's not in the room the apron screams, "I'm Fran's. Don't touch." Yet it fits beside Mémère's and Mom's. "This commute is terrible." Her face pinches as she changes into her clogs.

I fill her in on the trials and tribulations of the day. "I'm storing the milk, eggs, etc. in the back of the van. It's cold enough today, they'll keep. Mom's bringing over the coolers we use to take food to the cottage, and we can fill them with ice for tonight."

"Good idea." Fran reads the new menu based on the ingredients bought and salvaged. "You're a quick thinker."

I choose to omit that I called Mom. Actually, I called Dad first, but he said I had to talk to Mom. Apparently this happened last summer in 100-degree weather. I hate to admit it, but there's so much about this business I'm not aware of.

The bell rings at the back, and I open the door to find Mom and one rolling cooler. "The other two are in the trunk." She points her cast at Dad's SUV. "Julio, would you?"

Mom's here two seconds, and it's like she clapped a set of markers. The black-and-white image of the bakery transforms into full color like it's the Wizard of Oz. Julio gives Mom a one-minute hug before he tosses on his boots.

Fran adjusts her pins, wipes her palms on her apron, and extends her hand. "Mrs. Connor. Nice to see you."

"Ah, our Christmas miracle worker." Mom shakes Fran's hand with her uninjured one.

"I'm excited to be part of the team. You have a wonderful business here: my type of bakery." Fran tugs at the cuffs of her sweater. "I hope you're feeling better."

"Getting better every day." Mom faces me and wraps her arms around my shoulders. I sink into the warmth of her embrace. My pulse slows. I need the hug.

Mom taps her wrist against my shoulder. "This thing comes off in two weeks, and then I'm free."

"Mom." I untangle myself from her grasp. This isn't a mother-daughter reunion. We have a crisis on our hands. I clear my throat. "The repair man is on vacation. Is there an alternate service we can use?"

Mom gives Fran a polite nod and pushes me forward. "Let's chat in the office, honey."

We walk past Mom's apron hanging unused on its hook. Her gaze catches on it, but neither of us mentions what we must both be thinking. Soon everything will return to normal. Even if she only comes back part-time. Fran is the solution.

In the office, Mom takes a seat on the couch, as if a guest is all she is in the space that she spent six days a week in for the last thirty years. I sit behind the desk and bring the old computer to life. "Do you think they'll be able to come today?"

"No one is fixing the fridge." Mom presses her lips together.

I grind my teeth. "Okay, I get it. My expectations are too high. But I can't get the fridge fixed if I don't call someone."

"You aren't listening to me. The fridge is gone. The last time Felix was able to bring the ancient compressor back to life, but he said if the same thing happened again, he wouldn't be able to repair it. It's too old. They don't make the parts anymore." She leans her elbows on her knees and places her head in her hands. "What are we going to do?"

My neck stiffens and my brain is back to the frazzle of the morning. I concentrate on opening a browser window. "It'll be fine. I'll get another fridge."

Mom rocks her head. "I've been trying to do that for months. There is nothing used available in this city that we can afford."

"Well, we could get a loan."

Eyes laced with doubt meet mine. "We've already taken out a second mortgage on the house to cover the new display case we had to purchase when the glass cracked on the old one. There's no more credit." She sighs. "Unless you have some cash hidden somewhere."

All comfort from Mom's hug ebbs. I barely have enough in my bank account to cover this month's rent on the apartment I'm not using in LA. "I don't understand. How did it get this bad?"

"I'm not sure. When Mémère got sick, she became my priority."

My gaze lands on the strawberry-patterned vase on the corner of the desk, like I can pour the rising ache at not being here into the fine porcelain. I'm here now, Mémère. I'm here now.

Mom's fingers dig into my shoulder. "Sarah, your brother is right. It might be time to sell."

"I'm not giving up." I meet Mom's gaze. "Mémère wasn't a quitter. She went through hard times."

"True." There's a little more optimism in Mom's voice. "Once she got into a dispute with our flour vendor, and we ran out. We made graham cracker-crusted treats for a week. Discovered some gluten-free recipes we still make today."

"See? Good can come from difficult times." I think of Nick. If we'd spent the night together after we met at a club, I might've added him to the stack of forgotten flirtations, never thought of him again. If we'd met on an app as Nick and Sarah, I might've never known who he was hiding and why. If we'd never been roommates, I might've not realized how much I needed to keep everything, including him, under control. My chin trembles. Look at us now.

I put my arm around Mom. "We'll make Mémère proud." I hold in my sniffle. "I promise."

Twenty-Six

NICK

Blend is quiet. We're not supposed to use our phones inside the café or when not on break, but with one customer finishing his pastry in the opposite corner from the register, I give in and pick up Sarah's video call.

"Did you get your results yet?" Sarah is sitting in the office of the bakery.

My body heats at the memory of what we did in that chair, on that desk. One more week. One more week, and she'll be in my arms again.

"Not yet." I do know the grade will hammer the final nail into the coffin of my scholarship for next semester. "They'll be bad. Finishing my report on the plane ride home from Toronto wasn't the best idea. I don't even remember writing the last two pages."

"I feel awful." Her face falls, and my gut follows. "This is all my fault."

"What?" I lean my hip against the counter. "Me doing a shitty job on my paper has nothing to do with you."

"You flying between Toronto and LA was too much. I—"

"Don't say that. I'd fly every weekend to see you." I'd fly tonight, but I don't have two dimes to rub together. It's another homemade gift for her this Christmas at this rate.

Her mouth forms a straight line. One of my least favorite expressions on those lips. "How's Fran?" Fran is the solution. Fran brings Sarah back to me.

That gets a little smile. "Good. She's smart and a quick learner."

My sinking feeling gets a life ring. This'll work out. "A few more days in her probation, right? Then she's full time?"

"Yup." Sarah's eyes dart to something in the corner. "A few more days."

The door to Blend opens, and two girls skip toward the counter. "Customers. Gotta go. Talk tonight."

She waves at me, and the screen goes blank.

"Can I get a latte with a shot of caramel? On ice?"

That I can do without thinking. Thankfully. Because while my hands craft the sugary concoction, my mind is in Toronto.

The new barista wheels a mop and bucket into the back. "You would not believe the mess in there." Glad I'm the manager, and my clean-the-bathroom days are over. I should be glad about more.

The Silver Screen Showcase is days away and I feel the nervousness like before the Starlight Gala. Except Sarah's not here to brush it away this time.

One more week, then she'll be back. I'm bummed she'll miss the event on Friday. The missing piece to my family puzzle. Mike is still waffling over coming or not, insisting he won't show if Dad does. It was low, but I played the guilt card, asking him to not make me choose between my brother and my father. He grumbled about me being a pain in the ass.

Still, I can't shake this heaviness in my chest.

I should be making plans too, but the pieces that outlined a solid border of a doable puzzle for my life in November revert to a pile of a thousand fragments, and there's no picture to consult to put it together. Sarah keeps telling me she'll be home for Christmas, but Mike's words don't leave me.

What if Fran quits?

What if Sarah stays?

Browsing the catalogs of every university in Toronto that offers a degree in film has become my nightly activity. The city has a lot to offer. Although I won't be able to get into any classes for the spring semester, I could apply for fall. Plenty of time to help Sarah with the bakery. The skills I've learned working at Blend are transferable to work at Côté Fraise. I can run the front of the house while she's dealing with the back and the baking. This may not be a bad idea.

I stack more cups for the morning rush. Even the boss has to make sure there are enough coffee cups.

An alert beeps on my phone. The girls and their to-go iced drinks are out the door, so I open the email. My Econ grades are posted. I'm colder than when I was walking with Sarah in the snow of Toronto. Dread seeps into my bones.

I check the website, and my stomach lurches. The three cups of coffee I've had aren't happy with my grade either. The hammers of doom knock in my temples. There's no way I can keep my scholarship with this grade.

At least now I have a legitimate reason to not be happy. It's official, I'm losing my scholarship.

"Nick." Professor Takamado waves at me from across the register.

"Your usual?"

"Please." He taps on the glass display. "And the apricot Danish?"

"Coming right up." I don't even try to smile. My hands shake as I tamp down the grounds for his standard latte. Nausea hits me as I smell the warm milk in the frother. I must be sick. I add the foam to the coffee and pass it to Professor Takamado.

"And the Danish?"

"Right." I look at the cream cheese, cherry, and apricot ones. "Which kind?"

"Apricot." He narrows his eyes. "Are you okay?"

"Fine." I take the pastry and place it on a small plate. He always eats it at the corner table.

"You don't sound fine. Wanna talk?"

The shop is still empty this close to Christmas. I haven't taken my break yet. "I'll take ten," I shout to the new barista, who's back restocking the milks.

I plop into the seat across from Professor Takamado and take a sip of my water.

He breaks the Danish in two. "What is it? Is having your mom in LA stressing you out?"

"Mom?" Right, the last time we talked was before her move. "No. Mom's great. I haven't eaten this well since I left Chicago."

"What then?"

"School."

"Good." He shakes a hand in the air. "Sorry, not good. But I can help with school. Not so much with Mom."

"Not sure you can help with school either." I can't talk to Mom or Dad about this. They'll be too disappointed. "I'm losing my scholarship. I tanked my Econ exam. Even if every other exam comes back with a perfect score"—I rub my chin—"and they will not, there's no way I can get the final grade I need to keep the scholarship. Without it, I can't afford UCLA. I can barely afford it with the scholarship."

He frowns. "Can't your parents help you for one semester? I'm sure you can work on getting your grades back up."

"No. Mom doesn't have a job right now, she just started looking. And Dad"—I won't go there—"it can't work."

"I didn't think you'd quit so fast. Have you talked to financial aid?"

"Yeah. Nothing they can do."

"I'm sure the school wouldn't want to lose such talent. There are always ways." He sets down his coffee. "I shouldn't be telling you this, but I showed your Silver Screen entry to the dean. He's not involved in the judging or anything, but I wanted him to see what promise we have in you."

"You believe in me that much?" I catch myself. "I mean, thanks."

The corners of his mouth curve. "You're welcome, and yes, I do. You have an eye, Nick. A way of framing a scene. I'm not saying you're Tarantino, but what you did with Nazir's prison exit." He shakes his head. "I don't know how you got that on film, the loneliness and remorse when no one was at the gate to meet him. I wanted to go pick the man up. Then his face when his sister arrives. I'm strong enough to admit I needed a tissue."

"It was mostly luck."

He leans forward. "No, Nick. Don't do that. You have talent. We need to find a way to keep you hear at UCLA." He taps his chest. "I need you here."

TWENTY-SEVEN

NICK

The dean, Mr. Takamado, and several professors I don't
know stand on the small stage in front of the blank movie
screen. My brain serves me flashbacks of screening the final cut
of *Indigo* with the Blue Team and playing my confession to
Sarah this summer. Those moments seem a lifetime ago.

"These cards are to pick the audience's favorite." Mr. Takamado raises a rectangle of paper and a pencil in the air.

The seat next to me squeaks. "What did I miss?" Mike whispers into my ear.

When I invited him to see what Ms. Hansley, Dad, and I
accomplished over the last three months, I never got a yes. But
my big bro is here. Although he's not a perfect substitute for
Sarah's absence, my heartbeats soften. I relax my grip on the
brochure, knowing he made the effort. For me. Like he did
during the ten years Dad was absent from our lives.

"The showcase history." I pass the program to Mike. "Plus the dean listed a bunch of famous names. People who launched their careers by having the honor—the dean's words, not mine—to be chosen to star in one of these events."

"Good." Mike throws a glance to my left where Mom sits. Dad's on her other side, their hands interlinked like high school sweethearts.'

The missing Sarah part kicks back into overdrive, because if all were perfect in my world, she'd be here as well. The memories of her running out at the end of *Indigo* wouldn't seem so ominous. She came back then. She will come back again. Three more days until I see her.

I can wait.

"Please, turn off the sound on your phones and devices and put them away." Mr. Takamado highlights the four men standing by the doors. "The ushers will be walking the isles during the films to ensure no illegal filming takes place."

I take out my phone, text "Miss you" to Sarah, and tuck it into my jacket pocket.

During the two days after we finished filming the last bit, when I had my Econ exam, and the looming trip to move Mom, each frame I had to edit drained my patience and confidence. I was in the editing stage of the project where the only thing I saw were mistakes, inconsistencies, and changes I could've made if I only had more time.

My documentary that plays on the screen has little to do with that stage. If I saw it on TV, I'd believe the episode was directed by a professional. Each film today has a reason to be here. That's not the surprise. What sends my heartbeat into overdrive is that our documentary fits into the lineup. On par. Even above some of the other work in the execution.

Confidence is a skill, like any other. I puff out my chest and grin to myself in the darkness. Seeing my work in this forum and knowing it is not the worst, or here out of pity, but for the merit of it is the biggest boost to my confidence since I won the Best Director award for Indigo. My sternum sings with pride. The strong, edgy belief in myself is not arrogance. I have loads to learn and master, but I'm not a fluke.

The lights are back on and the dean reappears with his microphone in hand. "That was an impressive collection. Every year the Showcase surprises me in the best of ways and reminds me why I do this job. The new talent we foster within these walls will be the leaders in the entertainment world, and we found them first." His smile is broad, and I can't help but smile alongside.

He's talking about me. My cheeks hurt from all the smiling.

I'm happy even if I don't place. "Please, drop your ballots into the box the ushers are holding at the exit and enjoy the refreshments. We'll invite you back in about an hour when the judges have completed their deliberations, and we'll announce the winners."

Mike rises. "I know who I'm voting for." He scribbles on the paper.

"You don't have to vote for me because I'm your brother. Vote for who really liked." I follow him to the exit.

"I'm voting for you because I didn't realize what you did was *this*." We drop our ballots and walk to the room down the hall set up for the reception. "I was expecting"—Mike picks a glass of water from one of the tables—"not *this*."

I rub the back of my neck. When was the last time Mike saw something I filmed? Must've been my first photography and film class in middle school. "What did you expect?"

"I don't know." Mike's gaze freezes at something over my shoulder. Mom and Dad break our tête-à-tête.

"That's four votes for Nicky." Mom's excitement is palpable. "Those judges would be silly not to pick you." She wraps me in her side hug. She's biased but I love it.

"Thanks, Mom." Even though this is not remotely as fancy as the Starlight Competition Gala, having Mom with me makes this one of the most important events of my life. "Thanks for coming."

"There's no other place I'd rather be." Mike's turn to get his portion of Mom's hugs. "Celebrating the future. With my boys. The loves of my life." She swivels her gaze between Mike, Dad, and me. "Our family back together."

Mike's huff ruins the moment. "I'm not here for him." Mike juts his chin Dad's way.

Dad reaches into his coat pocket and produces an envelope. "I have something for you." He stretches his hand to Mike.

"Ten years of child support? You can give that to Mom." Mike crosses his arms on his chest.

"We aren't here to argue." Mom's conciliatory face loses its glee. "Let's focus on the positives for once."

"Agreed." Mike downs the rest of his water and slams the glass on the tall table we're standing next to. "I'm sorry."

Those are not the words I expected from him. Nor did the rest of our group, because all eyes turn to Mike. He turns to me. "I'm sorry I pushed you away from the film industry. I should've trusted you. Trusted Mom. I can't imagine wanting a career in something so creative and volatile, but I'm not you." Mike tugs on his tie. You can say that again. Mike is all business all the time. The only break he takes is his weekly video game marathons. Even his love for martial arts is a business now.

"What you've created, I would have to be blind or a fool not to see that this is the right career path for you. So, I'm sorry for being a stubborn older brother who wanted something safe for you versus something that you wanted to do." Mike puts his beefy arm over my shoulder and does his version of a side-hug. Not as comforting as Mom's but solid. Very much like Mike.

Stable.

Like he's been for the last ten years.

Reliable.

He releases me. "I'm sorry, Nick." Not Nicky, not little bro. Nick. I stand a little taller and a lot happier. One more of my wishes has come true. The warmth that spreads across my chest is not from Mike's body heat, but the love I know he carries for me.

"I'm sorry too," says Dad. He takes Mike's hand and places the envelop into it. "I hope you read it, because this is not the best place for me to tell you the whole story, but I'm sorry for all I've done to you, to Nick, to Chrissy. I'm not the same person."

Mike opens his mouth to protest, but Mom tugs on his sleeve, and his lips slam shut as he lets Dad continue.

"I know everyone says that." Dad's expression is somber. "But that's what I've been doing the last five years. I've been proving it to myself, so I could prove it to you."

Seeing him and Mike next to each other like this for the first time in years draws attention to how alike they are. "I hope you can forgive me, but I don't expect it. I only wanted to let you know. What you do with that I accept. It's up to you." Dad tips his chin. "Know this: I'm sorry, son."

Mike flinches at Dad's last words, stuffs the envelope into his pocket, and retreats. "I'll see you inside." He strides back into the hallway and out of our view.

If what the envelope has inside is index cards, if Mike reads them, if Mike believes Dad, if, if, if . . . There's a chance though. For the first time in years there's a chance for Mike and Dad to become father and son again. The ache behind my breastbone is for the years that Mike had to be the brother *and* the father, and for the night when Sarah held me in her lap, reading the cards Dad wrote for me.

"Are you Nick Stavros?" A short woman with large owl glasses and frizzy curls enters the spot in our circle Mike just vacated, her eyes expectant. I nod. "Oh, good. Colleen sent me your way. And you must be Theo." Her gaze moves to Dad. "The father and son duo that blew me away today." She switches back to me. "You got my audience vote."

Nice of her to let me know. I guess we are up to five out of what seems like at least two hundred people in the auditorium. Not a guarantee of success, but better than four.

"I'm Regina Davis."

"Mrs. Davis, I didn't know you'd be attending today." Dad's voice tells me he knows who she is, and that whoever she is, it's a position worthy of his "forced extravert" voice he employs with industry execs.

"The dean is right. I've attended the showcase for the last five years and without fail discover one or more students who have real talent. The kind I like to work with." She's talking to Dad, but her eyes keep flicking to me. "Colleen and I have just been chatting about the documentary. I thought she was the catalyst behind the project, but she insisted without your script and Nick's directing and camera work, she wouldn't have been able to produce anything remotely near the quality we've seen today."

The pink that spreads from under Dad's tight collar is a clear signal he's flattered. "She's been very supportive of the ideas Nick and I had."

"I'd love to take over the proverbial baton and offer additional funding and opportunities." She takes a card out of her purse and gives it to me. "I'm thinking a series. There are hundreds of low security prisons in the country. We can see what other facilities we can work with." She pushes her glasses up her nose. "If ice-road truckers and fisherman can grab audiences the way they did, I think you have something here. Send me an email with your schedule for the second week of January, and my assistant will find time for us to chat. See you then."

She leaves before I get a chance to unglue my lips to say thanks.

"Who is she?" I ask Dad.

"She is a Streamplus exec who runs IP acquisitions. I think we're the IP she's interested in."

Streamplus. He can't be serious. "As in they want to stream our documentary?"

"Unlikely. I think they'd want to option it and make a series of documentaries from it. And I agree with her. The audience will be there for it."

Streamplus. No matter whether I place at the showcase or not, I've won the opportunity of a lifetime. If we get a contract with Streamplus, that would mean money, and even if I skip a semester or two before I get it . . . I bump my fist in the air and shove aside the doom that settled over my financials.

What a day. I massage my face as I sink into Betty's driver's seat and throw my head back. If I were still six and believed in Santa Claus, I would've thought he brought my Christmas presents a couple of days early. The words tickle my throat, ready to burst. I slide my phone out of my pocket and push the button next to Sarah's name. It's past her bedtime, but in her reply text to my "miss you" earlier, she promised she'll stay up and wait for the results.

A loud yawn is the first thing I hear from her end.

"Did I wake you?" I ask.

"Nah. I'm still in the office, placing the orders for next week." The clacking of computer keys plays backup to her voice. "Fran is opening tomorrow morning, so I can sleep in and come in at seven."

Sleep in used to mean noon for her, now beginning at work at seven is a luxury. "Next week, when you're back, we'll spend the whole week sleeping in."

"Mmm. I want to hear about what next week in bed would be like, but I want to hear about the showcase even more. Did you place? Who won?" She sounds almost awake.

"I did." I don't quite believe it myself.

"Did what?"

"I won the damn thing." The judges called out my name. I got to hold the plaque in my hands onstage next to the two other people who placed second and third. When Mom, Dad, and Ms. Hansley hugged me a little too long in the hallway after the event was over, no amount of pinching would've made me believe it was true.

"Out of the ten entries, you got the first spot?"

"The scholarship is mine. No more money worries, at least where school is concerned." I take a deep breath. It doesn't cover the entire tuition, but close. "I get to TA for Mr. Takamado next semester too. Unreal."

"Unreal." She echoes my words, but with happiness instead of my wistfulness in her voice.

"That's not all of it."

"There was another prize they didn't advertise?"

"Sort of."

"Don't torture me. My hair will turn gray if I wait any longer. What is it?"

"Not related to the university, but apparently several industry execs come to the showcase every year to scout for talent."

"Makes sense." Her voice is breathy. "And . . ."

"And I might've been scouted."

"A studio contract?"

"Nothing is guaranteed, but we meet with Regina Davis in January to discuss."

"Regina Davis?" Sarah's definitely awake now. And she definitely knows who that is. "That's a huge opportunity." She squeals, and I move my phone away from my ear. "I'm so proud of you." She's back to her normal voice. "You're doing it."

"Doing what?"

"Living the dream. You're living the life you're supposed to live." She doesn't sound as happy anymore.

"I guess." I watch people get in their cars in the parking lot. The campus is still busy even at seven in the evening, but with all the people and even my family around me today, I'm lonely. "One thing is missing."

"An Oscar? You'll get there, just give it time." She forces a short laugh.

"A Sarah."

She breathes into the receiver. I don't dare inhale. I've always wanted her to say I love you to me in person, but at this point I'm desperate. I feel the tension crackling between us through the waves of the cellular connection. I hear her gulp air on her end.

"I miss you too," she says.

My chest falls. Close. Her reply has the right number of words, and the second word has the right number of letters in it, but they are not the letters I long for her lips to utter. "See you in a few days."

"Can't wait," she whispers.

I can't either.

Twenty-Eight

Sarah

I hug Natalie goodbye, wishing her a Merry Christmas and a Happy New Year. With a satisfied sigh, I flip the sign on the front door, lock it, and head to the cash register to do the last count of the year.

Out of the corner of my eye, I spot Grayson leaning against the wall in the kitchen. He's bubbling with energy, like before a final tournament game. I tip forward. He's talking to Fran as she proffers him a plate of macarons she made this morning. He digs in and closes his eyes, obviously enjoying her baking.

Good. I feel prickly and flushed. Now Grayson will have no reason to complain about her. She is the future of Côté Fraise. I feel it in my bones. The apparition of Mémère in the corner winks at me in agreement.

The till balances, and I stuff the cash into an envelope and twist the string around the tab to seal it. When I walk into the kitchen Fran's sunny smile has been replaced by a frown, and she's staring at Grayson.

"Stop bothering our newest employee." I shield Fran from my brother. This feud between Grayson and me will get resolved today, and I'll have my brother back. Tomorrow morning I'll be on a plane to LA and in Nick's arms by midday.

I'm tired of living with half my heart and I can tell Nick is too. Our chat last night felt . . . distant. Not being in each other's lives, there are pockets of our day you can't convey in a two-hour video chat. How did people do this before smartphones? I settle one of my hands below my clavicle, attempting to calm the fevered heartache. His mom recorded the showcase announcement, but it wasn't the same as being there, squeezing his hand like I did when he was nervous at the Starlight Gala.

Grayson holds out his palm. "Can I borrow your phone?"

"Again?" I slap it into his palm. Dad and Taylor picked up the new phone this morning, and after we give it to Grayson, I'm changing my passcode. I hate to think how many girls he's texted, never mind the prank ones to Nick. To keep up the ruse I add, "When will you buy a new one, or at least a new battery?"

"When I get some money." His voice is sharp, and the undertones leave a sour taste in my mouth.

Yes, selling the bakery would mean an influx of cash. Not worth the cost of losing the last part of Mémère we have left.

A smart comeback flits on my tongue, but the back door bursts open, and Taylor, Mom, and Dad shuffle in.

"Brrr. It's frigid out there." Dad helps Mom with her coat.

Fran pops off the stool she's sitting on. "I'll put on some coffee."

"Not necessary Fran." I gesture to the door. "You can head home now."

"Actually"—Grayson squares his shoulders—"Fran's staying."

I know he liked her baking, but this is a bit too much.

Mom rubs her hands together. "Family meeting, remember? I don't think Fran's interested in our squabbles."

Fran inches toward the exit. "I don't have to stay."

"Stay. Please." Grayson steps in front of her. "This involves you."

Fran's back stiffens, but she stops.

"I need the bathroom. Be right back," says Taylor.

My baby brother is always on the run when anything gets complicated or serious.

"Why does this involve Fran?" The funky churning in my stomach turns into burning acid.

Grayson gives Fran a should-I-tell-her-or-will-you look. I wrap my fingers around the base of my throat.

"Let's sit, and I'll explain." He heads toward the café.

My instinct is to plant my feet and not leave the warmth of the kitchen. Instead, I follow Taylor as he returns into the café, and we all pull chairs around the center table.

I tug on my earlobe. "We're sitting. Explain."

Grayson squirms in his seat. Eyes the same color as mine scrutinize the faces of each occupant and land on me. "Fran is part owner of B&B."

The floor drops from under me. The woman I'm counting on to save the bakery is not who I thought she was. I dig my fingers into the underside of my chair. Why does the truth always sideswipe me?

Mom's eyebrows knit together. "I don't understand."

I turn to Grayson. "You knew? This whole time?" I don't know why I ask, the evidence shadows his face. I turn to Fran. "I can't believe you lied to me."

To her credit, she maintains eye contact. "The truth is, my wife Everly's family owns B&B."

Truths and lies. The story of my life. The acid in my gut bubbles.

"But why?" Mom sputters. "Why would you pretend to want to work here?"

Fran spins the strawberry pin on her apron. "I didn't pretend. I do want to work here, wanted to learn the way you run things. To show you that you can leave the bakery in my hands."

"Your hands?" My brain short-circuits from the impact of her statements.

"Côté Fraise is the kind of business we'd like to include in B&B's portfolio. My wife and I have been talking to your grandmother for years at conferences, and on her trips to Montreal. Just like her, we love using fresh ingredients and doing things by hand. It's like fate brought us together for this moment."

Mom's fingers find mine. "You knew my mother?"

Fran adjusts her pastry chef hat. "Everly and I adored her hats. At a conference in New Orleans, we went shopping together and bought coordinating feather fascinators. We paraded around town in them for the rest of the weekend. Your mother knew how to enjoy life."

I almost smile at the story. Sounds like Mémère.

Icy truth frosts my lips. This woman is mistaken if she thinks her tale of knowing Mémère will make me trust her. Every word out of her mouth could be a lie. A ruse to take control of Côté Fraise. I struggle through the chill that fills my veins, and even the warmth of Mom's hand can't thaw me.

"Your grandmother built a great operation here." Fran addresses me. "Everly and I look forward to taking it to the next level."

"Not happening." I wag my finger. A Connor is taking Côté Fraise to the next level. I hold my chin high, like Mémère taught me. Like Mom reminded me to do the day Rod tested me on *Vampire Club*. I won that time and I'll win again today. "Start looking for another bakery to buy. This one is not for sale."

"Wait." Grayson holds up a hand. "You can't argue that Fran doesn't fit in. You yourself told me she's the answer to all our problems."

"That was before," I say.

Mom says, "You did praise her skills."

No, not you too Mom. I tug my hand from hers and grip the sides of the chair.

"She makes good éclairs, just like Mémère did." Taylor's attempt at conciliation earns him a death glare from me. He shrinks back into his seat.

Dad clears his throat, breaking the silence. "Is the offer still on the table?"

Fran nods. "Very much so. Now I've worked here, I'm more in love with Côté Fraise than ever. With a few improvements, we can make it shine again."

Improvements? Panic sets in my gut. I glance at the ceramic strawberry-shaped salt and pepper shakers that have adorned the tables for as long as I can remember. I press my hand to my queasy stomach. Will Fran throw them away? I shake my head. She won't get the chance to.

"What happens to Julio if we sell?" Mom's question startles me. Is she considering this?

"He's great with the customers and they like him. We'd definitely keep him on." Fran smooths her skirt. "We would keep Sandy as well, but she has her own opportunity, and I'm happy for her. There's an employee of ours who has expressed an interest in moving to Toronto, so we can start the new year fully staffed."

"But you'll raise prices." The venom pours out of me. "Those customers you love won't be able to afford eating here."

"There will have to be pricing changes." Sunny Fran disappears and business Fran takes over. "This isn't a museum, it's a business."

My fist hits the table. "And there you have it. She'll destroy Mémère's legacy." I turn to Mom. "You can't be considering this. Côté Fraise is your life. I'll help. Stay in Toronto like you wanted me to. Mother and daughter 2.0, remember?"

"What about your life?" Dad's smile reeks of sadness.

"I can write screenplays in my spare time. Now that I have some experience, I can apply for jobs here." Once I get the bakery running smoothly again, I can get a part-time job. Toronto is known as the Hollywood of the North.

Dad crosses his arms. "What about Nick?"

His words feed the panic in me. Dad must realize how I feel about him. "He'll understand."

"You know him best." Dad places both hands on the table. "But long-distance relationships are hard."

"We'll manage. You and Mom did."

"Actually, we didn't." Mom places her hand over Dad's and their fingers interlace. "You wrote a movie about it. That scene where Isabel left Rudo. Can you do that in real life? Even if Nick's one in a million, can he let you go?"

"You don't see how amazing Nick is." I raise my eyes to the ceiling to stave off the emotions. Beyond a million. The only man for me. What I feel for him can't be explained in words. Every time I try to respond to his beautiful I love yous, my heart expands so much it blocks my throat. "This is not about Nick. It's about Mémère. About honoring her."

Mom's eyes meet mine, and I freeze, not ready to hear the next words. People around me move in slow-motion. Blood whooshes in my ears. For a moment I think she might announce she wants to sell. I squeeze her hand, saying a silent, "Don't let Mémère die again."

"Fran." Mom turns to her. "Thank you for your offer. But Côté Fraise is not for sale."

The hurricane in my stomach and head settles. I knew Mom didn't want to sell.

"You think this is what Mémère wanted?" Grayson bucks out of his chair and storms out. "You're wrong."

"Excuse me." Dad gives an apologetic shrug and follows.

Fran's fingers unclasp and press on the edge of the table. "I'm sorry to hear that." She takes off her chef's hat, places it on the table, followed by her apron. "I'll show myself out."

"You did the right thing, Mom." I enfold my partner. "Mémère would be proud."

"I hope so." Mom pushes the hair from my forehead.

On the drive home, I pass row after row of houses decorated in candy canes, reindeer, and bright lights. Karen Carpenter croons a holiday classic on the radio. The lyrics touting there's nothing like home sweet home for the holidays. My eye ticks and I push the heel of my hand into it. The reality of what needs to be done next seeps in.

Twenty-Nine

NICK

I WAKE WITH A start, my heart threatening to explode out of my chest. Thump, thump, thump drowns out the sounds of traffic on the street.

Gray light filters through the window and robs the room of color. I press my palms to my forehead and force myself to inhale. Every morning I've had long cold showers because every night this week I've dreamt of Sarah, high hopes lacing my dreams. But tonight's dream was different.

It was the nightmare I had for weeks back in Chicago after Valentine's Day. Running after Sarah, her almost within my grasp but then slipping away. I swear, I can feel the fever from the pneumonia prickling along my skin, liquid filling my lungs.

It's just a dream.

Stiff as a board, I get out of bed and shuffle to the bathroom.

The apartment is mine today. Siobhan left for Ireland yesterday and Ryan is working a double shift at The Diamond Club. He declined my invitation to join my family for Christmas, saying the overtime at the bar would help him pay off his bills.

Cold water beats against my shoulders. I count to thirty and turn it to warm. The contrast shower helps with several ailments. My heart rate is almost back to normal. I'm wide awake and should be able to start my day, but I can't shake the eerie images.

I rescue Sarah's strawberry conditioner from its under-the-sink exile and reinstate it on the corner of the tub.

As has become my ritual, I uncap the pink bottle and pour a little of the liquid into my hands. Mixing with the steam from the shower, a cloud of strawberry surrounds me and at last my muscles release. Tonight, this shower will be filled with the real thing. I'll be able to touch her, hold her, kiss her. She can touch me, hold me, kiss me. I ache for her to kiss me again.

I shave the stubble I've been neglecting and head back to our bedroom. Except it doesn't feel like our room. Some of her clothes are in the closet but the scent of Sarah has faded. Yes, I may have stuck my nose in her outfits to be near her.

Another twelve hours, and Sarah will be here. I collect days' worth of clothes off the floor, stuff them into the hamper, and open the window to air out the putrid stink of my fevered dream. Should I ask Mom to borrow her van so we can have a repeat of my arrival to Toronto? No. We have the apartment to ourselves, and Sarah will want to drive Betty home.

The index cards with Mom's recipes I copied from Yiayia's cookbook are in an envelope on the bedside table. I flop onto the bed. My homemade gift isn't fancy, but making cupcakes together at Côté Fraise was one of my favorite parts of visiting Toronto. Food is how our families show love, and I want us to continue the tradition.

My phone lights up with a text.

Sarah: I'm not coming back to LA.

I snatch the glowing rectangle.

Me: Not funny, Grayson.

What a jokester.

Her brother and I have been texting since his prank on their parents' anniversary. I like the kid. Well, he's not a kid. He's my age. Sarah thinks he's goofy and irresponsible, but he surprised me with the conversation we had on her birthday. I know nothing about horses but his passion for them was palpable.

Like Sarah's was the night we met and worked on her screenplay at Griffith Observatory a year ago today. The night I found my girl. The night my life changed. The night my heart began beating the first time for real. For her.

Tonight, Sarah and I will have a drink at The Diamond Club—not an Old Fashioned—to celebrate our anniversary and her coming home. Back to me. I stretch on the bed and breathe in the fresh air. The bakery will be in good hands. She'll return to *Vampire Club*, maybe get extra hours from Dad, and I'll have my TA job, my scholarship, and a meeting with Streamplus. We'll make it in this town.

I can see our future together. Working on another movie together. Finding a place of our own. Me getting down on one knee like in my favorite love stories and making her mine forever. It's all right there in front of me.

Sarah: It's not Grayson.

I stare at the screen.

Me: Taylor?

Sarah: It's Sarah.

I hit the call button, and the phone rings endlessly until it goes to voicemail.

"Hi, it's Sarah. I'm not available right now." Her voice fills my ear. "Please, leave a message, and I'll call you back."

"Sarah, one of your brothers has your phone. Call me back when you get this."

I hang up. Dots move on the screen under my latest text. It's taking too long, and I collapse on the pillow, waiting.

Sarah: Things didn't work out with Fran. The bakery is in more trouble than I thought. There are debts that need to be paid, repairs that need overseeing, and I'll have to hire and train a new manager.

I might as well be back in the shower. I'm simultaneously hot and cold.

This is not Grayson or Taylor.

This is not a joke.

I struggle to type as quickly as my sweat-covered palms allow.

Me: OK. But isn't the bakery closed till the new year?

Sarah: Technically, yes. But there's so much to do.

Me: You can take a few days off. Spend Christmas here. You need a break. I need to see you. Then go back after a few days.

Sarah: No.

My mouth is dry. I stare at the two letters. What does she mean, no?

I hit the call button again. She thinks she's better writing words, but I need to talk to her.

The phone rings twice. There's silence, then soft sniffles.

"Sarah?"

"I can't do it."

Her whisper rattles me. I press my ear to the phone, as if that'd bring her closer to me. "Just come home for a few days. We can sort it out."

"Nick." She says my name as if a razor is slashing her. "I can't."

I clench my fist to stem the rising panic. The chills lose to the heat of the anger I refused to acknowledge. I'm not perfect, but I've done my best to be patient even though I hate our separation. I despise it. Being away from Sarah is not something I can endure much longer. It must end.

"Fine. You stay and finish this. How long do you need?"

"Nick."

"Another couple of weeks? A month?"

"Nick."

"What?" The loudness of my voice transmits my irritation more than my loneliness. The lid on the box I shoved all my fears and emotions into this past month rattles. The hinges creak and groan against the strain to keep calm, to not overreach. I pace to drain the rage from my cramping muscles. I must stay in control.

"You're not listening to me." Sarah sounds too much under control.

Fuck no, I'm not. I don't want to hear what she has to say.

"I'm not coming back to LA."

Not coming back.

The meaning trickles into my fevered mind. A lid blows and scatters the sharp pieces of my dreams to hold Sarah in my arms tonight. The stillness that follows is worse than the preceding explosion. My feet won't move, my heart won't pump. My mind and body are unresponsive. Numb.

"I can't keep hurting you like this," Sarah whispers.

"You're not hurting me." She's killing me. The monotone sentence delivers the emptiness inside.

"Don't lie." Her words slap me. Calling me a liar is the worst thing she could say after the not-coming-back bit she already used. "We're both hurting, and someone has to end it. So I'm ending it."

Except that. My legs buckle, and I'm on the floor. The room tilts and shadows spread on the ceiling. This can't be real. I must still be dreaming. I slam my hand against the solid wood dresser and pain radiates through my arm.

"No," I say past the lump in my throat.

"I . . ." Her voice cracks. She'll take it back. We can work things out. She can't keep making these one-sided decisions that affect both of us. I love her. She loves me. We'll figure it out. She's not thinking it through. "I've loved every minute we've been together. But our time is not now," she says.

It's a version of the words she wrote for Isabel when she told Rudo to leave.

My fingers dig into the phone. "Don't you dare. You are not your mother. I'm not your father. I'm not leaving you."

"No, but I'm setting you free. You deserve to be happy. Not split between two worlds."

I straighten. Solvable.

"Fine. I'll move to Toronto."

"Don't you dare," she says through her teeth.

I dare.

For her. For me. For us.

"Watch me." My empty bank account disagrees with my words.

"You can't," she yells into the phone. "You need to stay in LA. Your life is just starting. Things are happening for you, with Starlight and now the Showcase win. You earned that scholarship."

"So they give it to the girl who won second place. She'll be thrilled. I'll go to school in Toronto. They have a film course—"

"And do what for money? Sell coffee?"

The floor underneath me wobbles. I'm not betraying my dreams to follow her. I'm shifting the course of how I can achieve them. "You said Toronto is the Hollywood of the North. I'll find a job."

"But you have one. You earned that TA position."

I hit my fist on the side of the bed. I want to work with Professor Takamado, but I want Sarah more. I need Sarah more. "There'll be other opportunities. You have faith in me, right?"

"So much. That's why you can't leave LA. You're talking with Streamplus, Nick. Streamplus. People would kill for that opportunity." Her voice cracks on the last word and my heart follows. I can't stand that she's in pain. "If you pass that up, you'll regret it for the rest of your life."

"I don't care—"

"You do." She knows me too well. Better than anyone. "This is your dream. You told me so a year ago. I saw it then. I see it now. You should chase after it with all your heart."

Sarah is my dream.

"What about your dad?" There's a strange, muffled noise. My breath hitches, and I freeze. For ten years I yearned to be in the same city as him, be able to talk to him, share a meal with him. "You just got him back, and this would ruin everything. I can't bear that responsibility."

Even though she can't see me, I shake my head. "He and Mom can visit Toronto anytime."

"Nick . . ." Her voice trails off, and I see my opening. She's not resolute, this is solvable. I can find a way. I pull on the thing that brought us together a year ago tonight.

"What about you? What about screenwriting? Dad's project will need an assistant." I'm back on my feet, grabbing a duffel from the closet. I tear random shirts and pants off the hangers and shove them into the bag. Actions speak louder than words, so I'll shout at her by showing up on her doorstep. Then she'll hear how serious I am. "The next season of *Vampire Club*? Rod wants you to return."

The line is silent. My heart makes a tentative, hopeful beat.

Sarah takes a long breathe. "I told him I'm not renewing my contract." She did what? "It's up to me to help Mom keep Mémère's dream alive. I can't leave again."

"Don't do this." The back of my throat smarts.

"It's done."

"Sarah, please." I throw my computer into my backpack and yank the power cord out of the outlet by our bed.

"You are the most amazing person. The best boyfriend a girl could ask for." Her voice is stronger now. The conviction I hear in it cracks my ribcage open, obliterating the organs responsible for keeping me alive. "Maybe someday we'll meet again. Until then, live your life to the fullest. For both of us."

I throw the duffel against the wall and watch my underwear and socks scatter across the room. Words get stuck in my heart that lies bleeding on the floor among my clothes.

"Siobhan will pack my stuff when she gets back from Ireland. She'll sell Betty and send me the money. You won't have to do anything," Sarah recites, like those are instructions from a list.

I wish for the numbness to come back, because every sentence guts me. How long has she been planning this for?

"A clean break," she says.

Just when I thought I've reached my limit, she says something that hurts more. If she doesn't stop, I won't survive her next words.

"Don't call me again. I won't answer."

My insides rip to shreds.

The line goes dead.

I hit redial. "Hi, it's Sarah. I'm not available—"

I try again. "Hi, it's Sarah—"

And again "Hi, it's S—"

"Hi, it's—"

"Pick up," I scream into the phone.

"Hi—"

"H—"

I catapult the phone across the room and kick the scattered remains of my unfinished packing. The sunny December morning pricks my eyes when I stick my face out of the window and suck in a breath. I knead my temples and slam my forehead on the window frame, wishing for the physical pain to cure the torment in my heart.

I fail.

My head hits the floor and the fibers from the rug Sarah and I bought at IKEA together scratch my cheek.

What the fuck am I supposed to do now?

THIRTY

NICK

Despite the lack of her, reminders of Sarah are everywhere in this apartment. Ghosts of her haunt me in every corner. Staying here a second longer is impossible.

Toronto is where I need to be to fix this.

I check the airlines, but everything is so fucking expensive, and my bank account didn't miraculously fill with money overnight. There's one option left. I give up on thinking. I repack my duffel and head out the door. Driving Betty would only remind me of Sarah, so I run. When my lungs can't take any more, I walk.

My shirt is plastered to my back when I jog through the lobby of Mom and Dad's apartment building. I slap my hand against the wood of their door repeatedly, as if it is another object I can punish for the mess my life has become.

"What is so urgent?" Mom opens the door, slings a towel over her shoulder, and goes for the side hug I got addicted to as a kid.

I slide by her and avoid any contact. I'm not in the mood for hugs. Or words. Or anything. I shove my hands into my pockets. I shouldn't be here. I should be at the airport, on standby, trying to get onto the next flight to Toronto.

Driving Betty by myself, it would take five days to make it there. Even if I sleep in the car, don't spend money on hotels, and eat crackers and canned tuna from the back of the cupboard from home, I still need money for gas. A lot of money.

A flight to Toronto will solve this. I drop my duffel.

"I need to borrow money," I tell Mom.

Mom pokes her head into the hallway and looks both ways. "Where is Sarah? Is she running late?"

"She's not here."

"I can see that. When will she join us?" She closes the door and heads for the kitchen. "Angie is delayed too. I can keep the sole on warm, it shouldn't dry out, the salad is done, rice is in the Instant Pot. I'm so glad I didn't leave it in Chicago. That thing is—"

"Sarah is not coming," I shout. This is taking too long. I need a ride to the airport and money. "I'm not staying."

Mom spins to face me. "Slow down. Sarah isn't coming? Did you have a fight?"

"She didn't give me a chance to have a fight. If we had a fight, I might have actually had the opportunity to show her that I'm on her side. Instead, she just kicked me to the curb."

I dig my fingernails into my palm to stop from hitting the wall. "She insists she knows best. Why does everyone think they know what's best for me?"

"I can't say I'm following what's happening. Who's everyone? Can you start from the beginning?" Mom touches my elbow, and I don't jerk away even thought the contact burns. Mom means well, but I don't need coddling. I need to get to Sarah.

"There's no beginning. Apparently, this is the end." The words scorch my tongue but fail to cauterize my wound. I run my hands down my face. "She wants this to be the end." The metallic taste lingers, and no amount of rinsing my mouth would get rid of it. I meet Mom's gaze. "It's not. She doesn't get to decide. Not this time. I'm not letting her tell me what I should be doing with my life. It's my life."

"Sit." Her voice is soft and she's the epitome of calm, like when she told me my record from stealing the car to rescue Mike was not the end of the world. That it was in my power to change the course of the rest of my life. "What are you talking about? Did Sarah break up with you?" Her grip on my arm tightens, and she drags me to the sofa.

I grab a throw pillow and force myself to sit beside her.

"She told me she had to, had to stop hurting me. Her pushing me away is what's hurting me." I punch the seat cushion and jump from the couch. I can't sit here. I need to move. I need to get to Sarah. "All I need is money. Money to buy a plane ticket to fly to my girlfriend and persuade her that breaking up with me won't work."

The anger flashes through me again, and I squish the pillow to stop myself from punching something. "We are perfect for each other. If she needs to stay in Toronto, I'll move to Toronto."

Mom springs to her feet. "You're moving to Toronto?"

"I need to find a way for us to be together. There are other schools. Mike was right, the University of Toronto has a film program." As I talk, the plan I tossed around in the back of my mind starts to take solid shape. All is not lost. "I can apply for the fall semester there. I'm not giving up on my education. Just changing course."

"But your new TA job and your scholarship?"

"There will be other jobs, other offers. But there is only one Sarah." The alarm in my voice scares even me. I smash my fist into my other palm. "She doesn't get to decide this."

Mom fights through my hands, hauling me into her arms. "Nicky, I understand. Believe me. I was mad at your dad when he decided things without me. Not even telling me what he was doing, pushing me away during the proceedings."

She releases me. "And when he did finally ask, it was to divorce me and change our names to my maiden name. I was devastated, but now I can look back and see he did it because he thought that without him, we would have a better life. Wouldn't share the shame of his name, have it follow us to Chicago."

The similarities between Dad and Sarah shine through again. Are control and self-sacrifice required traits for screenwriters?

"What he didn't understand was I would've much rather stayed and been by his side through his journey. That him not seeing you all those years broke my heart." Her voice catches, and it's my turn to wrap myself around her. "I hated that he didn't give me a choice."

Just like Sarah. "Exactly. I hate this. I need to talk to her face-to-face. She's not answering the phone. My only choice is to fly to Toronto and have her listen to me for once." The burning beneath my sternum reignites. "But I need money for the plane tickets. There is a flight at 11:00 a.m. tomorrow morning. It's double the price of the red-eye, which is sold out. Or I can go to the airport, try to catch a seat on standby tonight or tomorrow if something opens up."

"Nicky." She rolls her eyes. Now she reminds me of Sarah. I love Sarah's eye rolls. Her act of frustration is cute. Mom's isn't. "You're not going anywhere tonight. Or tomorrow. You and Sarah need to talk, but you are in no state to do it. I have some money put away, and I can loan you enough to cover the ticket, but let's agree on something."

Strings, conditions, distance. Always something holding me back from what I want. I force myself to listen. Mom is willing to help. "What?"

"You need to let her have some time."

"I can't—"

"You can. You need to calm down as well. Go to her when you have a solid plan and facts. You want to be treated like an adult? Act like one. If you fly there tonight and throw your anger at her, shout at her like you've been shouting since you came into this apartment, she won't listen. Even if you are in the same city, it doesn't mean she'll see you or hear you out."

Mom's words throw a blanket over the firepit of fury I've been carrying since I picked myself off our bedroom floor this morning. "What can I do?"

"Here is my proposal. We look at the tickets together and choose something we can afford later in the week." Mom's gaze is steady, just like her. "You and I do a pros and cons list like we did to decide whether coming to LA for school was a good idea to begin with."

"Sure. I can do that."

"We look at the money. What can you afford here. What can you do and afford there. Create rows and columns so we can see what's realistic. Then we make a decision." She pats my knee. "You make a decision."

I make a decision.

The smoke in my brain clears. It would only be a few days. It's not like she's leaving Toronto. I waited months to get to her last time, a couple nights are nothing compared to that.

"This way you will have something solid to show Sarah." Mom caresses my cheek. "Something that says you are not doing it for her. Or not only for her. Not giving up on your dreams."

I get the sense that she appreciates Sarah's willingness to sacrifice our relationship for my future.

"That whatever you decide is a solid plan. From everything I've seen of Sarah so far, she'll respond to that a lot better than if you appear on her doorstep shouting in anger."

I nod. "She is sorta like you. Numbers aren't the first thing I'd go for."

"So like your father: act first, think later. But look at him." She waves her hand around at the apartment. "It took him longer than expected, but he had a plan, and it's working."

"Okay, okay, I get it. Let's do the spreadsheet. With Sarah, numbers and plans might just be the secret weapon to get her on my side."

This I can do. The numbers will work out, and I'll show her it isn't necessary to break up or quit anything.

I bury my face in my hands. "I didn't mean to shout at you, Mom. I'm just so angry, and so scared."

"Both valid feelings." She pulls my hands from my face. "I'm here for you and will always be. I'd much rather you stay in LA. But I realize what's it's like to love someone so much that moving to the other side of the continent is a no-brainer."

I'll be moving to a different country. I need to look up how long I can stay in Canada before they kick me out. Do I need a visa to stay long-term? I fumble for my phone.

Her support means the world, and what was the worst day of my life looks slightly less disastrous. "I love you, Mom."

"I love you too, Nicky." She stands and leaves me alone in the living room.

Mom's I love you is both a balm and vinegar. I'm beyond lucky to have a mom who gets me, who's on my side no matter what, even if she doesn't agree with me.

But her gentle I love you reminds me that I've never heard those words from Sarah. That she has never trusted me enough to give them back to me, even after the many times I've said them. I chew on the inside of my cheek. Maybe the reason it's easier for her to push me away is because she doesn't feel the same way about me as I do about her. The metallic taste of blood coats my tongue. Maybe I was wrong, and my certainty that she loved me was just me seeing the reflection of my love.

If Sarah needs words and numbers, I will give her words and numbers. Because I'm not ready to give up, but I won't force myself on her. If she truly does not want me in her life. If I misread the last year. If I fooled myself into thinking she loved me because that's what I wanted to see, I'll concede. I sink my hands into the soft cushion of the sofa. I'll acknowledge my defeat and let her live the life she wants.

My heart disagrees with the thought, slamming inside my chest, hammering out, "She loves you."

If I'm right, and she's pushing me away because she thinks that loving someone means not letting them help you and not letting them share your burden, I'll show her she can't quit on us. I rise. I'm stronger than she gives me credit for. I take in the combination of Dad's screenplays and Mom's recipe books on the shelf. Mom and Dad made it work. Sarah's mom and dad made it work. Sarah and I will make it work.

I pull my laptop out of my duffel and follow after Mom into the kitchen. I might be younger, but I'm an adult. I know what I want.

It's always been her.

Thirty-One

Sarah

"Merry Christmas." Mom shakes me awake.

Christmas morning or not, I can't face the world. My body doesn't want to move, begging to linger in the warmth of the feather duvet. I groan. Not like I have anywhere to go.

"Taylor insisted I wake you. Eighteen and still acts like he's eight. He wants to open presents."

I pull my sleep mask off my eyes. Even from my bed I can see mountains of snow outside. Off in the distance, a tractor blows snow off the driveway. Quite the storm last night. In Toronto. My new reality digs its claws into my shattered heart. Lying in bed without Nick is worse than venturing into the frigid room.

I'm not supposed to be here.

"Be right down," I say.

She shuts the door behind her.

I get up to change into sweats and a sweater. Nick's ring bounces against my chest in the same place his lips used to pepper me with kisses. The sharp jabs remind me of the gaping hole I created.

The pain that pierces me through and through started the moment I broke his heart during yesterday's call, punctuated every mile of my drive to the cottage last night, and woke me every couple of hours while I tried to sleep. When I think about Nick, my mind betrays me and hurtles me into a spiral of anguish over the loss of his love. Of him.

I perch on the edge of the bed and wait for the world to stop spinning. Ripping Nick out of my heart isn't possible, but ripping him out of my life had to be done. I roll my lips between my teeth. I'll get used to his absence.

Eventually.

I did the right thing.

With Fran.

With telling Mom I can stay.

With not returning Nick's texts and calls.

The weight of his ring presses on my chest. I should take it off, but I can't make my fingers undo the clasp. Hearing his voice would sooth some of my anguish, but I resist listening to his last pre-breakup voicemail for the hundredth time. He sounded happy. I hope he will be again soon.

One year ago, he walked into my bar and changed my life. A life in LA I was ready to give up. Until I met him. I swallow the memory of him draping his jacket over my shoulders. I don't have a choice. I can't rob him of his future, his chance to follow his path in LA. He'll hurt for weeks or months, but he'll agree with me years from now that me walking away was the best choice. I didn't do it to him. I did it for him.

Another stab incapacitates me. I wrap my arms around my middle to not split apart.

Sarah, you can do this.

My heart disagrees.

I cradle myself and take the punishment for the pain I inflicted on the man I love.

Moving seems impossible, but I do. Inch by inch. Time to pretend my heart isn't in tatters. I made a choice. Now I live with it.

I gather my hair into a ponytail and practice smiling in the mirror. Sunny Sarah is in the house.

"Are we playing Monopoly or Risk tonight?" Grayson has whipped cream stuck to the corner of his mouth.

I grind my teeth and try not to lunge at the traitor of our family.

Taylor taps his chin. "Risk. Grayson cheats at Monopoly."

Grayson cheats at life. Planting Fran in the bakery hoping I'd fall in love with her and change my mind about selling. Almost worked. I did fall in love with Fran.

"Do not." Grayson punches Taylor in the arm

"Do too."

I massage my temples. The throbbing headache that moved from the back of my head to take over every cell is either from the red wine I've consumed today or the constant happy face I'm maintaining. My brothers' bickering is not helping.

"Boys." Mom grins. The first authentic smile I've seen since returning to Toronto. She's off the pain meds and feeling like her old self. The mood swings are gone and so is the boot, replaced by an ankle brace. "I want to play Yahtzee."

"Dishes first." I pile the dessert plates and hope they start without me.

"Not it." Taylor touches his nose.

"Crap." Grayson drops the brand-new phone we gave him into his shirt pocket. "I'll clear the table, but you're on garbage duty."

Taylor scowls. "Not fair. I'll become an ice sculpture outside."

"That's for the best." Grayson rubs his stomach. "More dessert for me."

Dad stands up. "I'll help you, Sarah."

"No. You've done the hard work. I can do dishes." It's always been the deal. Dad cooked because Mom baked all day at Côté Fraise, and Mom cleaned up. I love how they share things, the good and the bad. Partners in everything. A mutually beneficial relationship.

I head to the hallway. My feet falter as a wave of missing Nick crashes into me. I lean against the wall in the kitchen to catch my breath. No amount of wine and no grade of headache can dull the debilitating pain in my chest. No more mutually beneficial relationship for me.

Not being with Nick is like the worst magic trick. Instead of separating me from Nick in a puff of smoke, it sawed me in half but let me live. I'm functioning, and my heart is still pumping, and I can talk and smile, but I'm not myself anymore. Acting happy when my insides are bleeding takes too much effort. I shove off the wall and bring the dishes into the kitchen.

Mom joins me and begins wrapping up the food, fighting with the cling wrap attaching to the bandage around her wrist instead of the bowl. She stacks a collection of containers in the fridge while I run the hot water and add suds to the sink.

"Do you need my help with New Year's dinner?" I say, because the only things Mom and I talk about today are food, entertainment, and how well everyone did on Christmas presents this year, especially Grayson's new phone. Mémère would've been proud. We ignore the elephant in the room. "I could make the rolls."

Tradition is to have a seafood feast on New Year's Eve. Mémère loved lobster and fish, and we'd get out the massive pot she bought in Montreal, melt pounds of butter, and bake the rolls we ate fresh that evening and then used the next day as bowls for our lobster bisque, classic New England style.

"I made reservations at Harbour 60." Grayson enters the kitchen with a tray full of dirty dishes.

I can't keep my mouth from falling open. "We can't afford that place." He was probably expecting to spend his newfound wealth at the swanky steak house.

"It's right beside the Air Canada Centre." He drops the dishes on the other side of the sink. "Give Mom and Dad a night off from cooking."

Mom picks up a platter and starts wiping it. "That sounds nice."

I rub the rough dark green side of the sponge against the crusted rim of the trifle dish and force the good little daughter smile back on to my face. The one I perfected over years of living under her roof. "So much for traditions."

Grayson slides up to the counter. "What's wrong with starting new traditions?"

"What's wrong with keeping the old ones?" My voice squeaks and I hate it. "Or are they not good enough for you now?"

"Stop." Mom puts down the dish towel. A new one with little horses Grayson gave her for Christmas, not the one with strawberries Mémère used. One of Mom's hands lands on my shoulder and the other one on Grayson's. She turns us to face each other.

I look at the sudsy water. "The dishes need doing."

"I'm not talking about the dishes." She detaches me from the sink. "Stop pretending you hate each other."

"He went behind our backs." I escape her grip and thrust my hands into the hot water. "Lied to us. All he cares about is money."

"You think—"

"Honey, that's not fair." Mom's fingers wring the new towel, creasing the starched cloth.

Grayson snickers. "You can't come back from LA and expect us to follow your whims. Our dreams are just as important."

"*Your* dreams." I grip the side of the counter and beg the suds in the sink to swallow me so I don't have to endure another lecture from Grayson. "You'd prefer to kill Mémère's dream."

Grayson's cheeks hollow. "How can you say that? Mémère is more than a bakery."

"I can't have this conversation again." I stomp out of the kitchen and into my room, leaving a trail of waterdrops. I should dry the floor so no one falls, but I don't have space in me to enter that kitchen again. Can't find the room to care. My feelings are working overtime.

Face down on my bed, I scream into it. My heart severs the last strands that were holding it together. Two halves do not agree, just like Grayson and I can't. Won't.

Mom, Mémère, the bakery—they're worth abandoning LA for. I can't be selfish again. I did it two years ago and lost Mémère. I don't want to lose what is left of her too. The rational, responsible, dutiful daughter half is at peace for the first time in a long time.

Yet, I long to be watching the LA lights from Betty's hood, celebrating the night I met Nick. This morning I should have woken up in his arms. The selfish and head-over-heels-in-love part of me wants to spend today, tomorrow, my whole life with him.

Nick.

Just thinking his name causes my body to shake. I jump up and run to the farthest wall, then back. The room is too small to contain my emotions.

I need a distraction. I gotta find something to do that doesn't hurt. I open Instagram. Couple after couple stares back at me. Ivy got engaged, and I can't even type congratulations. Siobhan's posts of her brother and his wife-to-be from their rehearsal dinner in Ireland mock me. I can't force myself to tap the heart button. I have no heart.

There's one single person who might talk to me.

Me: Are you free?

Karina doesn't disappoint. Her face fills the screen and I sit down, muss the hair I haven't washed in days, and pretend I'm not the total wreck I that am.

"Shouldn't you be out frolicking in the snow?"

I manage a not-quite-fake laugh. "Too cold." If I tell her about Nick, will I be able to keep it together? "How's California. Sunny?"

"Beeeeautiful." Her sing-song rendition of the word only makes it harder for me to maintain my smile. I shouldn't have called her. I can't spoil her Christmas with my pain. "Spent yesterday at the beach partying with some of the crew from *Vampire Club*. They say hi by the way."

"I miss them."

"They were shocked you weren't coming back. Rod told them he's not finished trying to convince you to be part of the show."

Her reminder that I've also given up the career I struggled for years to achieve and had within my grasp saps the last dregs of my energy.

"There's still time." Karina's bright eyes have the opposite effect, making me want to sink back into my pillow. "We're not officially back until January 10th."

"Thanks, but I'll be here a while longer."

She pouts, and I silently plead for her not to ask why.

"When you do get back in town, we'll go for a girls' night out, okay?" Karina doesn't disappoint.

I stretch my lips wider and hope my eyebrows are high enough to fake excitement. "Okay." It could be months or years before I get back to California.

An alarm beeps on Karina's end. "Time to get dressed and mosey over to my parents' place." Karina stretches her arms out like a cat soaking up the sun on a windowsill. "My nieces arrived this morning, and I made excuses to not join until after lunch."

We say bye and the screen goes black, and I'm alone again. Regret mixes with the thousand other aches in my chest.

I shouldn't have called her. I lie back on the bed and stare at the ceiling, listening to the compilation of pain running through my body.

The long creak of my door announces a visitor. I roll to face the wall. I don't want to deal with Mom.

Thirty-Two

Sarah

"Honey, can we talk?" Mom prods gently, like I'm five again and pouting over her donating my favorite doll. If I stay still, she might think I'm sleeping.

The bed shakes as she sits, and I scooch closer to the wall.

"Not everything is about my dreams.," says Grayson. I stiffen. Grayson's the one sitting on my bed?

Great, another ambush.

"You were Mémère's favorite." Grayson ignores my clear indication that I don't want any company. "You two had this amazing relationship and were as close as two peas in a pod. But she was my grandmother too." I put the pillow over my face. "Then you left for LA." His voice is muffled, but I hear every word. "Two years is a long time."

Without fail, the sharp point of their stakes sink into the portions of me that haven't been mangled by my breakup with Nick. They pin me to my bed and torture me with their truth.

I did leave.

I should never have left.

I should've been there by her side. I should've been working at the bakery. I chose the wrong path, and I don't think I'll ever be able to forgive myself. Tears well behind my eyes.

"But without you claiming Mémère's time, Taylor and I got to know our grandmother."

I never thought about that. Grayson was in high school when I left, still living at home.

"I loved her." Grayson sounds like he's the one who's about to cry and not me. "No more or less than you."

The way he pushed the offer to sell didn't look like my feelings for Mémère and his are on the same level. "Could've fooled me. Oh, wait you did," I say.

"She won't listen," Grayson growls.

"Sarah." Mom's fingers run through my hair, and my throat scratches. "Let your brother talk. He's trying to explain."

I give him my silence. That's all he's getting from me.

"You forget. I was in this house last year. I saw it all. Her slowing down. The effort it took to go to the bakery, to walk, to smile." He pauses. "Then the day came when she stopped going to Côté Fraise. I witnessed her fade away."

Tears come from my eyes, and the pillowcase soaks them up only for more to rush into the void. He pushes at my open wounds. Mémère's last days were without me, and that'll remain one of the biggest regrets of my life.

"Day after day, when Mom had to run the bakery by herself, I sat with Mémère. I stopped playing hockey. I read to her when she couldn't concentrate on books anymore. And we talked."

Grayson doesn't sound like Grayson. There's no cocky attitude, no joking or goofing off. His voice is low and . . . serious.

"We talked about her life in France and living in the countryside."

"You did?" Mom voices my thoughts.

"Yes. She shared stories from before she met Pops. What it took to come to Canada. Her father basically disowned her for marrying your dad." Grayson addresses Mom. "She told me about not having the support of her family and how much it hurt."

I knew the gist, but mostly Mémère liked to live in the present. She wasn't one to look backward.

Grayson shifts on the bed. "We also talked about her biggest regret." Mémère had regrets? This we never talked about. "Do you know what it was, Sarah?" My brother's voice trembles.

I don't answer him, not sure I want to know.

"Her biggest regret was that she didn't push you, Mom. To follow your own path in life." Grayson makes a noise like a cross between a growl and a huff.

"My path?" The mattress dips under Mom's weight, like this conversation is too heavy for her to hold standing.

"She told me about Pops, how he was on the road for long stretches playing hockey. At first she tagged along, but when you were born, the team frowned upon having children around, so she stayed in Toronto. You were her only friend as she learned to navigate the country she'd dropped everything to come to."

"I don't remember that." There's awe in Mom's voice.

I move the pillow away, listening to my mother and brother paint the picture of Mémère I've seen in the black-and-white photos Pops took of her. The movie of Mémère's life during her first years in Canada plays on the white wall of my bedroom.

I turn over as Mom rests a hand on Grayson's arm. "The summer after my high school graduation, the summer I met your dad in Vancouver, it was my first time away from her for longer than a week."

"Mémère hated it. Caught between wanting you to be independent, to find your way in life and wanting you to come home, desperately missing you," says Grayson. I feel like I'm eavesdropping on the secrets my brother spills. "She felt the same way when Sarah left."

She missed me. Why didn't she tell me? Every time we talked on the phone, she encouraged me to stay, like my being in LA was easy for her.

"When you came back to Toronto, Mémère was so happy to have her daughter and best friend with her again." Grayson's hand layers Mom's. "Ignored the dark cloud over you, how you sunk yourself into the business of the bakery and had nothing for yourself."

I wrote the scene where Mom left Dad, telling him to go back to England, pretending she could be just as happy without him. The riptide under my heart pulls me under. The reasons Mom broke up with Dad have nothing to do with my breakup with Nick, but I can't stop seeing parallels. If the pain of it renders me into a bundle of hurt and tears now, what was Mom feeling then? Goosebumps erupt over my skin.

Mom has always been a giver. I took that for granted, because being taken care of is one of the parts of my childhood I still treasure. I love her care. I love being loved by Mom. By Dad. By Mémère. Love surrounded me from birth till the day I left for LA.

Grayson sighs. "Mom, Mémère regretted stealing your life."

Mom gasps.

Mémère did no such thing. Mom wanted this life. She likes her life. Loves the bakery.

Doesn't she?

"She—" Mom starts at the same time as I say, "Mom—"

Grayson raises his hand to shush us, and I bite off the rest of the sentence. My happy-go-lucky brother's face is a mask of pain as his jaw clenches and unclenches. I've been there. I'm aware of how hard it is to get the words out.

I wait.

"Near the end." Grayson leans his elbows on his knees and rests his chin on his steepled fingers. "I think she knew her time was coming."

His voice breaks, and for the first time in my life I see my brother cry, not from laughing too hard, but because every memory, every syllable is as painful for him as it is for me. I'm not feeling more than him. He's just as wounded and damaged by Mémère's death.

My body freezes.

I don't have the monopoly on being hurt, on missing Mémère. Grayson, Mom, Taylor, even Dad, we all are injured by her absence. I can't deny it anymore. I leave my fortress of blankets and curl behind him. His back shudders at my embrace.

A vein ticks in his jaw. "Mémère made me promise. Taylor had to take school seriously. That part was easy. You and Mom though." He blows a long sigh through his teeth. "You are both so stubborn."

Just like you, I want to say.

"Mémère hoped you'd stay in LA and follow your dream." Grayson looks back at me. "When you didn't come home for Christmas, it made her happy."

Me being in Toronto with the family would've made her happier. Wouldn't it?

Grayson lifts his red eyes, watching Mom's crumpled shoulders. "She knew you wouldn't walk away from the bakery easily, Mom. Mémère asked me to help you find a new path." He wipes both cheeks with his sleeve.

"I tried to let you, Mom, figure it out for yourself when B&B came with their offer this summer. Wanted you to come to the realization on your own, so you wouldn't hate me." He shifts his gaze to me. I stare into his blue eyes that look almost identical to Mémère's, to Mom's, to mine. "But that's not what happened."

Grayson's guilt echoes against its many iterations in my soul.

"When Mom fell, I couldn't take it anymore. You wouldn't listen, so I had to show you. It was the only way." He studies his hands. "I did what Mémère asked me to. I reached out to B&B. She loved Fran and Everly. They will take care of Côté Fraise. Love it like they loved Mémère." He gives my shoulder a tiny shake. "You gotta let it go, Sarah."

"We have to sell the bakery," Mom croaks to my left.

"No." My tears muffle my denial. "It's all you have left of Mémère." All I have left.

"What are you talking about?" Mom's hand lands on my other shoulder. "Look around you. This cottage was built on the foundation of the love between my parents. Every board, every nail, every stick of furniture has a memory attached to it. Your grandmother is right here."

I bite my lip, but the pain is nothing in comparison with the lashes that grief rains on me.

"Exactly. See that dent in the wall?" Grayson indicates the spot by the door where the wood is outlined by an old silver frame. "We were playing knights and dragons, and you swung your sword too hard. We thought she'd be upset, but she hung the frame and said it gave the room character."

I laugh. That was Mémère, turning bad into good.

Mom touches the collar of Grayson's sweater, the circle of our arms complete. "She lives in the hearts of the people who knew her. The memories we share. Memories we're never gonna stop talking about. The memories you'll make with your children as they grow, spending winters and summers in this cottage."

"Playing hockey on Boxing Day," Grayson chimes in.

"Baking strawberry pies in June," Mom follows.

"Swinging swords in a house where creativity, bravery, and laughter are cherished. That's Mémère's legacy." Grayson continues the game.

The rolling nausea subsides, as I get in step with my brother for the first time since I came back here. We are no longer waves crashing against rocks. We're in the same rhythm.

"A happy family." I regard the room I've been using in a new light. I can see telling my children the stories of Mémère, how we planted the apple tree together and made sandcastles on the beach.

Children with Nick's chocolate-brown hair that curls when it grows too long. Kind eyes like his. I shiver. Nick, who's been getting close with Grayson.

My stomach turns. "Did Nick put you up to this?"

Grayson rolls his eyes. "I like Nick. He's a good guy. But this is about our family. About Mom. About you. I don't care if you ever see him again. What I do care about is that you don't quit your dreams."

Mom nods and smiles through her tears. "Being a screenwriter is your dream, honey. Your whole life, it's all you ever talked about. Telling your big stories, recounting tiny encounters, and turning them into heartfelt moments. Helping other people understand tough issues through your tales. You've been showcasing the beauty of everyday life in the way only you can portray."

The way Mom says it buoys me to the surface. My heart not whole, but able to hold enough blood to keep me alive.

"I don't care if you do it here, or in LA, or in France, or in South Africa." Grayson moves closer to me on the bed. "But you love it. Anyone within a fifty-mile radius of you can see that you love it. You come alive when you're writing your stories. Your face changes. You glow. It's what you're meant to do." He closes his eyes and pinches the bridge of his nose. "I'm sorry I lied to you, but you have to stop lying to yourself."

I flinch.

His words rip out the stiches holding me together. I've fought lies for so long. The scam that sidelined me when I arrived in LA. The fake name Nick gave me when we met. The truth Mémère hid from me about her health. I worry the sequins on the collar of my sweater. When did I start lying to myself? The sharp edges of the glittery plastic cut into my fingertips. How did I end up the biggest liar?

I wash my hand over my face. "I love writing. But I wouldn't forgive myself if I do what I love on the ashes of what Mémère loved."

"You are looking at it wrong." Mom grips my upper arms and pulls me into her. "Your grandmother wanted us to live our lives, not to spend them mourning hers. I know it, and Grayson knows it. Look around you. You know it too."

Mom's tears mix with mine. "Your grandmother told me not to tell you how sick she was, because she didn't want you to stay in Toronto for her. She wanted you to live your life for you *and* for her."

Grayson pats Mom and me on our backs as our sobs grow louder and ripple through our bodies.

"Let's sell the bakery," Mom whispers. "Go all in. Wring every ounce of happiness we can out of life. I deserve it. You deserve it."

How many times did Mémère whisper these words to me? "You deserve it."

We do deserve it.

I push aside the guilt of the past and try to live for today. "Do you think Fran will still talk to us?"

Mom crushes me to her, and Grayson's fingers relax their grip on my shoulder, his thank you a soft murmur. "I'll call her tomorrow."

The tears keep rolling, just like they did a minute ago, but these are different tears. They are full of hope, of not holding back, of overflowing love. "I love you, Mom." I lift my head and face my brother with a lighter heart. "I love you, Grayson."

"I love you too," they say in unison.

Thirty-Three

NICK

"The local time in Toronto is 1:22 p.m. It's a balmy two below Celsius with no snow in the forecast. We hope you enjoyed your flight and have a great stay in the 416."

The pilot's announcement stirs the butterflies in my stomach. I haven't been able to eat anything, and the coffee swimming in my veins fuels the anxiety that send my fingers shaking and my heart fluttering under my leather jacket Sarah loves so much.

The woman sitting beside me pats me on the arm. "I hope you find her."

I spent the last five hours pouring out the story of Sarah and me to this unsuspecting granny. She asked the reason for my trip to Toronto, and I couldn't stop talking. I even pulled up the spreadsheet on my phone that Mom and I created and walked her through the financials.

I'm ready. I have a plan. Things will be tight, but we can do it. Putting it on paper with Mom really helped. I can see a way forward now. I'm armed and ready to convince Sarah we can do this.

There's no one to greet me at the airport this time. The nerve endings in my back twinge at the sight of the guy who sat in front of me, scooping a woman into his arms and kissing her. I stop and stare at them making out.

That'll be me and Sarah soon. At least, I hope.

The airport is packed on the last day of the year. People coming home from the holiday rush. A family with three children wheels their luggage in front of me, blocking my way to the taxi stand. My plan is to try the house first. I hope the Connors are in town and not at the cottage. I was supposed to go to the Leafs' game with them tonight, so I assume they'll be there.

I step around the youngest child, whose princess-themed backpack is dragging on the ground, and aim for the door. Out of the corner of my eye, I catch a woman at the top of the escalator in a blue hat with blond hair. A déjà-vu moment of me in Chicago's O'Hare airport on Valentine's Day. Spotting a woman who I thought looked like Sarah, and I now know was her.

Another glance, but the woman is gone. My shoulder slams into the frame of the exit door, as if the building is saying don't go. Stay. Follow that girl.

I shake the ridiculous thought out of my head. It can't be her. My mind is playing tricks on me. Sarah is with her family. Getting ready to go to the hockey game.

"Are you in or are you out?" the father of the family asks. I step aside, letting them pass, and a blast of cold air hits me in the face. Even the weather doesn't want me to go out there.

"What the hell?" I mutter to myself. I turn around and take the escalator stairs two at a time to follow the blonde. This is a time-wasting errand. If it's not her, then I've lost a few more minutes getting to the Connor residence. But if it is her . . .

I bound off the escalator and peer over the mass of people on the departure level. Even with my height, there are too many to spot Sarah. This is a fool's errand. I turn to go back when the crowd parts to reveal a tiny form turning a corner. A tiny form the size of Sarah. A blue Maple Leafs hat.

It is Sarah. My heart screams it. My body follows. "Sarah!"

The nuns in front of me turn and stare. I crabwalk around them and run in the direction of my girl.

My legs are long, but the masses of people bustling to and fro impede my progress. "Sorry," I yell over my shoulder to the two ladies I cut off. I turn the corner I saw Sarah turn and continue running, scanning for her.

Up ahead, she's handing her passport to a security guard. "Sarah," I shout. She doesn't hear me and steps through the sliding doors behind the guard. I beeline for the doors.

A hand slaps against my chest. "Where do you think you're going?"

The man is dressed in blue, with a nametag that says Hashif. He pushes me back from the entrance. "I need to get in there. My girlfriend . . . forgot something." Sarah can't hold this small lie against me.

"Do you have a boarding pass?"

"No. But—"

"No pass, no entry."

The other security guard checks the passports of two young girls and they move forward, causing the sliding doors to open. The room is a winding line of passengers waiting to go though security. Sarah is right there.

"Sarah!" My heart pounds in my chest.

The doors start closing and Hashif steps in front of me. "Step back, sir."

"Sarah!" I yell as the doors shut.

"Do we have a problem?" The security guard looks me over.

I retreat and raise my hands. "No, sir. It's all good. I'll just text her." I move aside to let the passengers with boarding passes by.

Phone out, I type to Sarah. I'm pretty sure she's blocked my number, but I need to try.

Me: I'm in Toronto

Me: At the airport

Me: Don't leave.

I just need to get a boarding pass. My pulse plays drums in my head. I head toward the nearest ticket agent. My phone shakes in my hands. I'll buy the cheapest ticket and hope I can find her on the other side. This won't be a repeat of Valentine's Day.

"Mr. Old Fashioned."

My heart stutters. It's the voice I've missed. I almost don't want to turn in case I'm hallucinating. Don't want to waste precious moments when I need to buy a ticket.

"Nick?"

I do turn. And she's there. Leafs hat perched on blond locks, big blue eyes, the mouth I love to kiss. We stand staring at each other until a group of airline personnel passes through the space between us and breaks the trance.

And I'm running again.

She's running.

We're running, and we crash into each other.

My arms wrap around her, and the circuits close. Electricity flows between us. I come to life. Her cheek settles against my sweater, and my heart beats again. I crush her to me, my lungs taking the first real breath since the last time I saw her.

The scent of strawberries fills my world. A soft tendril of her hair tickles my chin. Her fingers press into the back of my neck. I blink away tears, marveling at how amazing it feels to touch her again. I'm never letting go.

Her body is shaking, and I worry she's cold. I put her feet on the floor. Not able to let her go, I bracket her sweet face in my hands. My fingers brush away the tears forming at the corners of her eyes.

"Nick." My name on her lips breaks me.

"Nick. I—"

I swallow her words, unable to resist kissing her. Her lips are like a balm to the anxiety, and pain, and suffering, and worry I've held on to for the last week. They float away like they never existed. Love, and adoration, and relief, and more love pours in to fill the gap. She heard my voice and came back to me. Hope fills the little cracks in my soul. Hope that we can work this out.

She presses into me, tilting her head back, asking for more. I give myself to her. This is not our last kiss, but I treat it like it might be.

It's not.

This will work. Once I explain everything, she'll see.

I wrench my lips away. "Don't say no."

"I—" She blinks. "No to what?"

"This." It hurts to remove my hand from her face, but I need my phone.

"Wait. I want to tell you—"

A horn beeps, and we both jump.

"Excuse me." A man driving an airport cart shoos us out of his way. "I need to pass through."

My fingers find Sarah's waist. I pull her out of the path of the cart. She brushes her hair out of her face, like she did the night we met, in the video I watched a million times.

"Nick, I need—"

"It's here—"

We talk over each other.

"Wait—"

"What?"

We do it again. One of us needs to listen. I gently put my hand over her mouth. "Sorry. But listen to me. I have a plan."

Her tongue licks my palm, and I can't help but smile. She's the cutest. "Let me talk."

With her nod, I remove my palm.

A metallic voice floats through the crowded airport. "Last call for passenger Sarah Connor. Please, report to gate forty immediately for boarding. Passenger Sarah Connor, your plane is about to depart."

"I figured it out. There's a spreadsheet." I drag my thumb over the screen of my phone and open the app. "I can move here, work at the bakery with you. That'd save time, but I can find a job elsewhere."

"I love you."

"I've looked into school," I say. "U of T, see I learned the lingo, they have a whole college, Innis College, dedicated to film."

She traces her finger along the line of my chin and tingles trickle through me. "I love you."

"This isn't a whim." I shake the phone. "I talked it through with Mom and Dad. My plan is solid."

She presses her mouth against my jacket, and my heart sputters. I stare down at the top of her head, waiting for her response to my plan. She has to see it can work. I need her to see the possibility.

Her voice bores through my clothes, into my chest. "I love you."

My mind catches up to my ears. What she said finally sinks in. Three words.

Not "It won't work" or "Go home, Nick." No.

The very words I've craved.

They sound as beautiful from her lips as I dreamed they would. No. They're better. They're perfect. My pulse skyrockets, and my heart threatens to burst.

Her blue eyes meet mine. "I love you. I love you. I love you."

"You do?" Dumb question, but I have to make sure she's serious.

"I love you."

I like this better than yes. Her I love yous swirl around me, forming an impenetrable wall of defense against anything this world can throw at us. Sarah Connor loves me.

"I love you too," I say.

She smiles and tugs on my shirt. I dip and just before our mouths meet, she whispers, "I love you."

I inhale the words, let them etch into my heart. My girl loves me.

We break apart, gasping for air. Sarah catches her breath first. "I love you."

I grin at her. "Will you ever stop saying that?"

She shakes her head. "I love you."

"I love hearing that. You have no idea." I kiss her nose. "They are my three favorite words of yours. And I've wanted to hear them for so long. But I like your other words too."

"I've loved you for a very long time," she says.

"Liking those words as well."

"I'm sorry it took me so long to say it. It seems silly now. I've been waiting for this perfect moment, like in the movies, with hearts, and flowers, and fireworks to tell you I love you. Trying to control everything. But I woke up this morning, and I couldn't wait another day to say it to you. The whole family pitched in, and I bought a last-minute ticket."

She shows her passport and boarding pass. "After our last conversation"—her eyes flit to a spot over my shoulder—"I had to tell you in person. That was the only thing."

I kiss her cheek. My lips can't get enough of her. "I couldn't wait either. I tried to get on a plane on Christmas Eve. But Mom stopped me."

Her mouth forms a big O.

"But I'm here now. Ready to move to Toronto. I told Ryan to start looking for new roommates."

"Not necessary."

"Sarah. I told you. I have a plan. It's solid."

"We sold the bakery."

I blink. "What?"

"Signed the deal this morning. They're keeping the name Côté Fraise, some of our family recipes, and plan to hang a dedication plaque in Mémère's honor. They promised to keep a set price for the regulars so Natalie and the others can enjoy their croissants and coffees."

"That sounds . . . fair. Are you okay?"

"Not sure. But it's the right thing to do. Côté Fraise was Mémère's dream. Just because none of us are getting up at four a.m. to make the croissants doesn't mean we've forgotten her. She's alive in our hearts."

I pull her close and inhale the sent of strawberry. The scent that to me will always be hers. No one else's.

"I'm coming home." Her words reverberate straight to my soul.

"To LA?"

"Yes, to LA."

I relax my grip on her. She's coming home. With me. "So," I whisper in her ear. "Did you bring the van?"

"No. They dropped me off and went to the game." Her eyes twinkle. "But the house could be ours."

THIRTY-FOUR

Sarah

NICK TWIRLS THE BORROWED hockey stick in his hand and checks out the stretch of frozen lake ahead. "I never skated on open ice before."

"Watch out for bumps. No Zamboni to make everything nice and smooth out here." I take his hand and we do a lap where Dad shoveled the snow this morning.

Grayson and Taylor pull out the nets.

"Nick." Taylor skates backward across the open ice, showing off. "Ready to lose your first real hockey game?" Behind him, Grayson juts his stick out, catching Taylor unaware. My youngest brother flies onto his butt and glides across the ice.

"We tend to play the game upright where I come from." Nick scoops me into his arms. "Will you be on my team?"

I tug on the lapels of his jacket. He ducks to my height and I plant a not-so-sweet kiss on his lips. "I'd love to. Oh, and I love you."

The grin on his face is magical. It irradicates the dregs of doubt I've felt since signing the papers yesterday. When Nick found me at the airport, I knew I'd made the right decision. A few minutes later and I would've been through the security gate. We would've missed each other again. But fate or someone else intervened.

"You're catching up fast," Nick whispers in my ear. "And I love you too."

After kicking Grayson and Taylor's butts, 8–4, we call it quits and make our way back to the cottage. My phone buzzes in my pocket. I tap the screen. "It's Karina."

"Girl." Flakes of what appears to be last night's sparkly make-up reflect in the California sun. Karina must have been out on the town last night. Her eyes widen. "Nick?"

Nick waves at her and stays close.

Karina bites her lip. "Just saw your message. Is it true?"

"Yup." I nod. "I emailed Rod, and I'll be there on the tenth. I'm officially back on the *Vampire Club* team."

"Eeeee!" The screen shakes as Karina bounces.

Grayson sticks his face in front of mine. "Keep it down, would you?"

"Hi, cowboy." Karina's voice drops an octave. "Snuck into any beds lately?"

"Is that an offer?" Grayson tilts his head. "Should I make my way to LA?"

I push my brother out of the way. "Stop bothering my friend." I turn back to Karina. "Let me call you back later when my idiot brother isn't hovering."

"Sounds good." She gets closer to the screen, as if what she plans to say is a secret. "I can tell you about the guy I met last night."

Grayson tosses his stick against the side of the cottage and drowns out Karina's next words "Can you repeat that?" I ask.

"I said, he might have an in at Sugar Tree Studios. Thinks they could be interested in our screenplay."

My day is getting better by the hour. "Really?"

"Don't get your hopes up. We were both pretty drunk. But"—she lifts her shoulders—"you never know."

We hang up, and Nick takes my hand. "That sounds promising."

I squeeze Nick's hand. "Maybe. Maybe not. Either way, it'll be an adventure."

The usual lump that sits in my stomach when promises are made in Hollywood is missing. Yes, I had a shitty experience. Yes, I let it taint my world and almost gave up on my dreams. Then I met this imperfect man who showed me there is good to be found, and bad moments can turn into good days.

Not everyone is a liar. There are honest and honorable people. People I can trust. I have a family in LA, not related to me by blood, but by choice.

In the living room, Mom and Dad snuggle on the couch in front of a blazing fire. "There's hot cocoa on the stove." Mom's head lifts above the cushions. "And a gift on the table."

My brothers beat Nick and me to the kitchen. Taylor shouts, "Last one in has to wash the mugs." They crowd the space and I elbow my way in.

I smell strawberries before I see the strawberry-shaped bowl wrapped in red cellophane, tied with green ribbon made to look like a strawberry leaf and stem. Mémère would've loved it. It's quintessential Côté Fraise. I barely get to admire the beautiful packaging before Taylor rips into it, revealing a collection of mini cupcakes, tarts, and bars.

Nick glides his fingers up my back and settles them on the base of my neck. "Who's it from?"

Grayson has the red glittery card. "It's from Fran." He hands it to me.

Inside is a handwritten note:

Only my first attempt. Your grandmother's recipes called to me, and I had to try to replicate the magic. Let me know how close I got. Fran

"Not bad," Taylor mumbles through a mouthful of strawberry tart.

I pluck the other half out of his hand, break it, and offer one piece to Nick. When the custard hits my tongue, the silky texture and not-too-sweet essence complements the flavorful strawberry. It's not exactly like Mémère's, but much better than the version I tried to make.

Nick watches me chew. I push his hand toward his mouth and he pops his portion in. He hums, and I can tell he likes it. Still, he doesn't say anything, waiting for my reaction.

"Good, huh?" I lick the residue of the sweet jelly off my fingers.

He nods, his fingers massaging the tense muscles below my ears. "As good as Mémère's?"

"Not quite, but Fran is close."

"So . . ." The massaging intensifies.

"It's okay. I don't regret selling." He raises an eyebrow like he doesn't quite believe it. On the drive here yesterday, he insisted on laying out the plan he had for moving to Toronto, showed me spreadsheets of financials on how he could make it work.

He'd do it too. Move here on a dime. For me.

My heart swells. "I love you."

There's that grin again. I will never get bored of the sight.

"C'mon." I grab his hand. "Let's leave the sweets to the boys."

My hand is under his shirt on the stairs. The shirt is off in the hallway. My lips are on his as I close the door to my bedroom.

It's a new day. A new year. A new set of holidays stand before Nick and me.

And I'll make each one count.

Eating chocolate-dipped strawberries for Valentine's Day. Kissing under the fireworks on Independence Day. Dressing in whatever costume he wants for Halloween. Amending for screwing up this Christmas by having our families together to celebrate. Celebrating two Thanksgivings, one Canadian, the other American. Drinking green beer on St. Patrick's Day. Munching on chocolate for Easter. Spoiling our parents on Mother's Day and Father's Day. Baking cupcakes on National Cupcake Day. Telling jokes on National Joke Day.

With Nick, I'll make every day a holiday.

**Thank you for reading Sarah & Nick's
year of holidays.**

Enjoyed their story? Spread the word.

Honest reviews persuade other readers to click on The Falling for the Liar Series and are a powerful way to support authors.

If Sarah and Nick entertained you, we would be grateful if you'd spend five minutes of your time leaving a review on their book's Amazon page.

Your review can be a few words or a few sentences.

Share your experience on the page of Distance, Love, & Us on Amazon.

Sign up for our newsletter at willadrew.com

Have you read Star Struck?

Falling for the Movie Star
Book 1

If you like an age gap, brother's best friend romance featuring LA's red-carpet glamor, Irish charm, and a reunion written in the stars, Siobhan and Asher's story is for you.

Turn the page for a sneak peek.

STAR
Struck
A NOVELLA
WILLA
DREW

Tonight on Extra

MF: Maria Fernandez here covering the prestigious Starlight Foundation Gala. On the red carpet with me is Asher Menken, star of romantic comedies like *Legally Hot* and the now-classic heartwarming historical tale *Tomorrow's Love*. Such a pleasure. It's been a couple of years since anyone on this side of the pond interviewed you. Where have you been?

AM: Thank you for the glowing introduction. Glad to be back in LA. I've enjoyed what the stages of Dublin and London have to offer, but I sure missed the California sunshine.

MF: We're glad to have you back. Hopefully, for good?

AM: For a while. My project—a collaboration with the winners of this year's Starlight competition—is the first movie my production company will take on. And I have my own reasons to stick around for the next nine months.

ONE

Siobhan

A CARDBOARD TUBE WITH a shred of toilet paper mocks me. Of course, I end up in the bathroom stall that's missing the key element. My parents ran out of Irish luck when they had me: I'm the only member of the Casey clan born on US soil.

"Can't open the flippin' holder." My best friend isn't her usual happy-go-lucky self. She's nervous for a reason. Months of hard work, and the possibility of writing for a big Hollywood movie comes down to tonight.

"Don't break your new nails. Just shove a bunch under the divider."

The coveted wad of white toilet paper and Sarah's undamaged red nails appear beside the spike of my stiletto.

"Got it." My voice sounds strangled, because I'm holding the bottom of my floor-length sequined dress between my chin and my chest.

"Good. Now hurry. We don't want to miss the opening number," says Sarah. "I hope we'll be celebrating more than just your birthday tonight."

The best birthday present would be hearing, "And the Starlight award goes to Sarah Connor." Ever since I met her two years ago when she moved to LA, Sarah's been the one with a plan: become a screenwriter. May have hit a few bumps (okay, craters) on the road, but my girl is making her dreams come true.

The Spanx I'm wearing at the insistence of Mrs. Marino, my boss who lent me this elaborate golden gown worth a year of my salary, don't want to go back up. How do people spend all night in these things?

"We were so sorry to hear about you and Leyla," the interviewer says on the TV in the lounge part of the restroom.

My ears perk up. I'm not sorry at all. I've been obsessing over my favorite romantic star's newfound freedom for weeks now.

"Well," Asher Menken's deep baritone loses its smoothness, "all I can say is—"

"Ladies and Gentlemen"—the TV switches from the pre-recorded interview to the real-time coverage of the awards ceremony—"welcome to the Fifth Annual Starlight Foundation Gala."

For feck's sake. The world is dying to know Asher's take on his ex. Okay, I'm dying to know. Even if I get a chance to see him, it's not like I could ask him myself.

"How much longer?" Sarah can't hide her impatience. "I don't want to miss anything."

"Just go." I wave my free hand at the closed door as if Sarah can see me. "I'll be in as soon as I can wrangle this tiny torture device back onto my crotch."

"You sure?"

"Aye, go already. Nick's waiting." Probably cursing me. Boyo is also nervous tonight, and we don't get along at the best of times. "Enjoy yourself. You've worked so hard for tonight."

A few clicks of her high heels plus the sound of the door closing, and I'm left alone with my tight beige nemesis.

I tuck the bottom of the dress into my décolleté. This is bollocks. I peel the undergarment off my thighs and balance on one, then the other silver strappy sandal as I struggle to free myself. Dress righted, I take my first deep breath of the night, ball up the offending material, toss it into the bin, give it the finger, and exit the stall.

A quick check of my stomach in the mirror shows it's as flat as it was with the awful contraption. I wash my hands and ensure my hair survived the battle of the bulge. The aquamarine dye I've been using this summer is starting to bore me. Might be time for a change.

The blue corner of the tattoo on the inside of my wrist is showing. I tug the long sleeves of the dress down, causing the neckline to plunge even more. Gotta make sure I cover up my body art tonight. While highly unlikely, Mum and Da might see pictures. They don't exactly know about this version of my artwork. My tastes run more towards black ink than gold sequins, but I do rock this dress. I blow myself a kiss in the mirror. Time to get this show on the road.

I reach for the door handle when the painted wood panel flies open and smashes into my shoulder. For a moment I teeter on my heels, sure I can save myself, but this battle I don't win. I land hard on the solid tiles of the bathroom floor.

"Bloody hell," I yelp.

The door slams shut, then opens again, and a tuxedo-clad figure enters the room. "Damn it, sorry, I didn't mean to . . . didn't know . . . are you hurt?" The crisp black silk of men's trousers crinkles as the offender crouches down and stretches his hand my way.

I blink. Then blink again. Wide pools the color of whiskey I've drooled over during movie nights with the girls peer at me.

"Are you okay?" An expression worthy of an Oscar nomination graces Asher Menken's face as he scans my body for broken bits.

I wiggle my toes, rub my shoulder, and swivel my head around. "All in one piece, no thanks to you." I've wanted to approach him since I first saw Ash on the red carpet a couple of feet ahead of us, but he was in the middle of an interview, probably the one I'd just been listening to. He and my big brother Owen are still best friends, but over a decade has passed since the superstar and I have been in the same room together.

"What can I do?" There is no spark of recognition in his eyes despite the fact that other than the long hair, I'm a mini copy of my brother. I wait to see if anything clicks, but his focus is not on my face. Rather, he gawks at my naked leg, exposed in all its glory thanks to the thigh-high slit in this fancy dress. His gaze travels up my leg and I follow, until we get to where the lace of my aquamarine thong is visible, no longer shielded by the Spanx. He looks at my hair, then my thong, and swallows.

"I still like matching things," I say.

"Sorry?"

"My hair matches my thong. Like my hair bows used to match my clothes, remember?"

His eyes narrow, and he tilts his head. "I think you might've hit your head."

"I'm Siobhan." I lift the sleeve off my left wrist and show him the tiny star, my very first tattoo. I got the memento as soon as I moved here seven years ago: my design, based on the one I drew for Ash a lifetime ago. "Réiltín?"

Another sweep of his eyes takes in more of my face as he scans me up and down, or left to right, or however the horizontal plane is looked at. "Owen's little sister?" His eyebrow raises.

"Aye."

"Unbelievable." He reaches inside his jacket, pulls out his wallet, and takes out a piece of paper. Ash sits next to me on the icy floor as I tug at the dress in a too-late attempt to cover up. He gives the paper to me. "My good luck charm."

I stare. In my hand is a faded copy of what I now have on my wrist. The original little star I drew for him when I was nine.

"You . . . kept this?"

Asher casts his eyes to the floor, and my pulse takes off. I mean, I've seen the expression before, both on and off the screen, yet up close and personal like this he's . . . gorgeous. Yes, the teeth are perfect, the chin is chiseled, and the hair—oh, how I want to run my hands through his hair to test if those strands are as tuggable as they appear. But this is more than the good looks. He's lit up from within.

I hand the piece of paper from the past back to him and will my heart to slow.

"Owen did say you lived here." Ash tucks the drawing carefully back in his wallet and puts it away. "Of all places to run into you." He smiles, and there's the "I'm sorry" smile that got him out of a trip to the police when he bumped into a car in front of us. The lady who owned the Peugeot let him go with, "What's one more scratch on this old heap of metal?" She would've berated any of my brothers for doing the same thing.

"I promised my friends not to get starstruck, but I didn't think they meant literally." I smile back. "Howeyeh, Ash? Can I still call you that?"

He nods, giving me the once over again. "Can't call you Little Star anymore. You're no longer . . . little."

My turn to swallow. The way he said *little* sends a shiver through me that I can't blame on the chill of the tile floor. My name is a puzzle for most people in LA. At work I heard a million attempts at my name until I came up with "she-Vaughn." Sarah shortens it to just Sio, "she." Back in Ireland my family calls me Shiv, and Mum insists on Baby Girl. But Asher's nickname for me, Réiltín, which means Little Star, might be my favorite. "I don't mind." He can call me anything.

"Réiltín it is, then." He runs his hand through the thick light brown strands he inherited from his movie star mother and rests his fingers on the nape of his neck. "We should probably get off this floor." He jumps to his feet, wraps his fingers around my wrist, and lifts me up. I wince in pain.

"Did I hurt you?"

"The shoulder is a bit tender." I lower the neckline and see a red line across my skin. Ash's thumb traces the mark from the door. His touch doesn't make the pain go away, but I'm both nervous and more secure with his skin on mine. His presence has always had this effect on me. The thrill and the comfort at the same time.

The first time I met him, my nine-year-old self didn't know what to think about Ash. He wasn't a famous Hollywood star then, just the nineteen-year-old friend my brother brought home for Christmas break because Ash had no family in Ireland to spend the holiday with. A breath of fresh air all the way from California to light up our middle-of-nowhere in County Kerry.

I fix my dress. "We should get going. My friend Sarah must be wondering where I am."

"Sure you're okay?"

"I'm tougher than I seem."

"You look"—he pauses—"great in this dress. All grown-up." His eyes stray to my cleavage.

"Yup." I straighten and push my chest forward. "Got me big girl boobs and everything."

"I didn't mean to . . ." His "I'm sorry" smile is back. "This isn't what I—"

"Just having a laugh." I tap him on the arm, like we're old pals. "Great way to start my next quarter century."

"Today?"

"'Tis."

"Well, happy birthday to you." He purses his lips, and his eyes brighten. "We could have a drink after the gala? Celebrate? Catch up?"

"Bang on." I don't jump up and down like I used to when I got to spend time with him, but I flash him my "thank you for a great tip" smile. Asher Menken wants to have drinks with me. I ain't saying no.

"Great. But"—he rubs the wrinkles between his eyebrows—"a favor? Could you check if there is a guy in a red velvet tuxedo hanging around by any chance? If he is, I'll stay here a while longer."

"Aye." I peek out of the door and see empty hallways. "The coast is clear."

Reporter 1: Did you see Asher on the red carpet tonight? No Leyla by his side.

Reporter 2: My heart broke when I heard about the demise of #AshLa.

Reporter 1: But he did look fine. Like, rebound fine. Any bets who the next lucky girl will be?

Reporter 2: One-night stand with Asher Menken? Sign me up.

TWO

SIOBHAN CASEY.

I can't believe Owen's baby sister scared my bathroom stalker off with foul language worthy of an R-rated movie. The creep thought he was clever hiding around the corner, ready to accost Siobhan and me on our way to the ceremony. Her vocabulary, among other things, has grown. In fact, there isn't much left of the little girl with a short bob, matching hair accessories, and hand-me-down outfits from her brothers. Although the eyes, those sometimes green, sometimes blue, sometimes gray eyes of hers, and Owen's, and their Ma's. I should've recognized those eyes.

When my publicist Jackson asked me to be part of tonight's ceremony, I almost said no. I hate these types of affairs. The fakeness. The shallowness. The constant vying for attention. I never dreamed my night would be like this.

I glance out into the sea of creativity, and the rush of youthful exuberance hits me like a tidal wave. My partnership with the Starlight Foundation was the right decision. This is the perfect project to kickstart my new production company. I already got the green light for two TV shows, and this movie, with the proper amount of press, will give me the cachet to do more.

Still, the best part is the opportunity to give back, do something worthwhile with the fame I've been lucky enough to achieve. And when the tall kid accepts his Best Director award, he's genuinely ecstatic. I can't help grinning like a fool along with him.

"That's Nick." Siobhan sits down after she finishes clapping her hands raw. An empty seat next to me had been an open invitation for the opportunists looking to pitch, but now I'm glad the organizers assumed I would bring a date. "He's been in LA less than six months, and look at him. I'm here seven years and keep slinging drinks."

"You want to be in the movie business?"

"God, no. Owen is the one with the acting bug in our family."

"Why LA then?" Owen refused to tell me the full story.

"Farthest place I could escape to with my American passport that met my criteria."

"Which were?"

"Far from Ireland, fun, sunny, and not an island." She winks at me. Good to see she hasn't lost her spunky attitude. "Had a string of jobs. Let's see, I was the Belgian waffle girl at Disneyland first. Girl's gotta start somewhere. Graduated to waitressing at a fifties themed diner. Gawd, that was horrible. They put that yellow American plastic they call cheese on everything. Who puts cheese on pie?"

Siobhan has the right to judge. Her family's cheese is the best I've ever tasted. Of course, I've had the privilege of stealing the stuff fresh from the cheese fridge when no one was looking. As a teenager I preferred to ask for forgiveness rather than permission. The bonus of performing in Dublin was that in three hours I could be at the Casey farm indulging in unlimited quantities of first-rate cheese. Well, and pretending I'm part of their large warm family. Owen is so lucky.

"Anyhow, now I work at a swanky resort bartending with my girl Sarah over there"—she swings her champagne glass in the direction of a group of young people, of which Sarah could be any one of three girls—"but the hours give me time to play artist."

"Well, lucky me. You saved me from being cornered by overeager fans and wannabe writers." And she saved me before. The first Christmas I spent at her family's farm, she saw me struggle to memorize my part for *The Little Prince*. I was ready to throw in the towel. Maybe the acting gene skipped a generation, maybe the tabloids were right and my good looks and family connections were the only reasons Trinity's theatre program accepted me.

Siobhan didn't let me give up. She ran lines with me, jumped up and down every time I got one right, and even drew me a picture of a little star, a réiltín, for good luck. The folded piece of paper with her design was in my pocket when I first went on stage and has been with me ever since, calming me when I'm nervous. And being back in the States has me super nervous tonight.

"He deserved the tongue-lashing. Shoving his script at you in the middle of the event is the worst way to get your attention."

"Hollywood is hard, I get it. But he was going to stuff the flash drive inside my jacket if you didn't interfere. I should've just shoved him off, but that'd end up in the papers with me as the unreasonable superstar, too stuck-up to talk to his fans." I take another sip from the flute the server keeps refilling. "The guy's face matched his red suit after you told him off. You're more effective than my bodyguards."

She laughs. Not the polite tut-tut of reporters reacting to my lame jokes or the light tinkle that warmed my heart when I managed to get Leyla to break character. No, this is a roaring, full-bodied, full-of-life laugh.

And I'm laughing along with her, feeling lighter than I've felt in months. No, years.

My real smile hasn't graced my face in forever. The world thinks Leyla and I broke up a few weeks ago. In reality, we've been apart for over a year. Our publicists timed the news for maximum impact, every step calculated to advance our careers. Well, her career. It's always been about her career. Every fight, a tug of war between her need to shoot for the stars and mine to settle down. In the end, our marriage came down to one thing: I can't wait to have kids, and she didn't want any.

"Gotta stand up for myself and those I care about," Siobhan says. "You know my older brothers; add waitressing in LA, and there's no better verbal self-defense school." She curls her arm and almost spills champagne onto herself. I catch the glass in time. "I know how to punch, too, if it comes to it. Owen made sure to teach me. And I always keep my thumb out."

She puts her glass down and demonstrates the proper fist technique. "Brothers." Her eyes widen. "Oh." She holds out her hand. "Give me your phone. Let's send Owen a selfie. It'll freak him out."

I like nothing more than pulling pranks on my best friend. My phone in hand, Siobhan leans in, her shoulder brushing against mine, and I inhale a mixture of honey and something spicy. "Smile," she instructs.

Easily done.

She plucks my cell from my fingers, her thumbs fly over the screen, and in a second, she flashes our smiling faces at me. "Check out who I bumped into," is written underneath our picture.

"Bumped into, huh." I chuckle at her play on how we met in the bathroom. She sends the text.

Siobhan opens my jacket, the gesture she berated the guy in the red suit for. "Done."

My body shrunk away from the rando's touch, but with my grown-up réiltín, I savor the contact. She puts my phone in the inside pocket and adjusts my sky-blue tie. Her eyes narrow, and she runs her fingers against the dots on the smooth silk.

"This tie, doesn't it remind you of the *Infinity* exhibit Yayoi Kusama did with the mirrors at The Broad a few years ago?"

I nod. "Like being inside a kaleidoscope." I took Leyla on a private tour of the immersive art installation at The Broad Modern Art Museum. We spent the evening lost in the multi-reflective rooms.

"Exactly." She smooths my tie one more time. The touch of her hand on my chest does things to me it should not. "Wasn't it deadly? Blows you only got five minutes in each room."

She's deadly. Real and beautiful. And alluring.

Gone is the little girl who doodled on anything she could get her hands on. Before me sits this vivacious, gorgeous woman. Her green—or are they blue—eyes twinkle in the low light of the reception hall.

"Did you study art?"

"I take classes when I can, but nothing official. I love to explore—oils, watercolors, sculpture, loom, pottery, print—tried them all. I even thought about costume design. But I think skin is my favorite canvas." She looks down at the star on her wrist.

This woman is a bright star in the dark night that has been my life lately. I can't look away; I won't, not when there's so much to see.

Even her dress teases by covering up practically everything yet accentuating her body in a way no garment should be allowed to. But I've glimpsed the secrets the fabric hides. Thinking about her long leg and how I'd run my hand up the curves to . . . I feel a twitch I haven't felt in a long time.

What am I doing? How can I be thinking like this? What would Owen say if he saw me ogling his sister?

Hey, boyo, don't even think about touching her.

Which is exactly what I'm doing. Thinking. And that's where I'll be stopping.

"So, you've traveled the world?" Siobhan reaches for another glass from the server walking by and our hands brush.

There it is again, the little electric shock like when I touched her in the bathroom. What is she doing to me? Am I having any effect on her? It's so hard for me to tell these days, reality and fiction always blurring. Is a woman truly interested in me, or is she just caught up in my fame and fortune?

It was easy when I met Leyla. We were both unknowns at the time, just starting out in the business. When our movie hit number one at the box office everything changed overnight. I was used to my parents' fame and seeing my face on the cover of tabloids wasn't new, but with my own fame, the frenzy reached a whole different level. Leyla and I relied on each other, bonded in the fire of chaos.

Siobhan is different. She knows me and doesn't have the starstruck expression my fans get. Talking to her brings the instant comfort I associate with my visits to her family farm. She taps her glass to mine, and I enjoy another brush of our fingers.

Her skin is cool. No, comfort isn't the right word. Connection? There's something here. We're on our third glass and I should be feeling the haziness of the alcohol, but instead, everything is crystal clear. For the first time in a long time, I'm alert and aware.

Four delicate fingers brush over the back of my hand, as if she's painting me with invisible watercolors. Her pupils dilate, and I'm sure mine do too. A slender index finger wraps around my thumb and slides up, down, and up again. If I'm reading her right, my year of celibacy is ending tonight.

She touches a sensitive part at the base of my thumb. "Wanna get out of here?" Siobhan's eyes confirm her invitation.

"Yes" escapes my lips before I even think about consequences. "Give me a minute."

As she walks away, I text my security detail to let them know I'm ready to leave and there's going to be a plus one. Hopefully, we can slip out the back door and not get noticed.

Across the room, Siobhan's talking to a short blonde in an even shorter silver dress. They hug, and my little star's walking back toward me. Her slender hips swing with the movement, glittering gold. My body reacts with more than a twitch this time.

"Where to, sir?" asks the limo driver.

"The hotel," says Siobhan.

"How'd you—"

"Know? Figured you'd be staying with your parents since you just got back. Their house is in Malibu, right? A tad too far for tonight."

She's too smart for me.

The hotel is only a short ride from the venue, and in no time we're in the underground garage. I hop out of the car hoping to open the door for Siobhan, but she's too quick for me too.

Leyla would've waited, expecting a grand gesture from me in case there were any cameras around. Always a show with that woman.

This girl—woman—however, pinches my security guard's arm. "Oh, you're a tough one." The guard sticks out his chest and eyes Siobhan up and down. "Spend every day at the gym, do we?"

I feel a pang in my chest. Jealousy? I jut out my arm. "Shall we?" Siobhan slinks hers through and leans into me. My temperature rises with the contact of her warm body as we make our way to the private elevator.

The metal doors slide together and once again we're alone.

"What is it about elevators?" she asks, a hand running down my arm.

"What d'you mean?"

"They're just so damn sexy."

"You think?"

She reaches up and tugs on my tie, giving me a low, breathy, "Yes."

I'm done for. Reason, propriety, and resistance are out the window. My lips crash against hers, one hand circling her waist to pull her closer, the other finally getting to touch the soft skin of the long lean leg she's hooked over my hip. My palm travels up her thigh and cups her butt.

The sequins of her dress scratch against my thin shirt as if they are clawing to get at me. She's amazing, and so alive. Her taste, her scent, her heat invade me, send currents through my body, and light me up like no other. The twitch is now a throb.

I don't have enough hands. I need to touch more of her, but there's no way I'm letting go of this luscious ass. I tear my mouth from hers and explore her chin, her neck. I pause, pressing my lips against her pulsing artery, the thump matching my own racing heartbeat.

The soft ding of the elevator indicates we've hit my floor, but I don't want to leave our little cocoon. Siobhan has other ideas and starts backing out of the elevator, my tie still clutched in her hand. I'm happy to follow, as long as I get to keep kissing those amazing lips.

We move down the hall, and I reluctantly break the kiss. "Wait."

"What? Bored already?"

"Not in the slightest." *More like alive for the first time.* "My room is this way." I clutch her arm and haul her down the hallway in the opposite direction, searching for my hotel room key with my free hand. I jam the card into the reader, the light goes green, and we burst into my suite.

Before the door closes, her fingers are undoing my belt.

"Careful of the gown. It's not mine."

The first time I roll a condom on, she doesn't even take her dress off.

Guess who ordered two burgers, not one?

Burger with Fries . . . $36.95

Burger with Fries . . . $36.95

Chocolate Cake . . . $22.95

THREE

Siobhan

FOR YEARS I WENT to bed ogling the poster of Asher in my bedroom in Ireland. Now I'm in America lying in bed with the real thing. I stare at his sleeping form, my fingers itching to trace the outline of his jaw, those plump lips.

"See something you like?" He peers at me through one half-closed eye.

"Lots. I—"

Ash's lips crash against mine, and my words are lost. Unnecessary. I open my mouth and grant him access like it's the most natural thing in the world. My lungs are screaming for air by the time he pulls away.

He doesn't go far. As if he can't stay away, he presses his forehead against mine. "I'm starved. Wanna order room service?"

Wasn't expecting that. The appetizers at the Starlight Foundation Gala were enough to sop up some of the champagne in my system, not replace a dinner. "I could eat."

Ash stretches across my body and slides the remote off the bedside table. My skin alights from the brush of his arm against my ribs, and I want his mouth back on me, charting a path along my side. I bite my lip instead. On the way back, Ash kisses my shoulder, the base of my neck . . . My brain argues with other parts of me. We are not going to get any sustenance if I don't stop this. "I thought you wanted something to eat."

"I do." His words are muffled as he savors my ear lobe. With a sigh, he pushes himself up into a sitting position and turns on the TV. "Let's see what they have."

The heat of his body leaves mine. I mimic his posture and pull up the sheet, so it covers our almost-touching legs.

While he rolls through the menu, his other hand settles on my leg. His thumb grazes my thigh, and I order my brain to concentrate on the food items scrolling on the TV instead of following my urge to grab Ash's hand and put it somewhere that thumb could be of better use. Cheese pizza, ravioli, pesto risotto . . .

"How about a burger and fries. France has decadent food, but they can't do a burger like here."

The only French food I've had is quiche lorraine at the bakery Sarah buys her butter tarts from. Must be nice to have had so much French food you crave a burger. How long has Ash been in Europe? At least two years. He followed his wife. No, ex-wife. Shit, am I his rebound?

That movie star smile flashes my way, and my heart skips a beat. So, what if I am. I don't care. I'll file away my time with him, from his hand helping me off the floor in the bathroom to what we did in this bed. Everything about this night, tucked away and treasured alongside the memories of him at our farm-house before he was famous.

"Add some chocolate cake and you got yourself a deal." I give him my most dazzling smile, because two can play that game. He stares at my lips, menu forgotten. I bring my mouth to his. "Burgers, fries, chocolate cake, and then I'm all yours," I whisper, with our noses millimeters apart. The desire in his eyes says he wants a bite of me much more than the food, but he leans back and completes the order.

The meal arrives blazingly fast. We sit cross-legged on the bed, the tray of food between us. Ash inhales the fries like there's no tomorrow, and I have to fight him for the last one. For a man who looks like he works out every day—scratch that, several times a day—watching him wolf down a burger before I start on mine brings back the teenage Ash I knew in Ireland years ago.

"I see your eating habits haven't changed much." He used to scarf Mom's meals and ask for seconds before any of my brothers finished theirs.

"I can pretend to be more civilized when I'm on display in public, but with family this is what you get." He winks and I forget to chew. "Dad enrolled me in etiquette classes when I was in middle school because he could not stand my table manners. Now imagine me, a short pimply teenager with braces in a room where I'm the only boy, surrounded by white tablecloths and a million forks and glasses, learning how to debone fish while looking cool as a cucumber."

"The latter part I can imagine, but you as a pimply youth? Impossible."

"Just wait until my mother sits you down with a stack of photo albums. You'll get to see more of my naked ass, and the array of pimples that plagued me for a couple of years in middle school." Ash runs his finger across my cheekbone, and I forget about the fries. I want his fingers to touch my salty lips, but he takes his hand away before he can get there. "I don't remember you having those. Any time I saw you, you looked like an angel."

"Angel? Mum would disagree. She thinks I was harder to raise then the boys." I lift my chin and show off my skin that Sarah thinks is flawless. "You missed my puberty years, but I'm the lucky one. Never had a problem with bad skin. My smile is a different story. I should've had braces, but that was not something we even considered." I smile wide and reveal my less-than-perfect teeth.

"So no embarrassing teenage photos of you at your Ma's place?"

"I didn't say that. Mom still drones on about my attempts at copying the latest makeup trends. I'm sure there are photos where I look like a cartoon character. Like my year 4 portrait. She won't let that one die."

"I have to see those." He laughs, and the sound is not like in his movies. It's lighter but deeper at the same time. "Next time we're in Ireland, I'll ask your Ma."

"I'm sure she'll do whatever you tell her. I'm surprise you don't know the combination to her safe. Unlike you, I'm my mother's worst nightmare. I moved on from makeup you can wash off to coloring my body with permanent images. Look at me."

He does, and there's that pull again as his eyes travel over my shoulder, under my right breast, and down. "They suit you. Everything I see when I look at you is beautiful."

"You probably say this to all your one-night stands."

He drops his smile. His gaze roams across my exposed skin, this time without the lust I've enjoyed seeing in them this evening. He's way too serious, and my skin prickles in anticipation of what he's going to say.

"I haven't done a one-night stand since I was twenty." His gaze finds mine and holds it. "I mean it when I say you're beautiful. You're so beautiful I have to touch you constantly to remind myself you're not a figment of my horny imagination."

I take his hand and place it on top of the blue cornflower tattoos on my rib. "Definitely not imaginary."

His thumb runs over the petal imprint. "Does it hurt when you get them?"

"Feck yeah."

"Why do it again if it hurts?"

"Because I love them so much. I can take pain if I know it's going to be temporary and lead to better things." After the first one, my little star celebrating my freedom, I swore I'd never get another one. The Celtic knot behind my right ear I got in a moment of weakness, of missing home. That pain was worth not caving in. "Plus, you sort of forget how much it hurts. Mum used to say women have more than one kid because they forget how much it hurts giving birth. If they remembered, we'd all be only children."

"Do you believe it?" Ash runs his finger through the leftover ketchup in little infinity loops.

"Sorta. I think if you want a kid, you'd go through any kind of pain to have one."

His finger freezes. "Do you want to have kids?"

"Absolutely. Maybe not four, like Mum, but a couple." I bop my head and point at my heart. "I'd be a cool hot Mom. The talk of the playground."

One side of his mouth hitches in a smile. "I can picture that."

"But I need to figure shit out first. My life is, well . . ."

"Like that ever happens." He licks the ketchup off his finger.

"It happened for you." I poke him in the shoulder, trying to get that smile back. I get a glimmer. "You're successful. You can have a gaggle."

"Might look that way. But money doesn't equal success. Or happiness." His serious expression returns.

I poke him in the shoulder again. "But it buys excellent chocolate cake."

"Let's hope it does." Ash takes the silver lid off the plate.

A slice of four-layered chocolate cake filled with chocolate ganache and drizzled with so much chocolate it forms a little lake on the plate is not what captures my attention. In the middle of the decadence there's a single unlit candle. A pack of matches with the hotel logo completes the still life.

"You remembered?"

"That it's your birthday? No way I could forget anything about you." He lights the candle, and in a quiet baritone starts whispering, "Happy Birthday to Réiltín." Each note lights a little candle in my chest. The heat builds until my heart is a puddle of tenderness. He ends with a breathy 'you' worthy of Marilyn Monroe and focuses on my lips.

I tear my gaze away and blow out the candle. My wish is for Ash to be my birthday present every year.

He removes the snuffed candle and digs into the top two layers with his fork. "Would you like some?"

I open my mouth to take the gooey chocolatey forkful, but he changes direction and shoves the cake into his instead.

"No way, it's mine." I lunge at the cake and snatch the plate away from him. He stabs in the direction of where the plate was, and I lower my mouth to the crest of the slice and bite the largest chunk I can out of it. I can feel the buttercream on my cheek, but I'm not letting him win.

Ash abandons the fork and brings his face to mine. He bites from the other side, chocolate icing smudging his perfect face. I fake taking another mouthful of cake and lick the goo off his skin instead. The bristles of his stubble rub against my tongue, and the combination of Ash and chocolate might be the favorite thing I've ever tasted.

I scoot closer, and the plate slides out of my hand onto Ash, coating his abs in chocolate ganache. "Oh shite. Sorry."

"The cake is good, but I prefer to eat it, not wear it." Ash pushes off the bed and places the tray on the table. "Be right back." He disappears into the bathroom, the door closing with a soft click.

I climb out of the ginormous bed, my limbs heavy with disappointment. I was hoping this was a refueling for more fun, not a goodbye treat. If I get one night with Asher Menken, I want it to last until dawn. That's hours away. I don't want to leave but I've been through this enough to know the signals. Hell, I'm usually the one doing the "bathroom time to leave" move.

Why would this time be any different? My stomach swirls and I regret the cake, but not the laughter. Nor the genuine warmth of our conversation or the ecstasy of our bodies together. He said he doesn't do one-night stands. Does it mean I'll see him again? Or was that the old Asher? Now that he's divorced, does he only want to play? Wouldn't blame him. Play is all I ever do.

I've managed to pull on my thong and silver sandals when the light from the bathroom falls on me.

"Hey." Ash leans against the doorframe. "Where do you think you're going?"

The way he's looking at me, I have an urge to cover my naked breasts. I straighten my back. "This was fun, but it's getting late."

He crosses the room. "It's not late. Unless you want to go." His fingers brush against my wrist then, circle it. His touch sends tingles to places I shouldn't think about if I want to leave this room. I don't want to leave this room. He traces the tiny tattoo again. "My little star." His whisper is like a benediction.

Ash raises my wrist to his lips and gently caresses it. Whiskey-colored irises scan my face from under long eyelashes, and my heart gallops out of my chest. He leans forward and presses soft kisses on the tattoo on my shoulder, his hands flutter at my hip, and the hotel room begins to sway.

He drops to his knees, those long fingers pulling at the string of my thong, his tongue licking the 'not easy but worth it' line of script on my hip. I place a hand against the wall to steady myself as he strips off my underwear, lifting one foot out of a sandal, then the other. As my toes hit the plush hotel room carpet, his hot lips suck on my inner thigh, and my legs begin to wobble.

I'm floating through the air. Literally. Ash throws me over his shoulder as he stands, and a giggle erupts from me at the swift motion. Then the softest sheets I've ever slept on touch my back as he returns me to our bed. I miss his warmth, his skin on mine for the moment it takes him to climb in with me, but it doesn't last long before his lips find mine. I sink my fingers into the silkiest hair in the world and pull. I'm rewarded with a moan that radiates through his lips into my core.

"Condom." He rolls onto his back, propping himself up on his elbows. "You do it."

Those intense eyes watch my every move as I tear open the foil, release the disk, and find the right side. His body stiffens as I roll it on, and a delicious thought enters my mind. I lean down and kiss his hip. My name escapes his lips in a low moan.

My tongue finds his abs, and they taste better than the chocolate cake. His fingers thread through my hair, and I sense his desperation. I feel it too. I find his lips, and he wastes no time as his body covers mine.

We fall out of time and space. Just Ash and I, together, as one.

Unlike our first or second time, everything is slow and sweet. Small movements cause ripples of pleasure I never thought possible. His fingers thread through mine, and the grip is anything but gentle, like he's afraid I might float away. I squeeze back, silently telling him I'm not going anywhere. I don't want to be anywhere but right here.

For once I'm not chasing the next high. Being with Asher is the high I want to ride forever.

END OF SNEAK PEEK

Read the rest of Siobhan and Asher's romance in

Star Struck

Available now

Acknowledgements

Dessert is served! It's appropriate on many levels that this last book in the Falling for the Liar series involves a bakery. First and foremost, because in case you haven't noticed, we both love food recipes. If you want a Willa Drew cookbook, send us an email at willadrewauthor@gmail.com and we will get to work on putting one together.

Sarah and Nick are how we created the Willa Drew Universe. Their meet cute was a little short story to keep Gala and DL occupied during lockdown. Thank you to the early readers of that story on Wattpad and especially our Sassy and Sexy Writers Squad Daria, Latty and Estelle, your words of encouragement inspired us to continue Sarah and Nick's romance to five books.

Essential to every recipe are the core ingredients that bring it to life. The same can be said for publishing a book. Thanks to our editors Julie and Victoria for being the vital staples. We thank Books and Moods for our amazing covers that captured the vibe of the five holidays. If you follow us on Instagram, you've seen the talented Maria Peña's portraits of Sarah and Nick.

The first taste testers prove is the recipe is a good one. Shout out to our ARC and Street teams for reading Nick and Sarah's stories back-to-back and encouraging us to give this couple the happy ending they deserved. We made you cry, we made you laugh, and we hope we made you fall in love with love. Thanks Hope, Melanie, Blanca, Ashley M., Tanya, Danielle S., Danielle M., Danielle W., Mashala, Thea, Kayla, Brittani, Ashley K, Claire H, Jennifer L., Jane, Brandy, Samantha, Katelyn, Amanda, Ally, Heather M, Abby T, Beth, Brittney, Dimitra, Elizabeth R., Tracey, Lisa L, Jordan M, Tami W. for making the effort to read the Falling for the Liar series and for stepping into the Willa Drew Universe with us.

To you, our reader. Thank you for taking a chance on us and reading this series to the end. Thank you for letting us into your lives, for spending your time reading our stories and for telling your friends, "You have to read this book." We write because our characters insist we tell their stories, but also because we want to bring the joy of romance into the world. Your hearts on our social media posts, encouraging emails, and book reviews mean more than you can ever imagine.

Writing as a duo brings two authors' experiences and creativity to our stories. While this series is by no means a memoir, there are countless personal references and experiences in these books that make Sarah and Nick's story near and dear to our hearts. Thank DL for the Canadian perspective, an obsession with movies, jewelry cameos, hockey references, and the matriarch of the Côte family, Mémère. Thank Gala for her fascination with characters who're immigrants, making the characters eat and drink things readers can cook or try as well, awkward meals with friends/family, constant mentions of coffee, treating objects as symbols of emotions, and child/parent conflicts .

Saying goodbye to the past, be it a business, a place, a book, or a character, is always bittersweet. While we're excited to give Sarah and Nick the happy ever after they deserve, we might not be able to part with them entirely. This first couple we wrote as Willa Drew might show up in future books, helping their friends find love and fulfillment.

Until we meet again, remember, as Mémère would say, "You're worth this."

DL: I'll miss writing Sunny Sarah, the Canadian who is not at all like me, but who I might want to be when I grow up. While she was originally a side character from my story Ruby Red, she came to life in our Falling for the Liar series. I adored writing her story and it makes my heart smile that she found love in such a wonderful, caring, and kind character as Nick. Thanks to Gala for trusting me to help craft, create and write Nick. I refer to Sarah as Sunny Sarah because she is a light in my life. I don't know if Gala realizes that many components of Sarah's personality are drawn from the real Gala I get to talk to almost every day. Gala, you are a light in my life and I'll be eternally grateful for you reaching out to me and asking if I wanted to write a story with you. Like Nick, you altered the course of my life over one holiday and my life is infinitely better for knowing you. Because like Sarah, I'm not good at saying the important things out loud and prefer to write them, I'm committing these words to paper so you always have them: I love you.

Gala: I love you so much, DL. And yes, I'm totally crying here. Because of all the I love yous that come with this book, because it's the final book in to Sarah and Nick's story, because it's a huge milestone, and because this end of the first series proves DL and me writing together is a special thing. We are magic. Nick was a stubborn and artsy side character, getting him, the youngest sibling, with Sarah, the oldest in her family, worked out perfectly. DL cracked Nick's heart and showed me and Sarah that he's a complete romantic. That's something DL and Nick have in common. Grateful doesn't quite cover how I feel for having my BFF (she l-o-v-e-s when I call her that, lol) write with me. She not only says yes to one adventure after another I drag her into but holds my hand when I fall into despair. DL brings optimism to my realism.

<u>Willa Drew</u> is not one, but two writers of fun, flirty fiction full of feels.

Lovers of emotional scenes (don't tell anyone: someone always cries as we write them), dramatic scenarios (don't blame us, the characters insisted), and the best the world has to offer like eclairs and butter tarts (don't ask us to share, but we'll point you to the recipes).

Our romances have every flavor. Angst? Check. Secrets? Of course. Risk taking? You bet. Expect slow burns, heart flutters, soul mates, first loves, and swoon-worthy kisses.

Hang out with us over on all the socials @willadrewauthor, visit willadrew.com, and sign up for our newsletter to get updates sent right to you.